DON'T LOOK BACK

A MACK & M MYSTERY

DON'T LOOK BACK

STEPHEN WINN

atmosphere press

Published by Atmosphere Press

Cover design by Marielena Andre

atmospherepress.com

For my son Colin Edward.
As John F. Kennedy once stated, "Life is unfair."

A portion of the profit from each Stephen Winn novel sold will be donated to a registered charity for the disabled.

PROLOGUE

The Discovery...a River West of Boston
A Few Years Ago

MACKENZIE SAMPSON, A TOP investigator and legal mind with Boston Homicide, stood surveying the murky river just below a sharp curve in the highway. With him was Lieutenant Detective Nik Lewis, who remained unusually quiet. Behind them on the large pull-off rest area, a small group of men and heavy-rescue equipment had been assembled by the Boston Police. It was spitting rain and cool just before noon. Like an old wolf smelling something unknown on the wind, Lewis felt a gnawing apprehension and let Sampson know for the first time in a long time he was lost for words.

Moments later, a burst of bubbles broke the rippling surface of the dark river. From his vantage point, Lewis immediately signaled the men, and they moved forward toward the edge of the river. A diver surfaced, removed his face mask, and shouted, "It's hooked up and good to go!"

The operator of the heavy-duty rescue tow truck moved into action. As he maneuvered the controls on the large crane boom, it lowered for a moment and then began to gradually rise. The cables attached to the crane quivered, sending ripples outward in the dark water as they grew taut. The boom rose slowly; the machine whined and buzzed. Then, like a great white shark, the trunk of a car broke the surface. Murky water cascaded down its sides as it hung suspended in the air—revealing a sludge-covered white Porsche.

Detective Steve Drakowski, Lewis's right-hand assistant, walked up to them and shook his head in dismay. "Geez, guys, what a shame to see such a beautiful car ruined," he said. "Most of us can only dream of getting a ride in a car like that."

Mack responded, while Lewis remained pensive. "Yeah. No one ditches a high-end Porsche—no one. They would sell it or cut it up in a chop-shop before they'd send it into a river. This whole thing stinks already." Lewis was certain he could smell alcohol on Mack's breath as he spoke, but said nothing.

Lewis looked around to make sure things were proceeding as expected, with everyone doing what was necessary to keep the site safe. There was a second heavy-duty tow truck on standby; three Boston Police cruisers; the Massachusetts State Police Underwater Recovery Unit; and two emergency vehicles, all with flashing bright lights that created a multi-strobe effect through the dense mist. Lewis glanced at the sky and saw the dark gray clouds hanging low, but it had almost stopped raining.

Curious onlookers were stopping and jamming up the highway. Police officers stationed along the shoulders were trying to get everyone moving. Two angry drivers were shouting profanities at each other from their car windows; both frustrated by the long delay and wanting to get past the other onlookers. They were only adding to the gridlock as people slowed to watch them.

Unable to shake his uneasiness, Lewis turned his attention back to the recovery. In the semi-organized chaos around him, the crane operator swung the long arm of the boom while raising the car high over a damaged and long-neglected guardrail. He carefully lowered the Porsche into a taped-off area set up to receive it. Four workmen grabbed the cables and guided the car to a safe landing while being careful not to touch it. The engine was missing from the Porsche.

As they unhooked the cables from the car, Lewis walked over to direct the rest of the operation. He could already see that the muck-covered car had been in the water for a long time—and it wasn't empty.

"Nik, how did this nasty business get started?" Mack asked.

Lewis popped a red lozenge into his mouth and cleared his throat. "Earlier this morning two fishermen spotted what looked like a white sheet of metal or something deep in the water," he replied. "One of them got his fishhook snagged, so they were trying to figure out how to unhook it. That's when they realized what they were looking at could be the vague outline of a car. It was too deep to be certain, so they called us. Good thing they did because as you can see it turned out to be significant."

Lewis and Mack circled the car, examining the exterior and commenting on the missing engine as Drakowski held back onlookers. Lewis was concerned that Mack looked unsteady as he walked, and made a mental note. "You know that cars get stolen, stripped and dumped in strange places all the time," Lewis added. "That's why our policy is always to send out a tow truck to assess the situation first. We've been using the same company since time began, and we trust them to scope things out for us. But this time the driver arrived on site and called dispatch, saying this thing was big and deep, so getting at it would be difficult. It was close to shore, but we'd need a diver to check things out and hook up cables."

"That explains this crazy circus around here," Mack said, pointing around him. "We even have a Porsche swinging in the air as the high-wire act."

"Mack, let's be serious—I've had a bad feeling about this whole thing, and it's been eating at me. Before the diver attached the cables, he went down to get the plate number and check things out. He thought he could make out a body behind the wheel. It turns out there's been a long outstanding search for this car and owner. I thought my head would explode when I found out the owner's name. I'll tell you more if he's the one in the car."

"And to think this started with a snagged fishhook—what a fluke," Drakowski said.

"A twist of fate," Lewis replied.

With the car on the ground, some members of the public who had pulled over to see what was going on moved forward to get a better look. Lewis shouted, "Hey, stand back! I need you people out of the way!" He finished circling the dripping car as Mack joined him. Most of the water had poured out, but a thick greasy coating of river-bottom slime covered it, causing the windows to be opaque.

Pausing at the driver's side, Lewis noticed a small area where the debris was scraped off the window, possibly made by the diver. He crouched to see inside. The grayish light of the overcast day barely illuminated the interior of the car with the windows so obscured. As he shifted his position to get a better look, Lewis felt his stomach tighten. Inside was a body slumped over in the driver's seat still held in place by a seat belt. The badly decomposed corpse was still wearing the tattered remains of a suit and tie.

Lewis turned to Mack. "I wouldn't want to be the medical examiner who has to deal with this mess. You need to take a look."

Mack peered into the vehicle, then stepped back quickly. "Man, that's right out of a horror movie," he said. "Who is this poor guy?"

"If he's the owner of this car, the plates ID him as Jack

Schroeder."

"Not *the* Jack Schroeder, the banker?"

"The very same. He was the head of one of the largest banks in Massachusetts. You probably remember that when he vanished a long time ago, there was a flurry of media coverage. Several theories about what happened to him were tossed around for a few weeks, but we had no leads, and then things settled down as I recall. After looking in the car, I see my first assumption about how he ended up here was wrong."

"Huh? What do you mean?"

"Using your circus analogy, I originally thought this was just another drunk or careless clown—but it's not. I checked, and there have been no repair works to the safety barriers in this area for several years. As you can see, there's no impact damage to the front of the car either. It looks like someone wanted this guy gone forever, so did a dunk job at the old boat launch and kept his Porsche motor as a souvenir."

They both squatted down and squinted through the window again.

"It's even worse than when I looked the first time, Nik," Mack said.

"Yeah. Damn it, Mack—we're most likely talking murder by drowning here. If he was shot or stabbed, we should know soon. The medical examination should tell us if there are any other less obvious injuries that could tell us of his fate, before the car was sent to the bottom of the river."

As Lewis turned to speak to Drakowski, he heard the car door open behind him. He spun around in a flash to see Mack had opened the driver's door of the Porsche without wearing latex gloves, and was leaning into the car.

"What the hell do you think you're doing? What kind of an investigator are you? Get away from there!" Lewis shouted.

"But...I thought I saw something on the seat and figured it might be a gun beside him. I...I had to be sure. That would be an important find, but there's nothing here! I also wondered if his foot was taped to the accelerator."

Nik lowered his voice. "I've smelt liquor on your breath since I first spoke with you this morning. You're supposed to be helping me investigate a crime scene, not damage it, damn it. I know you have personal problems, but you can't be a basket head case and expect to work for me. You should know I run a tight ship and always have. You've been warned before, Mack. You're out of here–fired!"

CHAPTER 1

Present Day Boston
A Sunday in Late May

"I DIDN'T WANT TO bother you on a Sunday morning, Mack, but..."

"But you did. It's okay, M, because I was up and frequent calls are what I would expect from a partner in my investigations firm. Isn't it good to know you're one of the few people on the planet who can get away with calling me this early on a Sunday?"

"You sound awful."

"I was up most of the night—hardly had any sleep since Friday. My mouth feels like I ate mud, and I probably look even worse than I sound. I'm afraid to go near a mirror—even my dog won't look at me. Hey, it was John F. who said life is unfair, wasn't it?"

"Kennedy? I think so..."

"His damn quote has been bouncing around in my head lately—I can't seem to shake it. Lewis said something like that when he fired me."

"That was a while ago, Mack. You've got way too much racing around in your head right now to worry about such things. Everything will work out, you'll see. You're the one who taught me persistence wins, remember?"

"Well, we can be as persistent as we want, but time is our enemy. If we don't find a new case soon, we might be forced to close our doors. There's no money left to fall back on and no way to take out another loan. The only other thing I can think of is to sell one of my collector cars, but I try not to think about that. I'm praying for a miracle. Anyway, enough about the good news—how come you're calling?"

"Because I want to tell you what happened last night. I was downtown and drove by the Old Tartan House pub. The cops had the entire parking lot secured, and they weren't letting anyone in or out."

"So, what's that got to do with us?"

"You're the one who taught me to check out every crime scene I come across just in case we might be able to offer our services. You never know—you don't try, you don't get, right? We should check out every possibility no matter if it's a long shot or not. Do you know who taught me that?"

"Okay, okay, I agree you did the right thing."

"I always try to think positive, Mack, and I'm always curious, as you know."

Mack paused to rub his temples. "You're making sense. Tell me more about what went on downtown."

"I spoke to Drakowski. He was waving curious bystanders away from the Tartan's lot. I found out it was about a Bentley owner and his car that had been parked there since Friday night. Unfortunately, Drakowski wasn't saying anything."

"Figures. That tough-ass Lewis must have told him to keep his mouth shut."

"I know you've still got hard feelings toward Nik, but you should leave your issues with him in the past."

"M, that's between Lewis and me, so..."

"So. Anyway, he's still the big cheese at Boston Homicide.

He was at the Tartan somewhere, but I couldn't spot him. Maybe he was in a squad car or something. Drakowski told me he was the guy in charge as usual. I decided to take a chance and ask Drakowski if he would do us a special favor."

"And what was that?"

"I gave him some of our business cards and asked him to try and get them into the hands of anyone who might need our services. He said if Lewis ever found out he was handing out our cards there would be hell to pay, but he knows we're in a tough spot hurting for work and wants to help. I remember he once told me his dad ran a small company while he was growing up and things were pretty lean for them many times."

"All right, let's check it out some more, as you suggest. I'm just worn-out and angry. We have no company money left, and that sucks. Things can't get much worse, so I might as well start looking up instead of down, right?"

"I think it's time you got on Lewis's good side and healed a few old wounds. It's been over three years since he fired you, hasn't it, Mack?"

"Yeah. Maybe this is meant to be the catalyst for better things to come. Who knows? I appreciate the info and your optimism, M, but right now I feel like crap. My head was pounding when you called, and it still is. I gotta let you go..."

CHAPTER 2

Saturday
Early June, Six Days Later

A COOL BREEZE WAS blowing in off the Atlantic. It was 10 a.m. on a Saturday morning with a clear sky and a temperature predicted to be in the low seventies. Anyone would enjoy being outdoors on such a beautiful day, but not Mackenzie Sampson. He was in a grumpy mood and in no rush to get to his office as he headed toward central Beantown.

His mind wandered, even as he drove in Boston traffic. The night before, he'd wanted to go out on a date, but couldn't get his mind off the Ellers case. He'd decided to stay home to consider his prospects—and drink. Myron Ellers was a sleazebag accountant who had embezzled money from a large retirement pension fund. He'd gotten caught with his greedy hand in the cookie jar. Myron grabbed a lot of cookies—almost $650,000 worth. The casework had paid well for the little Mack and M had to do, but now Mack felt anxious because the job was almost at an end. Were there more services he could offer the accountancy firm that hired him? If not, where would he find another project to keep his business afloat? The pressure was irritating and constant. He thought about government employees on a steady income. They had no clue what it was like to have to strive every day to find work—and worry about survival in the downtown jungle. It was yet another reason to justify his need to drink heavily and feel miserable.

When Jamie Lee, the love of his life, had died, he'd hit the bottle hard. He had met Jamie at a Harvard fundraiser. She was studying law there as he had previously, while she also worked as a part-time researcher for a Boston law firm to help finance her studies. Mack and Jamie hit it off big time.

Mack's hopes and dreams had come to a sudden and startling end when Jamie and her close friend, Cynthia, were killed in a devastating accident. A large vehicle sideswiped them while they were in Cynthia's Fiat, heading home on a rainy, dark night. The force of that vehicle striking the side of the small car caused it to veer head-on into a concrete abutment on their approach to a bridge.

Alcohol hadn't eased the repetitive anxiety attacks, so he also began popping Xanax like candy. His two growing addictions ended up ruining his professional life—a stellar career with Boston Homicide. He was forced to leave the force, a disgrace to the friends and family who had been so proud of him. Lieutenant Detective Nik Lewis had said he hated what he had to do—but Mack had received several warnings. He'd known his termination was imminent. The growing demons within him had wrecked his career. Now they were threatening to destroy his private life.

After his dismissal, Mack was left confused and lonely—a broken-hearted man in the depths of despair. Many times, he'd felt like giving up. But his heart yearned for fulfillment, and a last remaining spark of ambition instilled in him many years before continued to drive him forward. Upon his graduation, he had made a pledge to his father, Matthew, that he would use his talents and energy to help the disabled, injured, and others in need.

Mack's law degree from Harvard, and his police experience, helped him to secure his license as a private investigator. The money his father had left him in a trust fund had been his cushion to secure a home, and most recently pay for his PI courses, but now that support had dwindled to almost nothing. Mack was a failure at managing money—he had always had lots of it, but his careless spending habits finally caught up with him. He had developed a love—a passion—for investigation—a need to protect the innocent and make evildoers pay for their crimes. His vow to his dad became his guiding beacon as he walked through his valley of darkness. Even when nearly overcome with depression, he'd felt driven toward the light and renewed optimism.

Mack knew he had to keep his demons in check or they would consume him before he could build a reputable private investigation firm. It was a high mountain to climb toward his goal, but he felt determined it would be his redemption! Even so, only within the last few weeks had his desire for alcohol and drugs finally begun to subside, along with the hellish roller-coaster ride of his emotions. Although he still had bad days, he credited his improvement to his hope for a continuing relationship with Serena, despite her reluctance to get too close to him.

He shook off the painful thoughts as he parked in his familiar spot behind his office and opened the rear door of his SUV to let out Woof, his big chocolate Lab. He took his best friend with him whenever he could. Woof offered stable, nonjudgmental companionship he could always count on—and served as the anchor that kept him from drifting too far astray.

Mack looked up into the trees at the rear of the property, and so did the dog. He smiled as he spotted the two old gray squirrels once again, scampering through one of the big shade trees. From a small bag inside his vehicle, he grabbed a handful of peanuts and left them along the top edge of the wooden back fence. Both the squirrels and Woof watched his every move.

Then Mack headed inside the small house his associate, M, and his friends had converted into comfortable offices for Mackenzie Investigations. Several clients had expressed surprise to find no one lived in the cozy little place. He had secured Woof on the small back deck, and soon was seated behind his desk reviewing emails on his laptop.

A moment later Pauline entered through the back door, and Mack smiled at the familiar sounds he had heard so many times: purse dropped on desk, coffee maker started. She was an important part of the three-person office.

"Good morning," she sang, as she stuck her smiling face around the corner of his office door. "How's my dark, tall, and handsome boss today?"

Women usually noticed Mack's piercing emerald green eyes—his gaze was always intense—but today he knew his eyes were dull and red. Nevertheless, he thought he looked respectable dressed in jeans and a new burgundy shirt he wore untucked.

Pauline eyed him closely. "Are you okay?"

"Sure—I'm fine." It always made him feel good when they spoke.

Pauline had grown up in Western New York State. She was the eldest of five, having four rough-and-tumble brothers she'd helped raise while her parents worked. Everyone described her as a tomboy and abbreviated her name to Paul. At five-nine, in good physical shape, she had shoulder-length dark brown hair that she often tied back into a ponytail. Pauline seldom wore makeup, or if she did it wasn't obvious. This morning she was dressed in a long-sleeved white shirt with a light-yellow vest, skinny jeans, and yellow and white running shoes—comfort was always her first choice.

"What are you doing in this crazy place on a Saturday

morning, Paul?" asked Mack.

"M called me late last night after trying to get hold of you," Pauline said, as she stood in the doorway to his office. "He told me he thought we've got a shot at a new client, so I should be here this morning. Apparently, Drakowski called him to say someone from the Tartan Pub incident told him they would be in touch with him for a meeting Saturday morning."

"Could be my lucky day," Mack said, cracking a smile. "I hate to admit we're desperate for work, but that's an understatement."

"Try not to worry, because M sounded excited and told me to remind you to stay positive. He knew you'd be here Saturday morning as always, so thought a call just to me would suffice. M's bringing the guy here, but I'm not sure who the heck he is, what he wants, or what time they'll even be here. M never says much unless he's prodded, and I didn't."

"We'll need a fresh pot of coffee right away then, huh," Mack said.

"Bite me," Pauline shot back with a smirk. "Actually, it's already started."

A few minutes later, Mack came out of his office to use the photocopier and could smell the coffee.

"Paul, you're the best."

She beamed. "This is so true!"

Mack laughed as he returned to his desk, his hangover easing. *What would I do without her?* His stomach tightened as the fear for the future of his company arose. *I could never face having to lay her off...*

He greeted the many pictures of family, friends, and other mementos in his office, as he did every morning before having his coffee, then sighed as he got back to the many emails on his laptop. *The damn list never ends,* he thought. *Think positive like M says. Maybe there's good news in the air.* That's when he heard M's high-performance Dodge Challenger roar into the lot behind the office and park.

A moment later, M appeared in Mack's office doorway, accompanied by a stout, casually dressed middle-aged man. What little hair he had left on his balding round head was chalk-white, and his glasses had frameless lenses. As he approached Mack, his arm was outstretched for a handshake. Mack could tell by his facial expression he was stressed. He could see it in his tired eyes.

"Mack, I want you to meet John Whiting," M said. "You remember my telling you about the Bentley behind the Old Tartan House pub? Well, John wants to talk to us about that."

Mack stood up and his strong physical build and six-foot-four height quickly became obvious to the new guest. Mack was an imposing figure to most people he met, so he always made sure he greeted guests with a big, friendly smile.

"Forgive me for not shaking your hand, Mack, but since that COVID-19 mess started I decided to stop doing that, as have most people I know," John said.

"No problem. Nice to meet you, John," Mack said, as he looked him straight in the eyes. He liked Whiting's demeanor. "Please call me Mack, and by the way, I'm no relation to any large trucks."

Whiting chuckled at Mack's comment. "Nice to meet you."

There were three brass-tacked dark green leather armchairs set out in front of Mack's large oak desk, and Whiting sat in the middle one. Mack had inherited the office furniture from his father, who had died prematurely several years before. Mack sat in the fourth chair of the set behind his desk.

M located himself to Mack's right. He was only five-foot-five, close to a full foot shorter than Mack, but strong and lean. He was good looking with classic Italian features, a mop of black hair that he wore long, olive colored skin, and dark eyes. His muscular arms were his most noticeable feature. M preferred to dress all in black—normally jeans and a T-shirt, and low-rider black leather boots. This morning, however, he wore a blue polo shirt with black slacks.

Mack said, "It was good M was able to give you a lift."

"Sure was. All the way here I was curious about his moniker, but didn't ask him," Whiting said.

Mack grinned. "His name is Emilio, but as he grew up everyone shortened it to Em, spelled EM. Over time it just became a capital M. Now it's how everyone knows him. He's even got a few T-shirts with a giant letter M on them."

M rolled his eyes, but didn't comment.

"So, Mack and M," Whiting said.

"And there's Pauline out front," Mack added. "Can't forget her—she's important to this place. The good guys like her; the bad guys—not so much."

"I'll keep that in mind," Whiting said.

"Can I get you something to drink before we get started, John?" Mack asked.

"No thanks—not now."

"Then allow me to tell you a little bit about Mackenzie Investigations. We're bonded, insured, and licensed. We're also confidential, ethical, and reliable."

"Those are the things people like me want to know," Whiting confirmed. "It was good you were referred by a police officer at the Tartan who seemed to know you quite well. He gave me his card and yours, but despite his speaking about you in glowing terms, I had a friend of mine check you out just to be sure you would suit my needs. She said it appears you will do quite nicely, so that was good enough for me."

"We've helped many people out of tough spots," Mack said, with a calm nod.

Whiting hesitated. "I guess I'd better get to the point and tell you what I'm rattled about—but where do I begin? I'm not going to mince words. I've never had faith in our police—no disrespect intended. Maybe I've seen too many TV cop shows;

who knows? Real-life police officers always have so many cases and demands on them. Mack, I want one hundred percent attention to my case on a twenty-four-seven basis—no excuses. I have important reasons for needing immediate attention, and I'm willing to pay you very well for it."

While already counting the money in his head, Mack didn't want to sound too excited and risk losing Whiting's business. He replied, "We have a solid untarnished track record we're proud of, so I'm sure we can help you. But before accepting your case, I would need to know some details."

"Okay, fair enough," Whiting said. "I didn't tell M much on the way here because I wanted to save it for this meeting—repetition is taxing, and it's been tough enough as things stand. I haven't had much sleep in the last few days because I've been so damn terrified. My poor wife, Joan, is scared out of her wits. She's staying with her sister until we know more. My nerves are shot and I can hardly think straight, so I asked M to pick me up this morning because I didn't even want to drive. Thanks so much, M."

Mack knew it was best to encourage a new client to do the talking while he remained silent and focused on listening. While with the police, he had seen too many times when an aggressive officer kept talking over a person's efforts to explain the circumstances of a situation. That was always to the detriment of the investigation.

"John, it's always good to get things out on the table. I'm sure you'll feel better having done that," Mack said. "Tell us what's going on—what it is you need—how can we help you?"

Whiting answered slowly, his expression filled with pain. "There's a lot I have to tell you about my business partner and longtime friend, Bill Stewart. The police discovered his body last weekend, and a Lieutenant Detective Nik Lewis told me at the scene it was murder. I'm willing to pay you a contract fee of $100,000 to find out who killed my friend and why."

CHAPTER 3

MACK SAT PATIENTLY WITH M, waiting for Whiting to gather his thoughts and to continue talking, but his instincts were on high alert after Whiting's $100,000 fee offer. Was this heaven finally smiling down upon him—or was hell about to roar up with its deadly flames?

Something didn't feel right with this case, but he couldn't put his finger on what it was. Nik Lewis was no amateur—he wasn't one to make a hasty decision or ignore evidence, so his suspicions were likely correct.

On the other hand, there was no way Mack could turn down a shot at a cool $100,000 when he needed it so desperately for his fledgling business. Sure, there were a few minor cases to bring in a little money to keep the lights on, but this would be the motherlode. He imagined all the debts he could pay off, all the stress it would relieve both for him and his team, and the headway he could make with money like that.

In front of him sat a grown man doing his best not to break down. Several times Whiting found it hard to speak because he was forcing back tears—a tough thing for a man to do in front of other men. His grief seemed genuine, so Mack shook off his negative feelings to see what developed. It wouldn't be as if he was accepting this case under false pretenses. After all, there was no final coroner's report yet. Whiting clearly believed in his own instincts and was willing to forge ahead without police and trust he'd find out what happened to his friend.

"Please go easy on yourself, John, and tell us the way you see this," Mack said, trying to help Whiting regain his composure.

"Everything's such a blur," Whiting said. "Just like you and M are sitting with me now, Bill and I made it a habit of being in our office on Saturday mornings. During the week there would be a steady stream of people to deal with, and that was always our main focus. But come Saturday morning, we'd spend time together, slow down, and make some sense out of the chaos." He laughed as if remembering something fondly, then grew somber once again. "So, when Bill didn't show up last Saturday morning and hadn't called, I got concerned," he continued. "I phoned his wife, Maggie, who was worried too because he hadn't come home the night before."

"Did you ask her where she thought Bill might be?" Mack asked.

"I knew he went out with buddies every Friday night for cards and beer, but that he'd almost always head straight home. I asked Maggie if she had called his friends to see if he'd gone over to one of their places to crash. Once in a while, he'd have to sleep off a few too many. She said she made a few calls without success and planned to call a few more of the numbers she kept handy by the phone. I could tell she was becoming more and more concerned because this wasn't like Bill. I made calls to some guys to see if anyone could tell me Bill's whereabouts. I didn't want to say the wrong thing to Maggie beyond what I'd already told her. I didn't want to get him in even deeper crap with his wife than he was."

"Sure—you wanted to respect his privacy," Mack said.

"Also, I'm not his keeper. I'm his business partner and a good friend, so I always remember that. Plus, I didn't want to look like a wuss. I wanted to let him have his personal space. I don't know—maybe he ran into a curvy two-legged adventure that he couldn't pass up."

M was quick to pick up on that train of thought. "Did he chase women?" he asked. "That could be a motive for violence right there. Some men think it's their red-blooded, God-given American right to hurt, maim, or eliminate anyone who fools around with their wife, girlfriend, or daughter. You've always got to be careful."

Whiting smiled slightly and said to M, "I think Bill was very careful. To be perfectly honest, though, I could never figure out Bill's wife. She has a really hard side and was always sort of a mystery to me, but she's no pushover. I suspect she tried to keep tabs on Bill without him knowing about it."

"I think a lot of women do that," M said.

"I'd have a hard time believing he had another woman as a regular diversion," Whiting added. "He knew many women, but he'd have to hang out with someone for a while before he'd make a move. And it would always be a short-lived form of amusement. I've seen a woman on his arm from time to time, but only when there was no likelihood of Maggie spotting him. Hell, I'm sure I'd have known."

"What would she have done if she *had* spotted him?" asked M.

"I'm not sure I'd want to know the answer to that," Whiting said, frowning.

"So, he was smart enough to stay away from strangers—a lesson too many men fail to learn," M said.

Whiting took a deep breath and explained that Bill was what older men refer to as a *mover and a shaker*. He was just over six feet tall, good-looking, and kept himself in shape. He worked out regularly at a gym close to his home and always dressed sharp. When he walked into a room, people could smell the money. "Bill liked to be the life of the party," he said, "—especially on the dance floor. And he had the come-on lines and the moves to attract women." John added that he felt old and worn out compared to Bill, and that others thought the same way about him.

Mack got the picture. To John, Bill was a take-charge guy bursting with energy all the time—a man who could never sit still.

"Maybe this could be a jealousy killing because of Bill's roving eyes," he commented. "Can you tell us what he was up to that Friday night?"

"Bill met with his group of friends like he did every Friday night at the Old Tartan House downtown. All the guys call it the 'Old Tart.' There are lots of popular bars around there and many tipsy patrons roaming around, but it's not a seedy area. The guys he met with were a bunch of Scottish mates—all solid family guys with lots of money. They had a few pints together while cutting cards and making a few bets, and then would be on their merry way. Never any muss nor fuss."

"Sounds like a normal evening with buddies—happens all over America," M said.

"Sure, and every so often he liked to roll the dice elsewhere. He'd play blackjack, or take a few spins on a roulette wheel at a different place or two—no big deal as far as I know," Whiting added.

"Fine for any guy with lots of money to spend. So, the Bentley the police found at the Tartan was Bill's?" Mack asked. "M was down there last Saturday night and told me it looked like they were having a street party."

"Lots of action," M confirmed.

"There sure was!" Whiting stared at his knees, trying to avoid getting choked up again.

"You know, the make and model of a fancy car can be a

motive for the theft of parts, or even the entire vehicle," said M. "When I was young, I saw many cars heisted and sometimes the vehicle owners hurt. Most of that was in the rough neighborhood where I grew up, though."

"Bill drove a new Bentley Flying Spur," Whiting said. "He called it his '*British Beauty*.'"

M jumped in, "We're talking twelve cylinders—over six hundred horsepower! Turn that engine on and you'll hear those ponies snorting and neighing while begging to hit the road."

"Well, M, I don't think I've ever sat closer to more horsepower in my life than in the front seat of *your* car," Whiting said, shaking his head. "Your Dodge Charger is something from another planet."

M laughed, then said, "I'm really curious—is that Bentley over a quarter of a million?"

Whiting grinned. "Yes, with the custom options he wanted it was quite a bit more than that."

"Can we get back to Bill's disappearance?" asked Mack. "What happened next?"

"As I told you, I spoke to Bill's wife, Maggie, on Saturday morning, but she hadn't heard from him," Whiting said. "After three or four hours, I called her again. She still hadn't heard from Bill, but had made more calls as I knew she would. At that point, I told her I had waited long enough and was going to call the police. So, I went ahead and reported him missing. I told the officer I'd known Bill all his life, and it wasn't like him to take off without a quick call to his wife. But the officer didn't seem to care. The jackass cop I spoke to the first time told me they couldn't help me unless at least forty-eight hours had passed since the disappearance. Right after that I called a friend of mine who might know about such things, and he told me the police get on a missing person case right away before the trail goes cold. Maybe the officer I spoke to was feeding me a load of BS or was just plain lazy. I recall him telling me there were many reasons a man of Bill's age could go missing—at least for a short time. I was upset by then, and wasn't going to take any more of his guff—it was all I could do not to blow my stack! That's one reason why I have no patience with the police."

Whiting stopped and caught his breath. His brow was sweaty and Mack didn't want Whiting to collapse from exhaustion or a heart attack. It was obvious from the spare tire around his waist he was out of shape. The thought of having to give him mouth-to-mouth resuscitation wasn't a pleasant one.

"Are you sure I can't get you something? Ice water or coffee?" Mack asked.

"I think I'll take you up on the coffee—double sugar, double cream," Whiting said. Mack was ready for a fresh cup as well, but M seldom indulged in anything other than cold beer. Oh, and he had a weakness for port. Mack excused himself and walked out for a moment, returning with two steaming mugs of coffee.

"Please continue, John. What did you do next?" Mack asked.

"I went to see if I could find Bill's car. My first stop was the Old Tart. His car was still parked where he'd left it, far away from where other cars would park. I walked into the bar to see if I could spot him. Maybe there was something his wife wasn't telling me—did they have a falling out? The Saturday evening action was heating up by then, so I guess it would have been around eight thirty or nine. I asked the bartender and girls waiting on tables about Bill, but no one had seen him since he came in the night before. I'm a solid guy, Mack, but I've got to tell you I started feeling sick to my stomach at that point. That's when I called the police again and insisted someone look at Bill's car for signs of foul play. I guess I made sense when I stressed to the second officer who I spoke to that no one in their right mind would leave a beautiful new Bentley like Bill's in an unguarded downtown parking lot behind a pub for two nights in a row!"

"Man, you're so right!" M said. "Even one night is way too long."

"Yeah. That's when he told me he'd send a squad car to check things out."

"So, he finally listened. A Bentley owner's money talks—a poor man's pocket-change walks," Whiting said.

"Hey, I'm surprised the wheels were still on his car by then," said M.

Mack sipped his coffee and sat forward in his chair. It was time to ask Whiting the tough questions about how and when the police found his friend.

"When did a police car show up?" he asked.

"Ah...this is the part I've been trying to avoid," Whiting said, grimacing. He started to shake and stare at his knees again.

"Take your time—we have lots," Mack assured him.

After a moment or two, Whiting heaved a deep breath, then said it took about twenty minutes for the police to arrive. When they showed up, he went outside to the parking lot and pointed out Bill's car. They went to check it out, and the next thing he knew, one cop was shining his flashlight on the pavement underneath it while the other was shining his on the interior. Then they got in their squad car and appeared to be making calls. I thought they wanted someone to come and open it.

"Did they share anything with you at that point?" Mack asked.

"No. I didn't know if they were afraid of a bomb in the car or what was going on. I was shaking with fright and felt really chilled. I didn't want to stand outside, so I sat in my own car and waited for about what seemed like an hour. That's when a crew from Boston CSI showed up—they had bright lights, crime scene barrier tape, video and still cameras, special tools, testing equipment, and who the hell knows what else. I guess those two cops must've spotted or smelt something, but no one said a word to me."

"This is starting to make sense," M said.

Whiting said after CSI arrived on scene, he got curious and stepped out of his car. A few minutes later, a tall African American detective by the name of Nik Lewis from the Homicide Unit showed up and took charge. Next thing he knew, they had the trunk open and there was something large inside.

"What did Lewis say to you then? Anything?" Mack said.

"He asked who the hell I was, and what business I had being there. Then he wanted me to have a look in the trunk—one of the toughest things I've ever had to do. I'll never forget that awful scene. The terrible shock at the sight and smell of Bill lying there...well, that was too much for my stomach to take. I barfed my guts out afterward. While down and out, I heard one of the officers say he thought this might be a suicide. What an idiot!"

Whiting drank some coffee even though his hand was shaking. "A while later, Detective Lewis told me I shouldn't leave because he wanted to talk to me in his office—and no, I wasn't being arrested. He made it clear I should stay in town and the consequences of leaving could be dire. I said I'd be glad to share what I knew, but he still wanted to talk to me in his office."

"So, you went with him?" Mack asked.

Whiting explained that Lewis hung around the crime scene for a while and then drove him to his office. He said he was nervous about going because who wants to go anywhere with a cop? Lewis said the CSI team had a big job to do, so the fewer people milling around the better. While at his office,

Whiting said he told Lewis the same things he had been telling Mack and M. That included that he had called Maggie in the morning and again in the afternoon, that she hadn't heard from Bill, and that's why he had called the police. Lewis suggested he leave by cab from the police station. He said he'd have an officer drive Whiting's SUV to his home because he was in no condition to drive, and shouldn't leave his vehicle downtown. "So, I handed him the keys. All the while, Lewis seemed suspicious of me—me!"

"You know," M said, "at the start of every murder investigation everyone's a suspect—even you, John."

"It's just the way things have to be at the outset of any case," added Mack. "As Sherlock Holmes once said, and I'm paraphrasing, 'Eliminate the irrelevant factors and the one that remains will be the truth.' That's why we have to start the process of elimination right away. Anyway, did he share any thoughts with you concerning what might have happened to Bill?"

"Detective Lewis mentioned a thing or two in his car. Maybe he was just testing my reactions, but he said that the car showed no signs of forced entry. He said it was strange his people couldn't find Bill's keys anywhere on him or in the trunk, and also that Bill's wallet was still in his pocket. They found two $100 bills in it—he seemed surprised at that. Even his credit cards were untouched."

"Odd the cash was left behind," M said.

"I guess that's why he also asked me how mentally stable Bill was. When I asked him why, he said this whole thing smelt odd to him."

"There you go," Mack said, "—that explains why he said what he did. Did they find a weapon?"

"No."

"Wow. So, who told Maggie the bad news?" Mack asked.

"Detective Lewis, and thank goodness he took care of that!

He told her the Medical Examiner would have to hold the body for a while, given the circumstances. They needed to collect as much forensic evidence as possible and make sure any conclusions they arrived at were correct. I spoke to Maggie the next day—Sunday. The cops had woken her up late Saturday night—it was actually in the early hours of Sunday, and she hadn't had any sleep. I promised her I'd sort this out as fast as I could, and told her I didn't trust the police. I said I was planning to hire professionals to help investigate this thing instead, so that's where you come in. Also, I didn't like Lewis's silence. He obviously knew more than he was telling me—at least that was my considered opinion. He said until his people had the results from the autopsy by the ME, he had nothing more to add about Bill's death. He'd have to wait and see what he gets back."

"Did he mention if the pub had a security camera?" Mack leaned forward, eager for an answer.

"Lewis mentioned the Old Tart had security cameras focused on the entry and a few inside the pub. They intended to review that material, but they were disappointed there were no cameras pointed at the parking lot."

"Too bad," Mack said. "I was hoping."

"Yeah. They plan to get one or two installed now, but that's way too late for Bill," Whiting said, sounding angry. "Lewis also said it was unlikely there were any witnesses; if there were, they'd be unreliable because any good defense attorney could easily destroy the testimony of someone who had been drinking." He suddenly seemed to deflate, as if all the air had gone out of him, and he stared at his knees again.

"John, I want to compliment you on the way you've sketched this out for us. You've done a great job," Mack said. "Let's take a break now—this has already been a long and demanding session for you."

"It needed doing," Whiting said.

At that point, Mack offered to treat the three of them to Italian food for lunch. He said he'd like to continue their conversation because there was so much more he wanted to know about Whiting's business and his personal dealings with Bill.

"Italian is fine by me, but you don't have to..."

"Good, then it's settled. I sure don't have to ask M about his preference. John, there's just one more matter I need to settle with you before we leave the office."

"Sure," said Whiting.

"Please forgive me if this seems insensitive because I don't mean it to be, but it's time to discuss a contract between us, and—we'll need a deposit from you," Mack said.

"Fine. I'll write you a check for $25,000 to get this started and cover your start-up costs. You'll get two more similar progress payments and a final one upon solving my case. But it's on condition that you get started right away."

Mack and M almost choked in unison as they looked at each other.

"Great," Mack said, trying to hide his surprise. His usual deposit request on a murder case was $5,000, with billings based on time spent plus expenses—no advances. "Then we have a deal—I'll have Pauline bring in a contract for your signature." Whiting and M stood as Mack walked out to speak with Pauline.

"No offense," Whiting said to M, "but I sure hope you folks are up to what this case will require. I've had an ominous feeling something strange has been going on between Bill and some others behind my back. I can't understand why anyone would want to kill him, because I know he would never kill himself. I expect you can solve this thing and give me and his dear wife some peace of mind."

CHAPTER 4

AS THE THREE MEN walked out to Mack's vehicle after their meeting, John Whiting couldn't help but comment on the building.

"I hadn't expected to see you gentlemen in an office space quite like this. I really like how approachable it is, but it also conveys that you are down-to-earth and professional. That has certainly been my experience so far—you know your business, but are also easy to talk to and deal with. I appreciate that."

M started to say thank you, but before he or Mack could say another word, Whiting said, "And it's not often one gets to see such a handsome chocolate Labrador like yours—especially one so peaceful."

Mack was impressed. Whiting knew the breed and added with pride, "I appreciate the kind words. He's a ninety-pound Field Strain Lab, which means he has a more functional athletic build than the typical show dog type."

Whiting nodded his head with understanding. "What's his name?"

"That's Woof. When I bring him to work with me, he has all the comforts of home: a canopy to keep him comfortable, rain or shine, a roomy doghouse, a bowl of fresh water, and a copy of his favorite hunting magazine to keep him occupied." Mack laughed. "His nickname is Wonder-dog." Then he added, "I briefly thought of naming him Shark, but I didn't think it would go over too well if I had to call out his name at the beach!"

Whiting laughed easily, seeming glad for the reprieve from the more difficult conversation to come. "Why did you call him Woof?"

Mack said, "Shortly after I adopted him, I looked into those big brown eyes and asked him what his name should be. At that exact moment he *woofed* loudly enough to startle me, and I knew what to call him ever since. As far as I'm concerned, Woof is the only dog in existence to have named himself!"

Whiting laughed again and clapped his hands together like a delighted child. Then they all climbed into Mack's big black SUV with Whiting sitting in front, and M behind Mack. Pauline had work to do setting up the new case file, so Mack knew she would look after Woof until he returned. Plus, he knew her favorite takeout meal to bring her for later.

"Nice wheels," Whiting said.

"They're not for show. I'm six-four and spent too many long nights on stakeouts crammed into mid-sized and often smaller cars. I swore that would never happen again. Besides, bad guys don't expect a private eye to be driving a Cadillac SUV. I've always liked a larger vehicle because of the outdoor activities I enjoy, and I need the room for all of my stuff...and Woof."

"Makes good practical sense," Whiting said.

"If it's okay with you, John, we'll have lunch at Luigi's Linguini Restaurant. Great Italian—just ask M."

"Been to Luigi's only once a couple of years ago, so this is bound to be a real treat for me," Whiting said.

Soon a young attractive greeter had seated the three in a booth in the glass-enclosed dining alcove of Luigi's. Mack liked the privacy it provided because at lunchtime the alcove was used primarily for business meetings and important discussions. Although such meetings could be stuffy, the room was not. The natural light and pastel yellow walls enhanced the bright ambience of the room, as did the many live plants. The rich aroma of Italian food filled the air and traditional instrumental music played unobtrusively in the background. The rest of Luigi's was what M referred to as stuffy high-brow, with subdued lighting, dark wood paneling and furnishings, and expensive tapestries.

As they settled in, Whiting asked Mack, "You referred to your dog as Wonder-dog once or twice. Is there some meaning behind that nickname?"

"I'm more than glad to share that story too, John." Mack smiled. "I had barely started my investigations firm when I began work on a missing person case for a corporate client. The clues led me to track him to a remote area in the wilderness. As I was crossing a snow-covered pond, I fell through the ice. Instinctively, I called out for help, but there was no one around to hear me. My gloved hands were useless when I tried to claw my way out. Then I saw Woof inching forward toward me on his belly. He knew something was very wrong by my frightened calls. He got close enough for me to grab hold of him, and I was surprised and amazed when he began to back away from the hole—him pulling me out in the process!"

"Bloody smart dog!" Whiting exclaimed. "Amazing story!"

"He saved my life, and that's when he earned the nickname—Wonder-dog." Mack was quiet for a moment, then added, "You know, I saw first-hand that day how intelligent Labs are, and their natural skill at rescue and recovery. I've enjoyed reading many true wartime accounts of fallen American soldiers who faced imminent death on the battlefield but were saved by the brave efforts of trained Labs. They performed like champions on 9/11 and they've been four-legged saviors to people in all kinds of disasters. Labs have even been awarded numerous medals for heroic deeds. My Wonder-dog certainly deserves one for saving me!"

Whiting gave a weak smile, but soon appeared somber again, so Mack turned serious and businesslike. He asked his new client to talk more about his business associate while they were waiting to eat. "To investigate your case successfully, we need to understand more about you, Bill, and your business. You'd be surprised at how sometimes the smallest detail can be the most important factor in solving a case." Mack placed his notebook next to him on the corner of the table. "Maybe you could start by describing how you and your friend Bill made such a good living."

"Let me give you a little history." Whiting paused, and then emphasized, "Bill's full name was William A. Stewart, and he was always proud of his Scottish heritage. We have been the absolute best of friends since grade school. You'll laugh, but our ambition was to become famous actors. We attended acting school in Cambridge. Bill wanted to be in film, but my dream was to be in live plays on Broadway."

"It's a big challenge to get started in *that* industry," Mack said. "In fact, it's tough to even get a toe in the door in any part of the entertainment business. There are so many talented people out there all vying for a chance."

"You're so right, but we were confident enough to believe we had the right stuff. We were so different from one another, though; not only our looks and height, but as people. After we finished acting school, we couldn't find jobs, so we decided to start a small business together. I was the creative business brains behind most things, while Bill was the doer making things happen. We worked our asses off for a long time, but it finally paid off."

"How did you settle on a business and a structure for your company?" asked Mack.

"After a few false starts and no acting work, one of my business ideas showed promise—an import firm for luxury goods. Since it was one of my ideas, I claimed fifty-one percent and the title of CEO. Besides, I knew how to incorporate a bulletproof company since my dad was a corporate lawyer and advised me. This caused a serious argument with Bill—maybe our only one. He demanded a fifty-fifty split. But Bill ended up with forty-nine percent and the title of President, and he accepted it. I demanded final say or no deal because that's what my dad told me to do."

"Did anyone else get a shot at any stock?" Mack asked.

"No. We closely held all shares, which proved to be a smart strategy. Many start-up companies give too much away to minor investors in the beginning. That's because they're starved for seed capital and need every dollar. Later, they end up sorry when they start to make serious money, then realize they've given away too many shares for too little money."

"How is the business doing now?" Mack asked.

"It's been very profitable. We import artwork, rare collectibles, and jewelry—*lots* of jewelry. We've grown to have several showrooms in major American cities like New York, Chicago, Los Angeles, San Francisco, and Dallas. In Canada, we have outlets in Montreal, Toronto, and Vancouver; and in Europe, we're in Berlin, Lisbon, London, Paris, and Rome. In all locations we have private galleries on a *By Appointment Only* basis. That's where we store and show our valuable goods to prospective buyers."

"Most would be exclusive collectors I should think, so you'd have ultra-high security in each location for all of your valuables," Mack observed.

"Yes, we import special goods from all over the globe, even fine high-end automobiles. We sell them to select wealthy buyers, or auction them off in discrete advertised venues. There's even a division licensed to import German, French, and Italian wines. Rare ports come to us directly from Portugal."

"I love port," M said, a gleam in his eyes. "How did you raise the capital to get started with only empty pockets in the beginning?"

Whiting explained how he and Bill Stewart had well-to-do parents, but wanted to be self-made. They started when they were in college by importing hand-carved pipes—many of meerschaum—and select cigar brands for wealthy men. "So many people smoked back then—it was popular wherever you went. But our first big break came when we accepted a European shipment of valuable goods on consignment."

"Someone with clout trusted you?" Mack asked.

"Yes. We must have said the right things to someone important because soon we had our first major deal. We didn't question if it was all strictly legal. We were too damn hungry for business to worry about that. It was Bill's fast-talking talents that secured us the contract. He had the golden gift of gab, and he convinced the vendor we had access to people with lots of ready American cash."

Whiting took a sip of ice water and continued. "After doing research on our first shipment, we found there were artifacts in it from an actual ransom obtained from a king—a fourteenth-century treasure. I can't describe how excited Bill and I were! Man, oh man! We were fearful of the law, but hell, we knew we had to take risks to get ahead. We felt it was the start of the success we deserved! To honor the occasion, we called our company Royal Ransom Collectibles Incorporated—RRCI for short."

"What about your sources now?" M asked. "How do you get your inventory?"

Whiting described how it took them many years to find and develop their current sources—all legal. "We jealously guard several hundred of the best contacts and suppliers, and have more than anyone in our business could ever hope for. It's all because of the great reputation we built, and the niche market we carved out for them."

"Because of the upscale business you're in, and all the rich folks you deal with on a day-to-day basis, Bill's choice of a high-end luxury vehicle wasn't out of line then," M stated.

"Correct. I should explain that Bill was not only our President, but would assume the role of RRCI's Director of Sales whenever it pleased him—which was often. I can tell you that was much to the annoyance of our current Director of Sales, Lorne Harris," Whiting said.

Mack raised an eyebrow. "Did it ever get nasty between them?"

"Nothing rough or physical. It was hard to tell Bill not to micromanage our sales division though," Whiting said. "He wanted to have his hands in all things in that department because he lived and breathed sales and selling. Sometimes he stepped on a few toes and pissed off employees, so I had to settle down a few hot tempers and hurt feelings from time to time."

"Would there be others Bill might have upset?" M asked.

"Bill held things close to his chest. I'm sure he had one or two secrets he wouldn't discuss with me, but Bill was a grab-the-bull-by-the-horns kind of guy. He had an outgoing personality and he produced."

"And how did you handle *your* role?" Mack asked.

"As CEO, I was the head of corporate management. I loved Bill's really big sales numbers while I focused on the day-to-day administration—running the overall company. We both traveled often to our many branches. Bill was the showman who did his thing—a driven Type A personality. I was the reserved Type B, but it worked out well. There were issues, but every company has its challenges."

"Given the right circumstances, some disgruntled people

will do almost anything—even murder—to get their way and succeed," M said.

Mack spoke gravely. "John, is there anyone who would want to get Bill out of the way to ease their stress or improve their position in your company? If he got eliminated, then the game could change. That could have been to the advantage of certain players."

John shook his head vehemently. "But our sales would have suffered. As far as I know, the people we've hired are decent. I can't think of a single one who'd do something terrible to Bill, and that goes for outside the company as well. Our competitors have always acted respectfully, as we have to them."

Mack sat back in his chair and was quiet for a moment, then said he wasn't there to upset Whiting further, but wanted him thinking in new directions. He said it would be good if he'd call either M or himself with any thoughts or ideas that might arise later to help solve the case.

"Someone might not hurt Bill on their own, but might have hired someone to have your friend tuned," M said.

"Tuned?" Whiting asked.

"That's street-talk," Mack responded. "What M means is someone may have wanted Bill roughed up so he would sing a different tune, but it got out of hand. Maybe a situation Bill was involved in outside of your company went sour. It's pure speculation, but we have to cover all the bases."

"Well, you guys waste no time, do you?" Whiting replied, more a statement than a question. "Sign a contract with you two, and then buckle up for the ride. I like that."

"It's what we do, but sometimes it feels like a roller-coaster ride," M said.

The meals arrived at that point, so Mack took his notebook off the table and set it on an empty chair. He also made sure to order a dish to take back for Pauline, telling the waitress to remind him to take it with him when it came time to pay for the meal. They chatted about news and sports until they finished eating. Then three cappuccinos arrived with several dark chocolate pieces of biscotti. Luigi's had the best cappuccino in the known universe as far as Mack and M were concerned.

"Okay," Mack said seriously, "—let's get back to Bill again for a few more minutes. Anything else you can share with us? You've sure done a great job so far."

Whiting knit his brows. "Come to think of it, Bill loved his British Beauty car so much, he always parked it well away from everyone—like they found it at the Old Tart. He'd often say there are too many empty-headed, insane jackasses around. He'd get up on his soapbox and preach to high heaven about how envious, thoughtless, or careless jerks were and that they were the main reason the world was going to hell fast."

"Sounds like I would have got along well with Bill," M said, grinning. Then, using his fingers to suggest quote marks, he said emphatically, "Experience has taught me, 'nothing is foolproof to a sufficiently talented fool.'"

Whiting grimaced, "Bill would say it's the fools out there who worry him the most because they don't give a damn about his car or anything else that's fine or special."

"The fact is, too many people don't give a damn about anyone or anything but themselves," M said.

"Bill was right," Whiting said. "Few others care about *your* property—we see it in the way some of our shipments of valuables are rough-handled and damaged. We maintain a repair facility in Rhode Island to fix our damaged goods. It's expensive to run because of the range of special skills we need, and unfortunately, they get too much work."

After a long pause, Whiting added, "So you can see why a new dent or scrape on Bill's car would ruin his entire week.

He couldn't rest until they repaired every tiny scratch—ah, the pleasures of driving an expensive car. That's not to mention the smart-asses who will key-scratch your paint because they're jealous. It's because you have something special, and they'll never be able to afford one."

"There are many more of those bastards out there than most people think," M said.

"Anyway, have you got the image of Bill and his fancy car now, gents?" Whiting asked. "That's why he was so happy the Old Tartan's parking lot was well lit, and he could park in his favorite spot far away from everyone. He liked that the place was never full, even on a Friday night."

Whiting sighed. "Poor Bill. This awful event has been so complicated. It's spinning my head."

"If you're not confused by now, then you're probably not thinking clearly," Mack said. "That may seem like a funny or insulting comment, but hey, I'm not kidding! Many cases we deal with seem simple and straightforward at first, but it's not until you dig into them that you find out how complicated they really are."

Mack paid the check for lunch, thanked the waitress for remembering to give him Pauline's meal, and closed his notebook. He now felt he and M had enough information to get a good start on the case.

"Okay, I think we should get you home, John. I'll be contacting Lewis soon to tell him you have retained us to work on the Stewart matter as our client. Before I forget, though, I should disclose that I know Lieutenant Detective Lewis—he and I go back a long way. I was on the police force for a few years, but more recently, I'd call us friendly competitors."

"Well, I hope you're not too chummy with him because I don't like him," Whiting said as he stood up to leave.

Mack remained silent as he walked out of the restaurant, but thought, *Join the club, pal.*

× × ×

TWENTY MINUTES LATER, MACK was driving his SUV through an impressive gated entry into one of Boston's more distinctive residential properties to the west of Boston's core. The drive sloped upward past a long colonnade of mature trees to an all-brick traditional style two-story dwelling. The house was surrounded by over an acre of groomed lawn and well-kept plantings. Mack approached the long, low stone stairs in front of the home and stopped his SUV.

"Beautiful place you have here, John," he said.

Whiting beamed. "Isn't it? The property once belonged to a wealthy community leader in this area back in the nineteen-twenties. There's a brass plaque beside the front door with the name of the family who had it built. This home is not too far from Bill's place."

"I'm sure I'll get to see his home soon too. Anyway, it's been our pleasure, and I'll be in touch with progress reports," Mack said.

Whiting climbed out of the SUV, then held the door open as M moved into the front passenger seat. "Thank you for the ride and for being such good listeners," he said, but didn't turn to leave. Instead, he took a deep breath. "There is something else troubling me. I guess I should get it off my chest before I go. I'd decided not to mention this at your office or Luigi's, and I'm not sure how or whether it relates to this tragedy with Bill. I wouldn't feel right, though, if I didn't tell you about it. It's important you should both have the entire picture when you investigate this case."

"We're here to help you get through this as best we can. We can't do that if we only have part of the puzzle," Mack assured him.

"I'm done for today and can't talk more, except to say that a few weeks ago we had a confidential offer for RRCI from an anonymous buyer. The deal is still very much alive and on the table. The only other people who know about it are my wife, Joan, and Bill's wife, Maggie."

Mack asked, "How serious is the offer?"

"It's $55,000,000 serious," Whiting said, as he started to walk away.

Mack gave a low whistle. "That's an awful lot of money. Were you both planning to sell?"

Whiting stopped in mid-stride and turned slowly. "That's an important conversation we must have soon."

CHAPTER 5

Sunday

WOOF'S CANINE EYEBROWS RUMPLED with anticipation. He watched every move Mack made while cooking breakfast. He preferred tasty human-food morsels to be handed to him, but would spring into action if anything fell off the counter and could be intercepted on its way to the floor.

Mack and Woof had been best friends for over three years. Before Woof, far too often Mack felt his life was empty. Convinced he needed a companion to fill the void and go out running with, he had gone to the Boston City Pound to see what he could find. A number of puppies and grown dogs were available, but Mack noticed a young dog in a small cage that had been set aside. He could tell immediately it was a chocolate Labrador Retriever, but the paperwork clipped to the cage indicated the six-month-old dog was to be euthanized.

Mack asked one of the volunteers to find someone who could tell him more about the doomed pup. He knew Labs were the most popular canine breed in America and would normally be adopted quickly—why not this one?

A staff member came and told him the dog had just been picked up, and had been so badly injured by his violent owner that they felt there was no hope for him. They had given him something for pain and scheduled him to be put down.

Mack examined the dog more closely and asked what had happened. According to the report, the owner had been abusive—likely sadistic. He didn't know how to raise a pup, and would vent his frustrations and rage on him. Seeing the puppy badly mistreated, a neighbor called for help, but the last beating had resulted in cracked ribs and a fractured hind leg. Sadly, the staff member told him the shelter couldn't afford to treat such serious injuries. Also, most potential adopters would not be interested in such a damaged dog. He could require expensive veterinary care and no one could predict what long-term effects the abuse might have on his temperament.

Mack sat down on the floor beside the dog. As he moved near, he noticed the pup's tail was wagging under the blanket. Mack smiled because he was able to reach into the cage and pat his head gently. Despite the pain the Lab was in and the abuse he had endured, he must have sensed Mack had a kind heart and licked his hand while looking at him intently. Something deep within those dark eyes reached deep into Mack's soul...

Mack assured the female staffer the dog would be okay, and insisted he be permitted to adopt him. She walked away for a moment, then returned to say Mack could have the dog, but warned him of the potential issues and costs. Soon Mack was out the door with his new friend and on his way to one of Boston's most respected veterinarians. The vet took him in immediately, and after X-rays, told Mack there was hope...but the pup needed surgery on his hind leg and attention to other injuries.

She cautioned Mack that to have the best chance for a full recovery, he would have to follow her guidelines to the letter. Mack approved the surgery, then took three weeks off from work to nurse the young dog back to health. Later, there would be many people praising him for rescuing Woof, but Mack knew in his heart-of-hearts it was Woof who had saved *him*.

× × ×

SUNDAY USED TO BE Mack's hangover recovery day, but now it was his day of rest. Mack packed it full of things he loved to do, including spending time with his girlfriend, Serena, good friends and family, and his ever-faithful dog, Woof.

His hobbies were working on his four vintage automobiles, preparing gourmet food, entertaining, and enjoying fine wine. As for the great outdoors, he especially loved hiking in the woods, camping, and outings in a canoe or kayak. Any spare time of more than a few hours was a chance to get out of Boston.

Mack's objective was to get into top condition for the Boston Marathon. The last time he'd run it was over three years ago, and he was amazed to have completed the run among the top one hundred finishers.

Mack had met Serena when she was one of the main organizers of a large non-profit annual fundraiser—*The Run to Empower Women*. That had been many months ago, and they had grown close ever since. She had become his special partner in all things, and last night just happened to sleep over.

While in the kitchen preparing breakfast, Mack was pleasantly surprised when Serena appeared in the kitchen entry, rubbing her eyes. "Morning," she said.

Serena had been born in India, the eldest of two daughters. Her family moved to Boston when Serena was only seven and her sister, Xena, was four. Serena graduated from medical school as a family physician, and Xena graduated as an X-ray technologist the same year.

"So, when do you have to pick up Syd?"

"She'll call me when she's ready to leave Heather's—probably around one o'clock—but the real question becomes, can I separate her from Heather's cat?"

"Hey, my sweet lady—pets are good for kids. Anyway, after we shower together, can I give you a quick summary of my new case? I tried to tell you last night, but you kept interrupting me with kisses. My mind naturally wandered off to other places."

"Yes, it did," Serena said, as she broke into a smile and then winked at him. "Perseverance wins, you know. Do you want to try to tell me about your new case...again?"

× × ×

MACK'S HOME HAD BEEN formed from an extensive renovation of a garage and warehouse. It sat on a large property he had purchased after his dad died. His combination of creative architectural design ideas had resulted in a unique structure that drew much attention from the locals. It had plenty of space for his many possessions, including a fully equipped gym and a huge garage to hold his current SUV, four collector cars, a pair of ATVs, a flat-bottomed gunmetal gray duck boat, and a cedar canoe made by hand from an old friend. He also had an ultra-light fiberglass canoe and two bright green kayaks.

As for Serena, she lived with her daughter in a two-bedroom condo she had purchased close to her medical practice. She specialized in helping women with their problems, and got a great deal of satisfaction from the kind words she received from so many of them. She didn't mind the long hours and the dedication that was required. To her, it was all part of her important lifelong mission to do good for others. Her home was near to a private school for Sydney and a great mix of stores so mother and daughter could go shopping together—a favorite pastime of theirs. Her proximity to so many things she wanted access to in her life eliminated a lot of stress. She needed it to be that way.

Mack brewed a pot of Hawaiian Kona coffee for them after their shower. They sat in the living room to enjoy it and talk.

"So, what's next?" Serena asked.

Mack grimaced. "Well, I have to get hold of Nik Lewis early tomorrow and tell him I'm on the case with M."

"I thought you wanted to stay away from Nik—at least that's what you've always told me," Serena said.

"It's more like he wants to stay away from me—I think. Anyway, in my line of work, it's almost impossible to avoid him, and I'm sure I'd be more successful being on his good side. I've finally decided to make an effort to patch things up—it's about time. Besides, M has been bugging me and I know he's right. After all, it's been over three years now since I got the boot."

Serena offered a nod of approval. "As I've told you, most men will never acknowledge they're wrong. It's one of my tried-and-true proven facts. Once you become an exception and admit you were the guilty one, you'll start to heal."

"The mere thought of confessing that to him drives me nuts!"

"Sure, but get it done face-to-face with Nik, and you'll feel so much better! Anxiety attacks can be dangerous and Alprazolam...um, Xanax, is a powerful and addictive tranquilizer, as you've found out the hard way. I'm pleased you've been able to reduce its use, but you have to get away from it for good, Mack. Research has shown the natural scent of a live jasmine plant can help reduce anxiety, panic attacks, and depression. I'm going to buy you one or two."

"Nice. I'll be sure to think of you every time I look at one and breathe in its scent."

"That's my intention, Mack, and you should be proud of your progress so far. I know you realize it was the alcohol and drugs that led you astray. It wasn't the inner you, so that's all you'd be confessing to Nik. I'm proud of you, but you can't let your guard down. You have to keep fighting the good fight against that deadly combination of drugs and alcohol or it might kill you, and it will definitely kill our relationship. Do you understand what I'm telling you?"

"I do, Serena. Your smile makes the struggle worthwhile though, and I'm certain things will work out better going forward." He gave Serena a big hug and a few kisses. "It's great to get on track again–to have you with me, and to have new goals." Mack added, "The Stewart murder happened last weekend sometime, so I'm late to the horror show. I need to find out if Lewis has anything back from CSI or the ME because my new client, John Whiting, says he's positive it's murder. Lewis has it as murder as well, but I heard that at least one cop claims it's a suicide. I can't go nose-to-nose with Lewis unless I have hard facts to talk to him about. A good start would be to go down to the site of the murder with M and check things out."

"M likes to do that kind of stuff, doesn't he?"

"Yes, he loves it, and that's the main reason why he's so good at it."

Mack had a gulp of coffee, then continued. "I have to tell you, Serena, I think this murder case stinks. Nobody throws a hundred grand at you when they could work with police detectives and get most of the answers they seek for free. It seems Whiting doesn't want to be anywhere near cops. The details are sketchy, but here's what I know–Bill Stewart's car is fine, except for a little blood in the trunk. His personal effects were there–including his wallet with the cash and credit cards still in it, but not his keys. So, no way he died because someone wanted to take those things from him to buy drugs or break into his house. Stewart had lots of money though, so maybe something else was going on that's not jumping out at me."

"Throw the word *money* into the mix and the entire game can change fast," Serena said.

"You're so right—that's what I mean. Whiting told me there was no blood outside the car anywhere. That's why we can't assume how he died just yet. Maybe someone pointed a gun at him and forced him to get into his trunk, then smashed him in the head with something or choked him before slamming the trunk lid. If it was murder, that means he could have been drugged with a needle, put to sleep with ether, or incapacitated in some other way. We're not talking about a bunch of crazy kids wanting to take a joy ride in a very expensive car here. No siree...I believe this was something much more sinister."

"I hate to throw a wrench in the works, Mack, but if you're right and someone murdered him, can we assume it was a professional hit?" Serena asked.

"Maybe. Lewis concluded it was murder right from the get-go with Whiting. This entire case is strange to me though," Mack said, shaking his head.

"Well, as interesting as this conversation is, I have to pick up Syd now." Serena stood up to go, but met Mack's eyes. "I think someone wanted Mr. Stewart dead—very dead, but why? As you said, this wasn't duct tape over his mouth and throw him in the trunk while we go for a joy ride kind of stuff, or an opportunity to hold Bill for ransom. From what you've told me, this looks calculated. There was no blood visible around the car. His wallet with money in it was found on him, but no car keys or gun or other weapon." She paused for a moment then added, "And most importantly, because he was left curled up in his trunk, no one would find him for a while—though the answer to his whereabouts would be right there under everyone's nose smelling up the rear end of his expensive car. Why?"

"Serena, you just laid the whole scenario out correctly—and this whole thing stinks!"

CHAPTER 6

Monday

MACK GOT TO HIS office regularly by 8:00 a.m.—at least he did when he didn't have a hangover. But this time he wasn't sitting in his office. He was sitting in Lieutenant Detective Nik Lewis's.

"What the hell are you doing in here, Mack? And who the hell let you in?" Lewis was more than annoyed as soon as he saw Mack. "What the hell is going on? If you're here to apply for your old job, you can take that and stick it where the sun don't shine!"

"I'm not here to apply for another job, Nik—I've got a good one. I told the officer at reception I needed to see you on an important matter. She remembered my face as she stared at me through the bulletproof glass, so she buzzed me in. I made sure to give her my best smile."

"I'll be having words with her in a few minutes about your ugly mug and smile!"

"Hey, *please* don't give her a hard time. I'm sorry to surprise you, but I wanted to see you in person—we need to patch things up face-to-face. That's important, isn't it?"

"It appears to be a big deal *to you* after so long, Mack—but as for me, that depends. You should have called to book an appointment. I'm not sure I should even give you the time of day!"

Mack reached into the top pocket of his jacket and pulled out a small envelope, waving it in the air. "This is a peace offering—a white flag. I scored four baseball tickets for the Boston Red Sox versus the Toronto Blue Jays later this month. Are you free? Can you bring your boys?"

"I know damn well what you're doing, you con artist. You're punching far too low below the belt, Mack, offering me tickets like those. You're a sneaky son-of-a-bitch... Aah, you must want something? Yeah, I'm right, I know it! If it's not your old job, what is it?"

"Well, apart from making amends and patching up our friendship, I'm here to tell you John Whiting hired me. That's the whole deal."

"No, that's not all, Mack. I know you too damn well—deep down you're nothing more than a sneaky lawyer. There has to be more, so what is it?"

"Well, to be honest, Nik, I would like to know more about the Stewart murder. Whiting wants answers and is paying me well to find them."

"That would take some time, which I'm not giving you right now. You can't come in here and just assume you can totally disrupt my morning!"

Mack ignored his concern. "Whiting told me he's no fan of the police. I wish I was on this thing a few days sooner, but it is what it is. Any thoughts you want to share with me—please?"

"You never quit, do you? I always use my common sense on a case—something you had a severe shortage of when you worked here. According to my sources, Stewart liked to throw bundles of cash around, gamble big-time, and live the high life. The recipients of his gambling losses and rampant spending wanted to protect their golden child, so why would they kill him? And if this was about a woman and revenge, the antagonist would just come walking right up and start a fight or fire a few rounds—boom, done! We wouldn't have found Stewart in his trunk like we did, so that's why I'm holding back from saying too much, until I'm certain I know what I'm talking about."

"Have you changed your mind about what you figure happened to Stewart?"

Lewis shrugged. "Gotta go where the facts lead—and now they're telling us Stewart's death was no accident or impulsive act—it was a premeditated murder by a pro." He paused as if weighing how much to tell Mack. "For a brief moment I actually thought Stewart might have committed suicide. I can't believe I'm sharing that with you, but I always have to consider all the options right from the start. Anyway, there was no video on the lot where Stewart's Bentley was—that was a surprise and big disappointment. No fingerprints anywhere. There was only a small bit of blood inside the trunk. Stewart never even got into his car to drive it away, according to his investigators. More importantly, the killer didn't either. We found no DNA, no hair or cloth fibers other than Stewart's. Our CSI people were frustrated as hell."

Mack nodded his gratitude. "Nik, if it would help, Whiting talked about Stewart and their business relationship. If you want any of that, let me know."

"Hold on to it for the time being—right now, I'm up to my ass in other pressing case files. Your little stunt to surprise me this morning isn't helping!"

"Too bad things haven't eased off for you around here."

"It's the nature of the job, but having to fire your ass didn't help either—even with the frequent stress headaches you gave me! I thought I'd never get caught up after that because I couldn't hire a replacement given the budgetary cutbacks at the time. I shouldn't tell you this, but you did some impressive work in the few short years you warmed a chair in this building."

Mack took a deep breath. "Nik, I screwed up bad and I'm sorry for that. I liked working with you and learned a lot. I know I owe you big-time for all the grief I caused, and I'll make it up to you somehow."

Nik grunted. "You can't go back and fix it all, Mack—you can't. Keep working hard at improving yourself and move forward—that's what you gotta do."

"That's what Serena says too."

"I'm impressed with her already, and I haven't even met her! Drakowski told me he heard from M that you're dating an attractive doctor. You're a lucky man. Count your blessings she's still in your life. It's good you're trying to get back in the game—I'll give you that much. Serena may be a forgiving person, but I hope you know you won't get many chances at redemption from me. I told you I run a tight ship when I fired you, so I've got no time or patience for screwups—none."

"I understand, Nik. You've got a lot of people depending on you and a lot of stress to deal with constantly."

"Tell you what. I'll give you another shot now that you're a PI. But you have to play it straight, understand? If you take more of that Xanax crap you were on before, you better keep your ass a million miles away! And don't come traipsing in here again without my permission, or I'll have you shot!"

"Serena told me it's a long hard road to a full recovery; she's a doctor—so she should know. I'm being honest with you when I say I'm finally off the stuff, but it was a long hard road to travel."

"Well, keep going, Mack. I'm pulling for you just like Serena and M. But don't you dare come near me or my cases unless you're straight—I warn you."

"Thanks, Nik. Message received. So, are there any specifics

on Stewart's cause of death you have for me?"

"Boy, you've got big balls—I'll give you that. I should have thrown your ass out when I first saw you in here. You don't know how to stop, do you?"

"Nik, c'mon. Help me out here."

"You don't quit, do you? Come to think of it, that's the trait about you I liked best. Okay. The Medical Examiner says there was a single severe blow to the base of the victim's skull. Most likely a hammer; the strike zone on Stewart matched exactly. The ME said the brain stem looked like mashed potatoes, complete mush, so he was brain-dead right after he got smacked."

"I won't be eating any mashed potatoes for a while."

"We figure that immediately after he whacked Stewart with the hammer, the assailant put him in the trunk. Whoever murdered him figured the police would stop looking beyond finding his body, but they didn't. The angle of the hammer blow and the force of it looked to the ME like the killer was a lefty—and strong. Chances are Stewart was near the back of his car when the guy smacked him. His knees and pants showed he went straight down, so he probably dropped his keys right there. It wouldn't be too difficult for the killer to pick them up, open the trunk, and roll Stewart in."

"Were any keys found, Nik?"

"No, and it pissed me off. We thought they'd be in the trunk, but they weren't."

"Whiting said you told him there might be video covering the Tartan's entry and interior. Did you see any of that?"

"Sure, but the quality is lousy and the security system is an antique. The current pub owner figures no one had security cameras during the Civil War and the Tartan pub survived until now, so what's the need?"

"I hate when I hear crap like that," Mack said. "It would be a big help if we had better video right now."

"One of my team did spot something suspicious while going through the security footage shot last Friday night when Bill Stewart was in the place," Lewis said.

"Suspicious how?"

"There was a guy sitting alone on a bar stool, staring at the mirror behind the bar for a long while. That might not be so unusual until someone is murdered at about the same time. The guy was tall and skinny, and wore a ball cap with a long leather jacket. That made the ID job with the old cameras and crappy clarity even tougher because they couldn't make out any fine detail." Lewis snorted in frustration. "Seems they never clean the camera lens. The video looks like it still had haze on it from ten years back—maybe longer."

"I don't like it, Nik—none of it. This case gets tougher by the minute."

"The guy might have been watching a hot female—the spider waiting for the fly. But right when we see Stewart leaving the bar, this guy drops a fistful of cash on the counter and leaves at the same time without asking for his tab. We're still trying to get a make on him. We've been asking the Tartan staff if anyone had seen him in there before, or knows who the hell he is."

"I need to get on this fast, so I'll take M down there and check things out. I plan to interview Stewart's wife, Maggie, soon too. You talked to her yet?"

"Yeah, but I didn't get much. It's always tough with a new widow or widower. I spoke with her and was careful with my words, but only to tell her how and where her husband died. You know that's one of the worst things I have to do. She didn't want to be questioned right then, and I can't blame her. I tried briefing her on what our process is, but she wasn't of a mind to listen."

"That's understandable. It's impossible to predict how someone in a lot of pain will react to a police officer delivering such terrible news. You know that much better than I do."

"Well, I plan to talk to her again. Anyway, Mack, when you get to the Tartan—and I know it's been over a week since Stewart's death—you'll still see traffic cones and police tape where his Bentley was. We want to keep curious people out of there until we've pieced together the loose ends. I can't help but think there's something we've missed—like those damn keys."

"I should get going, Nik. Thanks for your time. You didn't have to be decent to me, but you were. Please be sure to say hi to your wife and those two up-and-coming ball players of yours. Oh, and before I forget, I'll pick you up at your place on game day at noon. That'll give us enough time to get to Fenway—the first pitch is at one o'clock."

"Sure. The boys will go nuts when I tell them we're going to a ball game. If it's a sport with a ball, they'll love it. Thanks, Mack, I'm sure it will make their day. Oh, and make sure you say hello to M and Pauline for me—and I'd like to meet Serena sometime too. As for the Stewart matter, let's get together over a coffee at Benny's. We'll do that when the smoke clears and we have time to talk—just be sure to remember my rules." Lewis paused. "One more thing, Mack—welcome back!"

× × ×

THE TARTAN HOUSE OPENED AT 11:00 in the morning, Monday through Saturday. The place was always ready to jump into action for the downtown lunch crowd, and then get prepared for more leisurely drinking and snacking after that. The carpets were rolled up at midnight, and the place was closed on Sundays.

Mack and M showed up at 11:45 a.m., then sat at the bar and ordered two club sandwich platters and a pitcher of cold draft beer. Once the place got lively, Mack checked out the other patrons at the tables and booths. By watching the mirror behind the bar, he realized the killer could have seen almost everything that went on in there that fateful Friday night.

"The chow's tasty and fresh, with large portions, and the beer is cheap," he told M. "I can see why this place is still popular and has survived for well over a hundred and fifty years. Who the hell knows when they installed the security cameras though?"

"Wouldn't be under the original staff, but one or two of them look like they've been here for a while," M said, nodding toward a waiter who looked old enough to be his grandfather.

Mack laughed and paid for their meals. Then he asked M to go out the door of the tavern and walk toward where Stewart's car had been parked on Friday night.

"I'll follow you out, but imagine you're Bill Stewart for a few minutes. You've had a few beers so you're groggy, maybe even a little tipsy, and you're searching for your keys while getting ready to open your car. There were traffic sounds in the distance like now, and probably other sounds and movements close around you."

"Okay, so if I hear something or see someone behind me, it's no big deal."

"That's what I'm saying. If you hear someone behind you like Stewart might have, you'd figure they're going to their car like you are and dismiss it."

M walked out, and a few seconds later Mack followed. As M walked toward the parking spot where Stewart's car had been, Mack was right up behind him in a few quick strides. They paused just before the police tape that still marked off the actual site.

"You see how fast I came up behind you?" Mack asked. "I'm sure Stewart was focused on finding his car keys and not on much else. He reaches the back of his car, pulls the keys out of his pocket, and *wham*. Someone hit him in the back of the head, likely with a hammer held in the killer's left hand." Mack mimed the blow. "Okay, now you fall down on your knees."

"Man, the weird and wonderful things I get to do in the pursuit of justice," M said, frowning. "I sure hope no one sees me because this is going to look weird. Do I get to put a new pair of pants on my expense account?"

"What expense account?" Mack grinned.

"Hey, if you don't ask, you don't get—remember?"

"Yeah—nice try. Anyway, imagine you're Stewart and you're right-handed. That means you fall hard on your knees after being hit by the hammer. Here, use my keys for the sake of this scenario. The ME said the blow would virtually have killed Stewart: no blood or brain matter was found outside of the car, so the skull must have been crushed inward and any splatter would have landed on the killer. So, you're on your knees, but you're out like a light."

Mack waited until M reluctantly got on his knees. "I'm the killer, and I've dropped the hammer on the pavement, so I have my left hand free. That's how I steady the victim on his knees—I hold his collar with my dominant left just like I'm doing now with you. I sweep up Stewart's keys with my right hand and open the trunk by pushing a button on the fob. Stewart was six feet tall, and my research told me the lip of the trunk on the Bentley is low, so I pull his arms and the top of his body into the left side of the trunk to take some of the weight. Then I grab him by his belt and lift while pushing the rest of him with my right knee. Awkward for sure, but doable. I push, shove, and roll him until he's lying in a fetal position on his left side—his crushed skull against the floor of the trunk. The murder sequence would only take a few seconds for a strong man."

"Okay, so can I get up off my knees now, huh?"

"Sure." Mack extended a hand to help M up off the ground. "Anyway, I've finished with Stewart, so my first priority is to get the hell out of here fast because my target is dead. Assuming I'm a pro on a contract, I likely got half my cash up front, so the next thing I gotta do is collect the rest from the person or persons who still owe me."

"I'm with you so far," said M.

"I see two alternatives here. Either the killer wants the scene to look like a suicide, in which case he realizes he screwed up—the car keys need to be in the trunk with the body. Or he plans to drive Stewart's car somewhere else and dump it or cut it up. Either way, he needs those damn keys. So, I ask you—why didn't he take Stewart's car if that's what he planned to do? He should have been able to do that with just the touch of a button on the fob."

"Because he had his own car nearby?" M suggested. "Or, for whatever reason, Stewart's car couldn't be unlocked with his keys. Maybe the remote on the fob didn't work or needed a PIN number. Or what if he dropped the keys and couldn't find them?"

"The killer stood right behind the trunk, didn't he? He might have dropped the keys on the ground to wrestle Stewart into the trunk. After closing the trunk, he might have reached down quickly to grab the keys with a gloved hand, but maybe his judgment is slightly off given the poor lighting. He's also in a rush to get the hell outta here, so maybe he even takes a kick at them to get them in better light so he can see them. His attempt may have failed, so at that point he decides to just take off before someone sees him."

"You're making sense, M. Hey, look over there—it's hard to notice, but there's a small storm drain."

To the left of the parking spot and in line with the driver's side rear wheel was a small rainwater drainage grate set into the pavement at about five or six feet from the car.

"You don't notice it because it blends into the pavement," Mack said. "As thorough as the police were, they might have missed it. You don't think—? I'll get a flashlight," he said, feeling a jolt of excitement. "We should look inside that grate. It might be a waste of time, but the steel hatching is spaced wide enough that a set of keys could have fallen in there."

Moments later, after letting Woof out of the SUV, they were on their hands and knees with a powerful beam of light focused through the grate. Woof sniffed everything, inquisitive as always.

"There's something shiny down there, M! Could be it's a broken piece of glass or something. There's a safety catch basin under this grate and there are a couple of things lying on it covered with grime. Go into the Tart and ask for a wire hanger."

Just then, Woof gave M a big lick on the side of his face.

"Ah yuck, Woof. Leave me alone, will you? Mack, your freakin' dog just slimed me!"

"He thinks you'll find him a treat, so he's being extra chummy...or he wants the rest of the pasta sauce off that pretty face of yours."

"What pasta sauce? Oh, I get it—picking on Italians today, are we? Ha—so funny. I'll be back with a hanger after I wipe your dog's goo off me."

M returned quickly, sporting a wide smile. "Got one. They had a bunch in a back closet."

Mack bent the hanger into a hook and slid it through the grate while M held the flashlight. After a long minute, Mack pulled something up that glistened in the light. With a shared expression of elation and disbelief, they were staring at a muddy gold key ring with what appeared to be car and house keys, and a name etched on it—STEWART.

CHAPTER 7

"I'M EAGER TO HEAR what you and M found out at the Tartan this morning, Mack," Pauline said. "I hope you realize I'm stuck here working like a dog and wondering what's going on while you guys are out in the field breathing fresh air. I'd like to be kept in the loop, please and thank you."

Pauline wore her dark brown hair in a tight bun that made her look stern. Mack knew her plan was to work out in the field with him someday—the sooner the better. But he objected to being pressured.

"Do me a favor and please knock it off, Paul," he said. "Did you get up on the wrong side of the bed this Monday morning? I know you're up to speed on Whiting's stuff because I emailed you my case notes."

Pauline said something under her breath and shook her head.

Mack gave her a kind smile, then went to his office to fetch a few notes and his laptop. In the corner of his office, Woof was sound asleep on his large dog cushion with his paws in the air. Although he was in a hurry, Mack paused and chuckled as he watched Woof breathing—savoring the feeling of peace it gave him. Before heading to the conference room for their first meeting on the Whiting case, he grabbed a cup of coffee, then sat down just as M joined him. Pauline walked in with a fresh bouquet of multicolored carnations and placed it in the center of the table, then sat as well. She knew carnations were Mack's favorite—he loved the spicy scent of them.

"Thanks for the colorful peace offering, Paul; very nice," Mack said, grinning. "Now let's get down to business. Before I call Lewis and tell him what we found at the Tartan, I want to put everything in perspective—figure out where we are and where we're going with this thing."

"A thought just came to me," Pauline piped in. "Maybe we should hold our next meeting in Honolulu." She grinned, then she added, "That'll put things into perspective very nicely. I know Keith will be excited to join us."

Mack and M laughed. Mack said, "Great idea, Paul. We solve this case and you never know; you just might be able to tell that craft beer-maker boyfriend of yours—that we're going! Tell you what—when I plan our schedule each month, I'll keep Hawaii in mind. Who knows? Maybe it'll become a reality. It'll give us something exciting to look forward to."

M leaned back in his chair with a dreamy sigh. "I like that, guys! In my mind, I'm already there. You lucky folks will see me do handstands on a paddleboard. I'll even do them using one hand."

"Show off!" Mack said. "I'm sure you'll do a few stunts on a hang glider too—am I right?"

"That would be the plan!" M said.

"It's fun to speculate, but let's get focused on Stewart so we can actually book that trip," Mack said. He paused, thinking about how he was going to phrase his thoughts. "You know I don't jump to conclusions, especially before I review all the evidence. However, what I believe we've got with the Whiting case is a botched professional hit."

"Really, Mack?" Pauline asked. "Why?"

"M and I played out the events we figure took place in the Tartan parking lot. We concluded the killer must have accidentally dropped or kicked the keys in through a drainage grate where we found them. With the wet leaves and paper in the catch basin, he probably never even heard them go in. Even if he had a flashlight, he wouldn't want to risk someone seeing him searching around Stewart's Bentley. Bad luck for the killer, but a great break for us."

"Why is it a great break for us? I don't understand," Pauline said.

Mack leaned back in his chair. "The original plan was likely to have Stewart murdered and make it look like a suicide. It may have been important to whomever paid for the hit that he be found quickly. But the killer probably was tempted by that expensive car and got greedy. He may have figured he'd throw it into the deal for himself. If he disposed of Stewart's body where it would be found easily, the police would know it was murder and that would trigger a massive investigation. For the person who wanted him dead, he was dead. No way he would want the risk of a big investigation. If the new Bentley disappeared, the police would assume there had been a carjacking and think the expensive British Beauty was in parts already, or on a cargo ship headed for some distant shore. It would have been a huge bonus for the killer—until he couldn't find the keys! But he couldn't spend time looking around for them; he needed to get the hell out of there."

"You see, Paul, it's a great break for us because now we have both the car and Stewart's body," M said.

Mack added, "And I'm sure it was a pro who did this evil deed given the skill the killer used. He's probably done this kind of thing before—maybe a few times."

"Yeah, but Mr. Slick must have started sweating and swearing as soon as he dropped those keys," M said. "He screwed himself big-time!"

"You're right," Mack said. "So, he wasn't so slick after all. Even a hardened killer would have a tough time getting a good night's sleep after losing those keys the way he did."

× × ×

MACK WANTED TO REST on this cool Monday night, and planned to watch football to keep his mind off his troubles. That meant he had to take Woof for a run at 7:00 p.m. instead of his usual 8:00 p.m. outing. He never ran with Woof on a leash anymore. He liked to give his buddy the freedom to stop and sniff anything he wanted along the route.

The sky was cloudy and gray with a temperature in the mid-sixties. Mack didn't wear the skintight runner's garb avid runners often wear. He preferred to keep it simple: a white T-shirt with silver-gray and navy-blue shorts—the colors of his favorite NFL football team—the New England Patriots. He always wore high-quality runners and never scrimped on footwear because, as a big man, he had to protect his feet against heavy pounding.

After running with Woof for a quarter of an hour, Mack experienced a peculiar feeling—kind of unnerving—as if he was being watched. He couldn't put a finger on anything specific, but he had learned from Nik Lewis to trust his instincts. Nik believed if something in your gut was telling you something was wrong, it probably was. Trusting that mysterious sixth sense had saved his life several times.

Mack began to pay more attention to everything around him as he ran along his usual route. There! He noticed it again—an older black pickup truck in his peripheral vision. So...it wasn't just his imagination! As he rounded the end of Checkerboard Park, a long narrow park shaped like a giant hockey rink where old men sat and played checkers, his angle of view changed. He was certain he had spotted the same pickup in two or three other locations. It continued moving and seemed to be following him.

As he watched, he saw the same vehicle again! He decided he needed to vary his route—to make him less predictable and vulnerable. He also made a mental note to call M about this experience so they could devise a plan to protect him—find out who was following him. Mack figured he may want to run the same route again to set a trap for the mysterious driver. He had learned long ago that being the bait in any plan could be nerve-racking and dangerous. Mack was hard to scare, but he liked to be prepared as he had learned in the Boy Scouts while growing up. It was much better to be safe than sorry.

× × ×

WHEN MACK ARRIVED BACK at home, he checked to see if that same suspicious pickup truck was nearby, but it had disappeared. He checked his security system, then had a quick shower. After putting on a clean T-shirt and comfortable old pants, he cracked a cold one. He also put water out for Woof, then sat in his favorite recliner in the den and called Serena.

"How was your day, sweetheart?" Mack asked, while sipping his beer.

"As usual, Mack, it was so exciting," Serena said, snickering. "I checked on the progress of toenail fungus for two older women; tried to talk some sense into a couple of teenage girls and handed out condoms and birth control prescriptions in an effort to help them; and dispensed my sage advice to the rest of my patients. The good news? Today's crowd will live to see another day."

Mack wanted to confide in her about his case, but the fact someone had just followed him was something he didn't think he should share with her. Doubtless she'd be afraid for him, and then for herself and Sydney.

"We're getting deeper into this case, and there's a lot of interesting scenarios to consider given the facts we've found," he told her. "Now I have to work at it like Sherlock Holmes—through a magnifying glass to sort out the tiny clues while smoking a pipe and wearing a deerstalker hat, of course." Serena broke into giggles at the imaginary picture she had of Mack looking like Sherlock Holmes.

"Serena, I'm sorry I can't talk longer. I have to set something up with M for tomorrow, so I'm going to say goodnight."

"No problem," Serena said, but she paused for a moment and then asked, "Mack, you seem tense—is everything okay?"

"Yes, I'm just getting tired as the wheels turn on this case. Have a good sleep."

"You too." He heard a kiss in his ear, and then she hung up.

He got himself another beer, peered out the window looking for anything unusual, then sat and dialed M. He picked up on the first ring.

"Hey, Mack, what's up? We just spoke a few hours ago."

"A little challenge."

"What happened?"

"Woof and I were out for a run when it felt like someone was following me. I saw the same black pickup too many times for it to be a coincidence. I doubt it was someone sizing me up for their Boston Marathon running team. When I got home, I checked to be sure my security system was on and my pistol was loaded. I've been looking out the window for anything unusual ever since."

"Could you see who was driving the truck?" M asked.

"No, it was that creepy feeling you get when you're being watched from a distance—a sixth sense kind of thing. The truck kept a steady pace behind me. I need you to help me get a handle on this. The new case is the only one that's active. If Whiting's been going around telling everyone he hired us, then Stewart's killer may have gotten wind of it and started stalking me."

"Okay, we'll meet first thing tomorrow and plan a strategy." M spoke in such a way that Mack knew he was already making plans. "Mack, we'll be proactive so don't worry—I know you're not the type to react without a good reason. In the meantime, stay safe."

Mack peered out the window once more before heading to the fridge for another beer. *Piss on it,* he thought, *it's just beer, not bourbon.*

× × ×

Tuesday

MACK, M, AND PAULINE were in Mack's office first thing while having another team discussion, this time about how to stop the stalker who had followed Mack the previous night.

"I've decided I want you to get photos of the guy in the black pickup with our office camera," Mack told M. "We'll also need at least one clear shot of the license plate and two of the entire truck in case the plate's a phony. I'll run the same route tonight. It'll be tricky to take photos and stay out of sight, but you know what we need."

Mack took a big gulp of his strong coffee and added, "I should call Lewis and give him an update on finding Stewart's keys. I'll have to turn them in. I need to tell him about this stalker too, but I can hear the wisecracks now—private eye tracks villain while villain tracks private eye."

"It'll be hard to show your face downtown after that," M agreed.

"Never mind that!" Pauline said. "Be serious! This crazy idiot could take a potshot at you!"

"Good point, Paul, and I appreciate your concern, but I've

done a lot of shooting over many years. You'd be damn lucky to hit me from the window of a moving truck using a handgun while I'm running. If you were up beside me as I ran by, that's different. It all depends on the skill of the shooter—but even then, the guy would be lucky to wing me. I wouldn't want to give you odds on it though, that's for sure."

"You don't want to find out, Mack," Pauline said. "Ever!"

"That's not a chance I'd consider taking either," M said.

"Hear me out, guys. I'll run the same route I did last time. I hope my stalker shows up again so M can shoot him—with our camera. And M, I'm sure you'd love to show off your talent with a handgun or other firearm, but set those thoughts aside. We just want to ID the guy and find out who hired him. Oh, and I don't want to call Whiting yet because I may want to plant some disinformation with him first."

"What do you mean?" Pauline asked.

"My best guess is Whiting told a few people he hired us to investigate Stewart's death. It's also my guess the killer—our very own Mr. Slick, as M calls him, heard about this. If that's true, he may be the one stalking me. Maybe he thinks if he takes me out of the equation, he'd have a much better chance of getting a good night's sleep. One option is to sneak up and surprise me from behind when I'm stationary—like he probably did to Stewart. That's assuming he's our murderer."

"You'd better stay alert and keep your eyes open," M said.

CHAPTER 8

MACK SAT WITH NIK Lewis in his office at Boston Homicide Division Headquarters. They were waiting for Detective Steve Drakowski to join them. Lewis had assigned Drakowski to assist on Stewart's murder case, and Lewis wanted him to sit in on everything Mack had to say. Soon Steve walked in.

"Hey there, Mack, how's the Harvard lawyer turned detective turned private eye doing?" Steve gave Mack a thumbs-up sign rather than shaking hands. He had a round, friendly clean-shaven face and wore a long-sleeved white shirt with a dark tie, black slacks, and black shoes. Lewis's clothes looked the same, except he wore a shoulder holster for his gun, while Drakowski kept his behind his right hip. Both men wore their badges on their belts.

"Hey, Steve, the man of many talents is doing fine," Mack said, greeting him with a big smile. "Thanks for asking. I wanted a face-to-face huddle because I came to give you an important update. I've got lots to tell you, but also want to hear what's happening on your end of the field."

Mack reached into his left jacket pocket, pulled out a plastic ziplock bag, and placed it on the desk. "And as you can see, I came bearing a gift for Boston's finest—the keys to Bill

Stewart's British Beauty. There's a grate in the pavement not too far from where the driver's side rear tire of Stewart's car was. Below that grate is a catch basin, and the keys were sitting on it covered with leaves. It was tough spotting them and even tougher removing them, but it's amazing what you can do with a wire coat hanger."

"But we examined that site with a magnifying glass—we checked every square inch," Drakowski said, sounding frustrated.

"I think it was a fluke we found them," Mack said. He wanted to make them feel better about the oversight and suspected Lewis realized that. "It doesn't matter who found his keys, Steve. We're working as a team here. The fact they were down that drain may help to confirm your feelings this was a pro hit, Nik. I figure it was an accident they fell in there. If the killer could have driven the Bentley away, it would be cut up in pieces by now or on a boat headed for South America. And who knows where or when Stewart's body would have shown up. As it is, we got damn lucky."

"Funny kind of luck," Lewis said. "But we're working it. And there's lots to do. We'll be looking into the insurance Stewart carried and we'll want a peek at his will too if he's got one. I also want to know if his company had a partnership policy on him. One never knows what one may find. The big question is—who wanted Bill Stewart dead?"

"Somebody had a motive for killing Stewart. There may even be several people involved," Drakowski stated.

"Mack, you got hired by Whiting last Saturday, am I right? Have you spoken with him since?" Lewis asked.

"No, I haven't. But right at the end of our meeting he dropped a bombshell on us. He said he and Stewart had received a recent anonymous offer to buy their company. That offer is still active and on the table."

"How big was the offer, Mack?" Lewis asked.

"Fifty-five million," Mack said. "I didn't get details at the time because he said the offer was confidential and it was obvious Whiting didn't want to say more. But we're talking huge money and murder in the same sentence. I want to dig into that issue much deeper, and soon."

"All that money could be one hell of a motive for murder," Lewis said.

"These guys had almost equal amounts of shares in their company. There are no other owners," Mack added.

"What about Stewart's wife?" Drakowski asked. "Had any words with her yet, Nik?"

"Very few. Maybe she'll be able to get some of the grieving behind her so things can be a bit better when I call her again later. For what it's worth, Whiting seems to care about her."

"Any chance Mr. Whiting has got his hands in this killing somewhere, Mack?" Lewis asked.

Mack shrugged. "Then why would he hire us? He's been told we're good investigators, so it makes no sense...unless he heard about my problem with booze and figured we'd probably fail because of that. He seemed genuinely broken up while talking to us at our first meeting, so he deserves the Academy Award if he had a hand in Stewart's death. If I'm wrong, I've been a chump. M and I would have to throw in the towel and sell the bat cave along with every one of our fabulous bat toys."

"Well, I had to ask," Lewis insisted while laughing.

"Sure, fair enough," Mack said, joining in. Then he grew serious.

"Guys, last night when I was out for a run with my dog, someone tailed me in an older black Ford F-150. It had tinted side windows and a bull bar on the front."

"A what?" Drakowski asked.

"It's what my dad used to call a pipe bumper. Farmers call them cow catchers and hunters call them deer guards."

"Okay—got it," Drakowski nodded.

"Anyway, the guy driving the pickup kept his distance, and I gave him no reason to think I spotted him. I'm sure it was a tail, so I need to find out who the driver was and what he wanted. I plan to run the same route tonight, but have M out there with our camera just in case he returns."

"Need any help?" Lewis offered.

"Thanks, but the two of us should be able to handle this—I want to keep it low-key. I want photos of the driver, but they may be hard to get due to the window tinting. We'll try for some of the entire truck and the plates as well. I'm eager to see what they'll tell us, and you'll be the first ones to see them."

"Mack, be careful. We don't want to see you laid out on a cold slab like Stewart," Drakowski said.

"And for heaven's sake, Mack," Lewis added with his commanding deep voice, "we don't need an ex-lawyer ex-cop private eye like you shooting up our city streets!"

"That was a mouthful, Nik," Mack said, grinning.

"I mean it. I don't want you to start a new exercise craze in Boston called *jogging with a gun*. We've got enough trigger-happy and explosive-fixated crazies out there."

"The only shooting will be with our trusty camera," Mack assured him. "That's scout's honor, buddy."

× × ×

WHILE OUT ON HIS next run, Mack wanted to be sure M had two separate chances to shoot pictures of the driver—just in case. He felt certain tonight would be the night. One problem they were facing, however, was that M would be trying to get the badly needed photos while standing in one spot. Mack planned to run faster than before, knowing the black pickup would follow him. M was an expert with almost everything he touched, but could he use their professional grade camera well enough under such conditions?

The two-chance problem had Mack stumped for a few minutes. Then it occurred to him that he ran around Checkerboard Park as part of his route—a long narrow park that featured lofty shade trees and flower gardens. There were numerous large bushes and shrubs and lots of picnic tables and park benches. A four-foot high wrought-iron fence surrounded the park with an entrance in the center of each long straight side. Mack and M were standing at the park entrance on the long side that Mack would run by first.

"Right here is where I want you to be when I run past. You'll be able to hide from view in the shrubbery as the pickup comes toward you. Work your magic with the camera here at position one. After that, hightail it straight across to the other side entrance over there. I'll run along that side soon after, so you should have enough time to get your butt over there."

"Cool plan, Mack—it should work. I was wondering how I'd run after you with the guy tailing you, and take more pictures all at the same time. This plan is simple but doable."

× × ×

MACK WAS AT HOME putting on a black T-shirt and gray running shorts when his cell phone rang—it was M checking in. It was 6:20 p.m., and M was standing ready with the camera by the first park entrance.

Mack didn't want to keep M waiting too long, so he put on his runners. Woof knew the signs of another run with his master, so jumped in little hops with his front legs, his big paws bouncing on the floor. Mack had just finished tying up the second shoelace when his cell phone rang again.

He decided not to take the call, but it was tough. The caller ID told him it was Serena, and he imagined she was calling to tell him not to go out on his run. The phone reached out to him with each ring. He struggled to avoid answering it until the last of the imploring rings ceased. He felt bad he hadn't answered, but had to get going. *Sometimes a man's gotta do what a man's gotta do,* he thought.

As he left his place, he could see stragglers coming home late from work. The evening was cool and overcast, with a slight breeze. As usual, Woof stopped to get sniffs of many things he encountered. Each time he did, it took him a few seconds to catch up to Mack again as they ran. They weren't long into the run when Mack got that strange, eerie feeling again. He realized he had left his cell phone at home because his mind had been on avoiding Serena's call, not on the need for it during his run. Dumb mistake.

Attentive to everything around him, he spotted the black pickup pacing him like last time. It wasn't long before Mack could see Checkerboard Park coming into view. Few people were on the streets and the sky was darker now, threatening to rain. The pickup continued to follow Mack; this time much closer. It traveled along the side of the park fence for a few seconds as Mack headed toward M, who was standing by the first side entrance. That's when he heard the loud roar of the truck engine as it sped up, followed by a *thump thump* sound. Looking back over his shoulder, Mack could see the truck up on the sidewalk speeding toward him, and no Woof! In a split second, the roaring engine closed the gap between him and the front of the truck!

Mack dove over the arrowhead points along the top of the four-foot wrought-iron fence. He cleared them as he tucked and rolled. Loud crashing and screeching sounds filled the air as metal scraped metal along the length of the fence behind him. He realized if he had waited a second longer, he'd be dead.

Mack's first commandment as a private investigator was, *'Never let them scare you.'* Well, forget that. He was terrified.

The incident could have been deadly, and he blamed himself for misjudging the murderous intentions of the pickup driver. He lay on his back on the cool grass, listening to the roaring engine of the pickup as it raced away. Woof! Where was Woof?

Reality hit him as he struggled to sit up with his chest heaving. He had jumped over an entire section of wrought-iron fence smashed down by a pickup truck driver who aimed to kill him. A large portion of the fence lay on the ground nearby. He had almost jumped head-on into a big tree, and had narrowly avoided goring himself on the pointed wrought-iron fence toppers. The next thing Mack knew, a big warm dog tongue was licking his face. "Oh, Woof! Am I ever glad to see you, pal!" He wrapped his arms around his dog's neck and gave him a big hug.

"I'm glad to see you too, but I'm not getting down there to lick your sweaty face, buddy," M said, with a relieved chuckle.

"I feel as if someone tackled me in the end zone after a full speed run down the field. One little problem—no one gave me any equipment to wear before the game. I'll be sore in a bunch of places after this, never mind the dirt, scrapes, and skid marks on me. Nothing feels broken, though."

"Alive and in one piece is good. Here man, give me your hand—it's much better being helped up by one, than being carried in a long wooden box by six."

"You sure got that right. Runners often say: *Don't look back because you might see someone gaining on you.* This time, thank heaven I did!" Mack took a few more deep breaths, then said, "Please tell me you got good pictures of what happened. Please tell me that."

"I only had one chance at this maniac as he sped by. I snapped as many shots of that slimy bastard as I could, so we'll see what Lady Luck gives us."

"While I catch my breath, let's walk over to that picnic table yonder and have a quick look at the photos." Mack hobbled over to the picnic table as Woof followed, wagging his tail.

Two onlookers who had heard the loud crashing and scraping sounds came over to offer their help. Mack assured them he'd report the incident, so they need not bother to call 911. He asked M for his cell phone and called Lewis's office. It was already 7:00 p.m., and Lewis had left for the day. He spoke to another detective after a short wait and described the incident. He asked to have a police car sent to the scene, saying he'd fill out a full report.

"Please ask Lieutenant Detective Lewis to call me as soon as he can. It's important he knows what just happened at Checkerboard Park. Thanks, and out."

M sat with Mack at the picnic table for a moment, and then M turned on the camera. They both watched the bright screen on the back as M searched through the photos. He had succeeded in taking several good shots of the entire front of the vehicle. When he enlarged two of them, they could see the driver wore a ball cap that partially shaded a thin hawkish face. But the eyes were visible, staring back at them with black pupils set in deep, dark, hollow sockets.

"Great shots, M! That could be Stewart's killer right there! Look at that demented piece of shit! He looks as if he slithered out of a horror movie."

"No one wants to face a creep like *that* in a dark alley," M said. "Not even me."

After a deep breath, Mack snickered. "He'll piss himself when he finds out we have these detailed shots of his ugly mug. One problem, M, there's no license plate on the front of the truck, so do you have any good shots of the back? *Please* tell me you do—"

"I kept shooting like a fiend. Keep your fingers crossed and we'll have a look!"

Several of the shots were blurry as the truck crashed and

screeched by. At the end of the series of shots, one photo displayed a bright image of the license plate. It was a good one—the only one they needed. Even though it looked as if the back plate had been intentionally obscured by dirt, they could make out the Massachusetts license number. No way the naked eye could ever have caught it without a good camera to freeze the movement.

"We're in business, buddy!" Mack said, as he slapped M on the back. "Fantastic!"

"At least we've got what we need! But I'm emailing these photos to our office computers as backup."

"Super job well done, M. You don't know it, but you're a few hundred miles closer to Hawaii right this minute!"

Mack began to laugh, but it wasn't because of his comment to M. It was elation and relief that he and Woof were unharmed.

CHAPTER 9

MACK RETURNED HOME EXHAUSTED but safe. The police had arrived at Checkerboard Park to see the mess the black pickup had made in that perilous instant when Mack could have died. They took statements from Mack, M, and the two other witnesses who had offered their help. Mack handed over their camera with explicit instructions on how it should be handled. He considered the entire camera and its digital images important evidence not to be tampered with. He shuddered to think the photos on it could have recorded his death.

The Stewart murder had occurred just a week and a half before this attack. He cautioned the police officers that the photos could be evidence in both the Stewart case and for his own attempted-murder. He insisted the camera go straight to Lieutenant Detective Nik Lewis or Detective Steve Drakowski in Boston's Homicide Unit—no one else.

When Mack arrived home, he wanted to call Serena and update her, but didn't want to upset her. He knew it was best to calm down, count slowly to at least one hundred, and get his ducks in a nice straight row. After feeding and watering Woof, he didn't feel like eating because he was sure a mild case of shock had set in. Cold and shivering, he put on a thick hoodie, made a cup of hot chocolate, and decided he'd tell Serena the whole truth and nothing but the truth. His face brightened with a smile as he placed the call.

"Your number appeared on my cell phone as I was leaving for my run," Mack said. "I was in too much of a hurry to answer. I feel I owe you a big apology."

"I was going to beg you not to go, Mack."

"It all worked out fine, so try not to worry. M was lucky enough to get good photos so the police can ID the truck and driver we're interested in. Serena, I'm sure it was the same old black truck and driver that I saw watching me the last time I went out for a run—the one I suspected at that time was planning something bad, but I had no idea what it was. Good thing I made the decision to include M this time, along with our trusty office camera."

"Were you or M hurt?"

"Um...no—shaken up, though. We're both fine and Woof is too, thank goodness. After the guy drove off, I called the police. We gave them our camera with the precious photos M took. I'm sure they will compare our photos to the video of the mysterious stranger in the Tartan pub. We suspect he's the same guy who followed Stewart outside the night he was murdered. If they're the same person, we could be on our way to solving the case."

"I hope it works out for you—I shouldn't keep you on the phone," Serena said. "Besides, Syd has to get to bed; it's way past her bedtime. Be sure to call me tomorrow and tell me how you're doing. Good night, my brave soulmate." There was a pause, and then she said seductively, "I wish I could be there to tuck...you...in. Sweet dreams."

All Mack could say as he hung up was, "Oh, baby."

× × ×

Wednesday

"JOHN WHITING CALLED A few minutes ago for an update on his case," Pauline said, as Mack walked by her desk headed for his office. It was a cool sunny morning, so Mack was wearing a green tartan flannel shirt and jeans.

"I don't want to talk to Whiting right now...but I guess I should. Mum's the word on most of the stuff we've found out so far, but I'll come up with something to tell him. Paul, that guy who followed me in the black F-150 the night before last—remember him?"

"How could I forget?"

Mack then described the previous night's incident, saying he was lucky to be alive.

"I want you to tell me you're okay. Are you?"

"Yes, I am, Paul. I don't feel good enough to wear a tie, though," he said with a smirk. Then he tried to change the subject.

Pauline knew Mack and M never wore ties. "Oh, Mack, for the life of me, I can't decide what silk tie might go best with that oh-so-sexy tartan flannel shirt you're wearing this morning," Pauline said in a high voice, obviously trying to cheer him up.

Mack laughed out loud at her playfulness.

"When I looked in the mirror this morning, I decided there was no tie in the universe that could match this shirt," he said. "Then I thought, oh what the hell...something strange happens to me when I put on a tie anyway. I figured it must cut off oxygen to my brain. After that, I'd be finished for the day, so that's why I didn't wear one."

"Keith often wears ties. That probably explains why he acts so dumb sometimes," Pauline said, chuckling.

"Who? Keith, the luckiest guy in the world—that Keith? Not only does he have you for a companion, but he's part-owner and sales manager of a growing microbrewery. Why would he even consider wearing a tie? Beer guys don't wear ties, do they? Since when? They wear big promo buttons with sayings like, *Drink More Beer!* and fun stuff like that."

"Well, he's both marketing and sales," Pauline replied, "and he calls his company a *craft brewery.* It's the term he prefers. He feels he has to wear a tie when he's out on the road promoting products because he thinks it makes him look more professional."

"Ah, poor guy–gee. Well, be sure to thank him for those last few samples you brought in for me. Superb stuff his place is making–nice and strong. M and I enjoyed them."

"Keith will appreciate that. He knows how much you and M love good beer."

"In my case, it's way too much, I'm afraid. Well, I'd better get on the phone with Mr. Whiting."

Mack tried several times, but failed to get hold of his client. He didn't want to leave a message, so decided to call later. In the meantime, he'd catch up on reviewing his long list of emails. He found a recent one with the subject line: *An Imperfect Plan,* which gave him a jolt. The message read: *An imperfect plan failed. There WILL be another.*

Mack tried to check the sender's email address but had no luck. He suspected the sender used Tor, a dark web program to assure anonymity. Mack was aware that Tor transmitted emails through a worldwide network of thousands of relays to conceal the sender's location, usage, and identity.

The NSA would sure love to close that sucker down, Mack thought to himself. He continued to go through the rest of his emails looking for other threats, but found none. This slimy bastard will get what's coming to him–I swear it on my dad's grave, he thought.

× × ×

IT WAS NOON WHEN Mack tried to call Whiting again because he hadn't received a response. This time he finally heard his voice.

"John, it would be best to talk to you in person, not over the phone. Can you meet me at my office in two hours? I've got a few things to take care of before that, so I'll give you an update then."

"Sure—I'll see you at two," Whiting said.

Mack decided he'd meet with Whiting in the conference room. It would give a professional impression and save him from tidying his messy desk. M was working with Pauline on completing a few pressing matters, so told them he'd meet with Whiting alone.

"Nice to see you again," Whiting said while shaking Mack's hand. He had arrived right on time.

"Likewise, John. It's been four action-packed days since I last saw you, and several things happened you should know about. Off the top, there's good news and bad news. I also have two questions for you."

"I could use a little good news, so let's start with that."

"The police couldn't find the keys to Stewart's car, but we did. They were in a rainwater drain in the parking lot at the Tartan, a few feet from Stewart's vehicle."

"Someone took them to break into his house and clean the place out?" Whiting asked.

"Possibly, but I doubt that was the intention."

"Then we can discuss the issue of his keys when there's something definite to consider. As if the death of my friend isn't enough bad news, you've got more?"

"Yes—someone tried to kill me last night."

"What the...? How? Where?"

Mack recounted the events of his near-death experience, leaving out the fact that M was there taking photos.

"Thank heaven you're all right! Did you see who did it?

Who was the driver? Can you find the vehicle?" Whiting asked.

"Great questions. It was gray and overcast and I was running, so it was difficult for me to see the black pickup coming up fast behind me. That's when I dove out of the way and the truck went screeching past, tearing down the metal fence where I was."

"But can't you or the police find the vehicle? There must be a way—"

Mack cut him off. "Fact is, John, Boston is a big city, and black pickups are everywhere you look. There's at least one on every residential block in America. It'd be like finding a needle in an acre of haystacks."

"Well, this guy is the proud owner of big balls or he's insane! Trying to run over a private investigator in broad daylight—that's incredible!

"I'm so sorry this happened while you were trying to help me. Hell, why would someone want to kill you?"

"I guess he thinks I know something important. So...here's one of my questions to you, John. After I dropped you off on Saturday, who did you talk to about hiring me?"

"Not too many—um, there was my wife, Joan, and Bill's wife, Maggie. That was on Saturday night over some wine. I spoke to our Director of Sales, Lorne Harris, while having Sunday morning breakfast with him. When I got to work on Monday, I convened a small meeting with Harris and his main assistant, Bethany Williams. Then I spoke to her staff member Royce Tomlinson, when I ran into him in the hall. That's it. I wanted to keep this to the Boston sales department, so told them to keep it quiet until I found out more."

Mack cringed inwardly at the lengthy list and chided himself for not instructing Whiting to tell no one. "It could be that someone in that group mentioned it to someone outside of your office," he said, "because right after that someone tried to run me over, probably the same person who killed Stewart—he must fear I'm a threat."

"No one in my circle would go blabbing to some crazed killer—no way!"

"John, I'm not accusing anyone, but my experience tells me it doesn't take much to circulate a secret, a piece of news, or gossip. As the saying goes, something is no longer secret if more than one person knows about it. You told five people and if each of those tells someone, then that's ten people who know—and that could happen fast!"

"I hadn't thought..."

"There's something my dad, Matt, told me a long time ago that's worth repeating here: *You're only six people away from someone who knows anyone in the world.* He called it *Six Degrees of Separation.* For example, you tell Lorne Harris, and he tells his best client, who is in the market for a yacht, and that person tells a Greek tycoon who is visiting his mistress in England, who is having tea the next day with the Queen—and now you are connected to the entire Royal Family."

Whiting gave a low whistle. "I see what you mean. Guess I better watch what I say to others from now on."

"News and gossip have traveled between people by word of mouth for hundreds of years. Not too long ago, there were no phones or email. Word of mouth was how messages got around, and as I just said, that could happen fast. Just think about Paul Revere..."

"I'm worried I said the wrong thing to the wrong someone, damn it!"

"Maybe someone you know has a big mouth—or is just thoughtless. Not good news, but we must consider all the options because that's what you're paying us to do. If I have to follow each of those trails to the ends of the earth while chasing this slimy bastard, then you'd better believe that's what I'm going to do."

CHAPTER 10

M AND PAULINE FOCUSED on Mack's every word as he told them what had occurred earlier that afternoon with John Whiting.

"I didn't tell Whiting much. I worried about where the info might end up, so I didn't mention I gave Stewart's keys and the photos to the police. That crazy pickup driver must think we're not holding any high cards, but I wonder if he ever heard the saying, *'Never play poker with a guy named Doc.'* Well, I've got a new saying for him: *'Never try to deal a dead man's hand to a guy named Mack.'"*

"Not a good idea from what I've seen," M said. "He'll never figure out what crappy cards you'll deal him in return, that's for sure."

"As I was leaving the meeting, Whiting asked me what our next step would be. I told him to tell Harris, his Director of Sales, I'd like to see him tomorrow. I said I want to know what they do and how they do it. That'll give me a chance to sniff around and ask a few questions about their setup and operations. We'll check out a few other things while we're at it."

"Just keep sniffing around until we smell something rotten—turn over a few rocks to see what crawls out. Guess who taught me that?" M asked.

"Right. You gotta sniff around even if you don't know what you're sniffing for. Sure as shootin' something will show up—often when you least expect it. I'll call to set up a time. I want you to come with me, M."

"You should both go carrying," said Pauline.

"After that near-miss the other night, I've decided to go armed from now on. Paul's right, M—I want you to carry your piece too. This is personal, and it's war!"

"I sure won't feel sorry for the skinny creep when you get him," Pauline said. "I've seen what you can do, so it's not *if* you'll get him, but *when*."

"Thanks for the vote of confidence, but I'd worry more about what M will do to him if he gets his hands around his scrawny neck."

Pauline laughed out loud as she gave M a thumbs-up.

"I told Whiting to tell Bill Stewart's wife, Maggie, that I want to see her over the next couple of days. I hope I can arrange it if she feels up to it. I have to keep in mind she's been through hell."

Mack stood up to end the meeting as Pauline's phone rang at the front desk. She ran to answer it, grabbing it by the fourth ring.

"Man, can that girl ever move when she wants to," M said, smiling.

"No kidding," said Mack. "You never want to be in her way when she's in a hurry."

Pauline called to Mack to pick up the phone. She said it was Nik Lewis on the line. Mack wanted to take the call in his office and asked M to join him.

"Nik, how are things?"

"You'll want to get here ASAP. I'm serious."

"M and I are out of here—see you soon."

As Mack and M rushed by Pauline on the way to Mack's

SUV, he told her they were headed to see Lewis. "Don't wait up—and please remember to feed Woof." Pauline just huffed out a mumbled response—something about how he and M get to have all the fun.

× × ×

A UNIFORMED POLICE OFFICER showed Mack and M into Lewis's office. He was part of the divisional security force that kept the police building safe.

Steve Drakowski was seated in Lewis's office when they walked in, and he stood to greet them. Both officers had bright eyes and wide smiles—a pair of Cheshire cats.

"You didn't break the law when you came speeding down here, did you?" Lewis asked.

"My driving instructor taught me never to speed, Nik—at least not without a good reason—and not if I could spot a cop car anywhere," Mack said, laughing. "Please tell us why we're here. You gents appear downright bubbly for overworked and underpaid officers of the law."

"I think you guys better stand on a plastic sheet because you're gonna piss yourselves when I give you the news."

"Better get a bucket," Drakowski said. "Nik's not kidding."

"We got a match on your Checkerboard Park photos with the guy in the video sitting at the bar at the Tartan pub. And we got an ID on the bastard. Congratulations!" Nik said.

There were whoops and laughs and high-fives as the room went electric. The four were acting like a group of teenagers at a football game after their team scored the winning touchdown.

"This is the first huge break we've had. If I could give you each a shiny merit badge for service above and beyond the call of duty, I'd do that right now!" Lewis said. After a few moments of ecstatic celebration, the four men sat to discuss their results further.

"So, who is he?" asked Mack.

"His name is 'Fast' Eddie Venn." Lewis answered. "He's well-known to us, and we've got his prints in our system from way back. You guys have probably never heard of him, but he's a regular Mob contractor and enforcer for the Vitale family. His handlers, the Vitales, are nasty thugs who are into everything. We're talking extortion, illegal gaming, drugs, prostitution, grand theft auto, chop-shops and more. The list goes on and on."

"And attempted murder on me," Mack added. "Any priors or jail time on Venn?"

"Eddie's made of Teflon; I swear. Every time we've had him in for questioning or on suspicion of something—which has been a few times—his heavy-duty Mob lawyers are here within ten minutes. Gucci Lupino is their lead defense attorney. He's a senior partner with Marino, Hawthorne & Sharp. I heard he's ninety-nine percent spotless on his cases and his clients walk—full stop. What pisses me off is he's smug about it and always makes it look easy."

"So, what are you thinking?" Mack asked. "Gonna arrest Venn?"

"Not yet," Lewis replied.

"Good," M said, cracking his knuckles. "That'll give me a chance to find him and rip his head off. That's less than the bag of slime deserves after trying to take out Mack the way he did. I suspect he was the one who sent Mack a threatening email after he screwed up trying to run him over!"

"I don't blame you for feeling upset, M," Lewis replied. "You've got a lot of reasons. Hey, Mack, maybe there's something in that email that can be used as evidence against Venn. I'd appreciate a copy so I can have it checked out. The photos and paint scrapes from Venn's truck on the Checkerboard Park fence will prove attempted murder on Mack, but we still have nothing on him concerning the Stewart murder. Venn was at the Tart that night, but there's no proof he killed Stewart. We have no prints. What we need to know is what Stewart was hit *with*. Can we find a hammer with his DNA? If it's in Venn's possession and Stewart's DNA is on it, then bingo, he's our guy. After that, smug Mr. Lupino can go screw himself."

"Are you saying we don't arrest him right now for the attempted murder of Mack?" Drakowski asked Lewis.

"Right. I don't want to tip him off so he can hide evidence. I want to nail him on Stewart's first-degree murder charge. We need to know where he lives, where he hangs out, and where he slinks and slithers. We have to find the black pickup truck and hammer—or whatever it was. The weapon he used may be at the bottom of the Charles River, in the harbor, or even in his truck. Who the hell knows? This creep might keep his trophies for all we know. Maybe he's a sicko who carves notches on the handles of his murder weapons."

Lewis turned to the PIs. "Mack, you're a hot item to him and most likely M is too. He knows what you both look like, where you hang out, and what you drive. I'll bet he even knows the name of your pooch, so leave the detailed search for the murder weapon to us. It's clear he wants to hurt you bad."

"No problem," Mack said. "Someone has a motive for wanting Stewart dead—and apparently me right along with him. My guess is Venn was contracted to whack us both. Unless he has a personal motive for killing Stewart? Did he step on Venn's toes in the men's room at the Tartan or something?"

Lewis said, "Ha, that must be it, Mack! I don't want to tell you your business, guys; that's never been my approach. But I need your help to find a motive—one that's better than a few sore toes. If you can get a lead on this for us, you two will earn more shiny merit badges than you can imagine. Sound good?

Hell, by the time I'm finished pinning badges on you, you'll think you're back in the Boy Scouts."

× × ×

MACK DROPPED M OFF at his condo in the North End and headed back to his place with Woof. He was wrung out and hadn't realized the trauma welling up within him after the attempt on his life. He had Woof to comfort him, but there must have been a greater shock to his system than he thought, and he felt like he needed a few stiff drinks.

Mack had several special security features installed in his home, and he armed them. He wasn't taking any chances with Venn or any of his crooked pals sneaking around. After a quick shower, he put on his favorite football team shirt and a pair of shorts. Then he walked into the den in bare feet, carrying two ice-cold cans of strong beer. It wasn't long before he had started a small fire in the wood-burning fireplace and leaned back in his favorite recliner.

"Sorry, Woofster. No run for us tonight because that last one was a doozie, and it's been a long day. I promise I'll make it up to you, though." Woof lay stretched out, looking too tired to go for another run anyway.

Mack took a few swigs of his first beer, feeling troubled he hadn't spent time with Serena since Sunday. He needed to assure her he was fine and to know she and her daughter were okay. He dialed their number, and Sydney answered the phone with her sweet young voice.

"Oh hi, Mack. When I heard the phone ring, I thought you were my friend, Heather, but then I saw it was you. Mom and I came home a few minutes ago because I went swimming. Mom picked me up after her work. I did a bunch of laps. It was lots of fun! I love going there!"

"Hey, I'm proud of you, sweetheart. That's great you're

learning to swim. Show me how good you can do laps sometime."

"Sure. Wanna talk to my mom?"

"Okay, Syd."

"She's right here, so bye."

Serena came on the line filled with excitement. "Hi there, stranger. I'm glad you called. After the day I've had, it's nice to hear your friendly voice. Here's hoping you can work some magic and take the edge off of my nerves. I had a few nasty cases today."

"Serena, I can't imagine what you've been through."

"Well, for example, it's never easy to tell a fourteen-year-old that the reason she's been feeling sick in the morning is because she's pregnant. It's the last thing she expected or wanted, and it's even worse when she has mean parents."

"That may be the main reason she got pregnant. She needed affection and found it elsewhere."

"Lots of tears and tough questions to answer. It's also hard to tell a long-time patient in her early seventies there's no known cure for what she has. I mean, seventy isn't so old anymore. People are living much longer these days—seventy is the new sixty."

"I thought seventy is the new fifty."

"Trust me, that's a stretch perpetrated by those trying to cling to more years than they'll get, Mack."

"Well, you've got a good heart, Serena. That's one of the wonderful things I love about you."

"Speaking of hearts, did I mention we women live longer than you men? It's a medical fact, so that's why we end up with all of your money." Mack could tell she was starting to feel a bit better.

"You never miss an opportunity to get in a good dig, Serena. What if I told you women live longer because men work harder, huh?"

"That's nasty, Mack...and very unfair!"

"Hmm. Try being a roofer applying hot tar in a sweltering humid climate, or installing furnaces in new homes in Alaska in the dead of winter. You'll see why many men have shortened lives."

Serena sighed. "There are many men *and women* getting mistreated constantly. It's like they're nothing more than beasts of burden to others with money—poor souls."

"So true. For so many, work is just paid slavery. Anyway, I guess you want me to face the facts about my impending demise as a male and write you a big check for everything I own right now—is that correct?"

"Ah, it's so nice to hear you sum it up like that. Will that be a bank draft or a cashier's check? Should I come and pick it up, or will you drop it off?"

"Man, you're some piece of work," he said, laughing.

"So...do you miss me? Tell me how much," she said, teasing him like a teenager.

"I miss you so much. I'm planning to take you and Sydney to a comedy show, and it comes with a dinner included. It's on Saturday night after this weekend."

"Gee, it's bound to be a nice treat for us. I can't wait."

"It's over a week away—I wanted to give you and Sydney something to look forward to. There's a great lineup of well-known comedians, Serena. No vulgar language and there's no age restriction, so Syd can come with us. I was lucky enough to get three tickets from a most appreciative female client of mine. She dropped in to say hello to Pauline and left the tickets for me, a gift basket with lots of fine chocolate treats for her, and even a pair of tickets to an auto show for M. I recall when I worked on her case, I mentioned my girlfriend has a daughter. That's why she left *three* tickets—how thoughtful is that?"

He took a long draw on his beer and continued. "The gift of the tickets reminds me of a recent case of ours. Do you feel up to hearing a short story right now? It should only take a few minutes."

"I'd like to hear a good story right now. It might take my mind off some things I had to deal with today."

"Well, consider it a bedtime story with a big bow on top—a true story from the recent Mackenzie Investigation case files. You can't wait, am I right?"

"How did you ever guess?"

"I thought so. Okay, here goes: A guy looks out the window at his driveway and notices his car is missing. He's shocked! No way he left his keys in it, so he wonders how it disappeared. None of his kids live in the same city, and his wife was at home having dinner with him. He calls the police, and they tell him they'll keep an eye out and stop by his home to get a statement and do a report. Two hours later, he's at his window again, and this time sees his car! He can't believe it! He and his wife rush outside to examine it for damage, but not a scratch can they find. On the dash there's an envelope. He thinks, *Ah, the hell with it,* and opens the envelope instead of waiting to give it to the police. Inside is a pair of tickets for private box seats to the Shakespearean play *Hamlet,* live on-stage at the King's Theater. There's also a brief apology in the envelope stating there was a medical emergency. The car thief and his wife needed a car because theirs had gone in for repairs. The race against time was of the utmost importance—they had no choice but to *borrow* a car and give away their own precious theater tickets as a thank you. Someone signed the note—*A neighbor who was too damned embarrassed to ask for a favor."*

"How did they start the car?" Serena asked. "I don't understand that part."

"No one knows, but many car thieves have special tools. They can drive away with just about any car they want—locked or not—in no time flat. If you lock your keys in your car and call your auto-club, someone will come out and open your car within five minutes. Getting it started requires a higher level of skill and practice, but it's often done without much effort. It depends on vehicle age, make, and model of the car. The higher-end ones are tougher, but that's how so many vehicles are stolen each year."

Mack took a final swig of his first beer, then continued his story. "So, they called the police right away to say the car was returned by a neighbor—no harm done. Then they went on their way, happy for the receipt of the *Hamlet* tickets. The tickets turned out to be worth hundreds of dollars, and scarce. Every performance had been sold out for weeks given the star-studded cast and great reviews."

"I can see why they were happy to be given those tickets," Serena said.

"Right. So, they're thrilled to attend with such fabulous seats. They have a wonderful time and complete the evening with a few cocktails before returning home. Later that night, they arrive at their residence, walk into the place and are horrified to find it has been emptied out, wall-to-wall. No note of apology or free tickets *this* time."

"Oh, what an awful story! Did they get caught?" Serena asked.

"Well, as a matter of fact, they did! It was the mixture of evidence from the police and our little firm that got the thieves a lengthy jail sentence for their repetitive illegal antics."

"I'm impressed."

"From the outset, M and I worked hand in hand with Boston's finest to bring this case to a head. I don't want it to sound as if we deserve all the credit. The thieves were careful and smart. They could clean out an entire large home in less than three hours with their experienced crew. The crafty sons of bitches always waited twenty minutes before starting to empty a home just in case the homeowners forgot something and returned."

"What did they do with the stolen goods they didn't want?"

"Great question! The leader of the gang thought he was Robin Hood or something. They made anonymous donations to poor street people of items they didn't want or couldn't fence. Stuff like clothing they found in dressers and closets, for example. Street people avoid the police like the plague, so no chance they'd tell who gave them the goods."

"What a shocking story."

"Serena, the conclusion is that it's often a small slip-up that will trip up even the most skilled crooks. This time it was a registered license plate on one of the moving trucks a curious neighbor spotted. Good thing he made a note of it—I'm fortunate to have talked to the guy later and that gave us a critical lead. So, that's the end of a true recent case file. The police are still following up on other leads they've received on how the goods were fenced, and by whom. They told me to expect more arrests soon, but our role is complete, and our fees have been paid in full."

"That was quite a story..."

"Well, hang on...there's one more important thing. I should tell you it was the couple with the vandalized house who gave us our comedy dinner-theater tickets for next Saturday. I don't think I have to worry about my place being cleaned out when we use *these* tickets."

"What lovely people. It was a great short story, Mack, and I'd appreciate it if you'd tell it to Syd on our way to the dinner-theater. It will be an education for her and add significant meaning to the value of our evening together."

"I'm happy you enjoyed your bedtime story, Serena. Next time, I'll have to tell you one in person. Goodnight, sweetheart."

CHAPTER 11

MACK COULDN'T SLEEP. A parade of many challenging questions cried out for answers in his head. A Xanax would help him relax, but he knew taking the pills was dancing with the devil and he was determined to stay off of them for good. He was determined not to touch them because Serena had warned him if he did, it would cost him his relationship. More stress. Beer was his crutch, and he knew he shouldn't have another...but he got up anyway. *To hell with it, it's just beer,* he thought.

Woof followed him into the kitchen. Mack grabbed a beer and one of Benny's dog treats, and walked back into the den as Woof jumped and squealed. There he spread out an old blanket so Woof could enjoy his treat to his heart's content without leaving a slimy mess to clean up. Labs drooled badly around food.

Satisfied he had taken care of Woof, he sat and had another swig of beer as he thought about the threatening email that he believed was most likely from Venn. *That bag of dirt—if it was his message, how dare he!*

Eddie Venn was a cold-blooded killer, and it was clear he wanted a piece of Mack. Mack knew the email was meant to throw him off his routine. Venn wanted to get him to do something out of character—out of the ordinary. That way, he could gain the advantage on Mack when he was vulnerable. Lewis had confirmed that for him: *"Fast Eddie is a pro who knows ways to get under your skin. Be very careful, Mack!"*

Part of the relentless stress Mack was feeling was due to confusion. In most cases, Mack and his team discovered the major motive for a crime fast. Then they found the doer—the perpetrator or perpetrators. In this crazy murder case, they had identified Venn as the doer, but still had no idea of the motive. He had his suspicions, and a $55,000,000 offer was the primary one. A criminal cover-up was secondary, but likely as well. He mused as he sipped his beer.

Either Venn had acted for an unknown personal reason—unlikely—or someone had contracted him to do the Stewart hit. Nik had said Venn was a known contractor and enforcer for the Vitales. Why would Drago, the Vitale Mob boss in Boston, order a hit on someone who did sales administration for an importing company? *It makes no sense...*

What did an exclusive company for high net worth buyers have to do with this, anyway? A drug import cover-up or the old trick of stuffing valuable statues with heroin or jewels? *You can bet that would make those rare statues more valuable.* And a big piece of $55,000,000 would be tempting. *Who would get that money and how would they get it? My dad always said to follow the money...I wonder what the Lewis team has found in Stewart's insurance policies and will—assuming he had them.*

Many more issues came to mind as Mack drank: Who gets Stewart's forty-nine percent of the company? Was there any partnership insurance? Would the company get paid out for Stewart's death? How will Maggie get paid for her husband's shareholding? Will Whiting sell the company now that he doesn't have his buddy, Bill, around to help him? Is he even considering selling, or will he be forced to sell to cover the impact of the huge payout of Stewart's current share value? And how will the company do as it moves forward? Bill Stewart was a veritable electromagnet for their overall sales at Royal Ransom. So...who will replace him? Mack's head was spinning with so many unanswered questions.

He finished his third beer as the jazz continued to play. Woof was crunching away at his large beef bone, trying to get at the marrow. Mack knew the feeling of trying to get at the meat of something, that's for sure.

But he crossed an old line when he cracked open another can of high-alcohol beer. He told himself this time things would be different; it would be okay. It was this crazy Whiting case that demanded new avenues of thought—new approaches. Besides, he needed to relax without pills, didn't he? The beer was helping to ease the terrific shock of almost losing his life. Or was he just making excuses—going into an old mind-space where he knew he shouldn't go? He went to the fridge and returned to the den with two more cold ones, but this time Woof remained in the den focused on his task.

"Woof, I need to explain something to you about my drinking, buddy, so listen up. I need to get this off my chest. See, I drink beer when I'm happy, but also when I'm sad. I drink beer when I'm alone and when I'm with friends. Sometimes I drink beer when I'm hungry...and yes, even when I'm not. Other than those times, I have no desire for beer at all... unless I'm thirsty—like right now." He sat back and smiled as he took another gulp of beer. Woof hadn't looked up from his chomping.

CHAPTER 12

Thursday

AFTER AN INVIGORATING EARLY run with Woof, Mack's headache was gone. He glanced ruefully at the sextet of beer cans in the recycle bin. *Gotta cut down.* He made a healthy breakfast of granola that included dates, seeds, and nuts, supplemented with a colorful array of fresh fruit. After a shower, he dressed up a notch from his usual work attire, donning a gray sports jacket, white dress shirt with an open collar, black pants, and new black loafers. He felt upbeat and a neat, well-dressed look gave him a mental lift—the edge he wanted to start his new challenging day.

He made a call to the number John Whiting had given him for Royal Ransom, and was patched through to Lorne Harris. He was surprised to get a meeting for that morning, so after the call he began to plan his questions. As he did, he hummed the old tune "We Are the Champions" by the rock band Queen, one of his favorite non-jazz songs. It reminded him persistence wins, and if you believe in yourself, you'll succeed—two great life lessons his dear dad had taught him.

He figured he was on a roll, so he called Maggie Stewart to book an appointment for the following morning. She agreed to see him at 10:00, but few words had passed between them. Mack sensed she was not in a talkative mood, so he didn't want to push it.

Mack wanted M to be with him for the meeting with Harris, and later with Maggie. M had an unbelievable sixth sense for BS—his special sensory talent. In fact, Mack considered M street-smart beyond the imaginings of most humans, a rare and hard-earned ability. As a skilled hand-to-hand fighter, he could read nonverbal communication signs and body language better than people who write advanced papers on the subject. He'd learned to read nonverbal signals out of necessity to survive, starting when he was young.

When M arrived in the office, Mack advised him of the upcoming meetings, and said they'd be leaving together soon for Royal Ransom.

"There's one important thing I don't want to forget to tell you. Harris is not to know that Whiting told us he and Stewart had issues. I'm assuming Whiting still wants to work with him, so I'm sure he will want to keep the waters calm."

"Count on it," M assured him.

"Paul has the day off and asked if she could spend it with Woof, so she picked him up before I left the house. That was really nice of her. Oh, and given she's away, you're the lucky one to be on phone duty until we leave."

"Ugh."

"Remember the blue moon the other day? That was my turn at phone duty, so now it's yours."

"Well, it's so good you had a turn," M said sarcastically.

× × ×

ROYAL RANSOM WAS HEADQUARTERED in one of the new office towers in the vast Boston financial district. Known as the Selector Tower, it was near Government Center, not far from Chinatown. The building featured an impressive polished pink and gray granite smoked glass lobby. The security officer at the guard station near the high-speed elevators told them that to gain entry to the tenth floor, they needed security clearance. After calling up to Royal Ransom, the guard unlocked the tenth-floor elevator button to permit access.

Mack told the security guard he was an ex-cop turned PI and asked about the security measures in the building. With a commanding tone, the guard said that among other classified security measures, they protected access to the tenth floor from the ninth and eleventh floors using a high-tech laser grid. Mack and M had never heard of a security measure like that.

As they stepped off the elevator on the tenth floor, Mack was surprised by the bright soft-white lighting, rich art deco surfaces, and quality furniture. He'd expected something starker and more minimal, but he admired the recurring geometric curvilinear forms and bold colors—raspberry, lime, and blueberry.

A young woman greeted them. She had classic-styled short red hair, and dressed as though she had just stepped off of a fashion magazine cover. She introduced herself as Angelica and told them Mr. Harris would join them shortly.

Lorne Harris soon walked in. He reminded Mack of himself—tall, about the same age, but better dressed. After gesturing to Mack to follow and giving M an odd look, he showed them into his impressive office.

"Great view you have, Mr. Harris," Mack said, eyeing the impressive floor to ceiling smoked glass. "We appreciate this opportunity to meet with you on such short notice."

"Please call me Lorne. Well, John briefed me and some others here on your role with this Stewart mess. He mentioned I should expect an interview. No sense holding you up in your efforts to get the son-of-a-bitch who's responsible for this, so how can I help you?"

Apparently, Harris liked to get straight to the point. Mack noticed he didn't offer a tour of the place, which was often a common courtesy.

"Lorne, is there anyone who wanted to do Bill harm? Are there any dissatisfied clients Bill might have had an outstanding issue with? Anyone Bill might have told off in anger?"

Harris made a temple of his fingers as he leaned on his desk. "Please understand we always make it a point to handle things as professionals here. If someone isn't happy for any reason, we'll want to meet them right away to get to the root of the problem rather than let it fester. Then we'll do our utmost to get it resolved immediately, if possible. We know if a purchaser is pleased with their experience with us, they may tell two or three others, and that's good for our business. If they're upset, they may tell ten or more, and that's bad. We have to protect our outstanding reputation because we meet a significant number of influential people daily. We often see a diplomat, politician, senator, or even a member of a royal family gracing our head office here. We have offices in several other major cities too. So no, to answer your question, I don't believe we have any dissatisfied clients."

"So...what about you?" M asked Harris, fixing him with a blunt stare.

Mack realized his partner had intended to sound rude. He was likely irritated that Harris had snubbed him when they first met. The surprise open-ended question was designed to catch Harris off-guard and possibly intimidate him—a part of the good cop/bad cop approach Mack and M sometimes used to get at the truth. M often played the bad guy role.

"What about me?" Harris responded, sounding contemptuous.

"M's wondering what your working relationship with Bill was," Mack said, smoothly.

"I had enormous respect for Bill because his sales skills

were incredible. He could sell people ice at fifty-below." Harris looked back at Mack as he responded.

"Are you the head of the sales team?" M asked.

"The Director of Sales, yes." He persisted in speaking to Mack.

"Who ran your department until now? Was it you or Bill?" M asked, trying to open a wound with Harris.

Mack and M already knew the answer to the question from what Whiting had told them. M was trying to see how honest Harris would be with his answer.

"Most of the time, Bill made the important decisions," Harris stated while avoiding M's stare.

"How did you handle that on an ongoing basis?" M asked. "I mean, any senior executive worth his salt would want to change that fast...or beat a path straight out the door."

This time Harris addressed both of them. "Don't be too sure about that! When I first took this job, Bill's micromanagement style bugged the hell out of me. His nose was into every little thing I did, and I felt like punching the walls when I got home from work sometimes. My wife is the one who deserves the credit for showing me some good old common sense. Thank goodness for that!"

"In what way?" Mack asked, puzzled.

"She told me I'm a fool, simple as that. I couldn't understand why she called me that; no man likes to hear an 'f' word coming their way! But once my blood pressure returned to near-normal, she told me I should realize I had it made in the shade. She said with the way things worked in my department, Bill did the toughest selling, worked the longest hours, and dealt with the toughest problems."

"She told you to open your eyes, lighten up, and appreciate the advantages you have working here," Mack said.

"Right. Let me put it this way—Bill had share-ownership privileges that I would never have. But I got paid big bucks to manage many nice people without too much stress—if I could just adapt to Bill's intrusive management style. I received full credit for half the work I'd otherwise have done if Bill didn't micromanage."

"Gotta hand it to that little lady of yours, Lorne," M said. "She's an intelligent woman, telling you not to let your male ego and pride get in the way."

"That's what she helped me realize, yes. And I also have first dibs and wholesale price privileges on a majority of the valuable rare collectibles that come through here. At the very least, I also have a great addition to my resume if I decide to pack up and split. I'm waiting to see how things go for a while, though."

"With Bill gone, you'll run the sales show for the entire company. Is that right?" Mack asked.

"I expect so—I don't imagine John will hire a big-hitter to replace Bill. I wonder how company ownership issues will be dealt with given that Bill owned almost half the company stock though. As I see things now, I get to do a heap more work for the same pay."

"Are you in line for any stock?" M asked.

Harris shrugged and swiveled in his chair. "No, probably not. I'm guessing John will want to hold this as a family company from here forward. I have no way of knowing, though, because John and Bill never discussed share-ownership with me or any of the other company directors. There have been several back-room discussions—that issue was at the top."

"Did any director have a serious issue with Bill?" Mack asked.

"No one. I don't think the guy had any enemies, and a lot of people will miss him. Anyway, I need to get back to business, gentlemen, so we'll have to end this interview right here."

"Well, sir, here's our card," Mack said. "Please call anytime if you need to. Oh, and one more thing; I will want to interview your staff members Bethany and Royce in the next few days. Right now, we'd appreciate spending a few minutes with Angelica. Is that okay with you?"

"Angelica? Why?" Harris asked, sounding surprised and concerned.

"How long has she been here?" Mack said.

"Just over a year and a half, and she's great; she has a master's degree in sociology. She wrote her thesis on human interactions in the workplace. We've trained her well in our business operations and needs. That's so she can qualify for a better position with us in the future. I assume she wants to stay and grow."

"Well, as your receptionist, she might have seen or heard something about Bill that you didn't, Lorne—no offense intended. That's because she's had a different perspective and field of view than you," Mack said.

"No problem, but I need my office," Harris said. "Assuming she's okay with talking, you can meet with her at the front desk. We're not expecting any guests for a while."

Lorne left his office for a moment. Soon, he was back to confirm Angelica would speak with them. They shook hands and Lorne led them to Angelica's desk at the front, then left.

"Please take a seat and tell me how I can help you," Angelica said, smiling.

"We're here representing Mackenzie Investigations. John Whiting hired us to look into the murder of Bill Stewart. We work closely with the Homicide Division of the Boston Police Department. I should mention that Lorne Harris speaks well of you."

"Thanks for telling me. He keeps to himself and sometimes I've wondered what he thinks of me."

Mack offered Angelica his friendliest smile to get her to warm up to him. Then he delivered another compliment. "You make a strong first impression for this place."

Angelica inclined her head, obviously pleased.

Mack added, "You asked how you could help us, and I appreciate the question." He wanted to use open-ended questions to see what Angelica might say, so he started with a general one: "What was Bill Stewart like to work with?" He chose to say *work with* rather than *work for* to elevate her status.

"It was good—he was direct and respectful," Angelica answered. "As long as I got him what he needed, things went well. Bill was no pushover, always demanding, and focused on making sales for the company. He had a one-track mind for sales, so I used to call him *Mr. One-Track*. But everyone told me he was great at what he did, and I respected that."

"Everyone says he knew what he was doing, but I got the impression he often stepped on toes," Mack said.

"Oh, you must mean Lorne and Bethany. Royce always got along well with him—at least that's the impression I got. He and Royce often huddled together to whisper about things."

"What things?" Mack asked, casually.

"I couldn't overhear much, but most of it concerned the private sale and shipment of goods. I didn't understand it to be honest, and I didn't dare ask. Who wants to be thought of as nosy? I got the impression something important was going on, but I don't think they wanted anyone to know."

"The key question is who wanted to harm Bill?" said M.

"No one I'm aware of—the people here are all so nice. The odd times there have been harsh words between Lorne, Bethany, and Bill. I always thought it was regular business chatter—nothing to be concerned about. Besides, I didn't want to pry or meddle."

"Did Bill ever confide in you about personal stuff in his life?" Mack asked. "Maybe use you for a shoulder to lean on? After all, you worked together for a year and a half."

"Well, sure he did, and I guess I can talk about it now that he's gone." She sighed. "It's still so hard to believe. Anyway, when I was first hired, he used to tell me about his Scottish friends he went drinking with downtown on Friday nights. He was a proud Scotsman, for sure. After a few months, I could see he needed to relieve stress, and he eventually told me about some gambling troubles he was having."

"Did you get the impression those troubles were serious?" asked M.

"At first, he made it sound unimportant, but later I could tell it was serious. It impressed me that he told his wife, Maggie, some of it. He felt he had let her down, and I know she was angry, but I told him I respected that. Most men would never say a word to their wives for fear of inhaling their pillow while they slept."

"Spitting out parts of your pillow in the morning is no fun," M said, smiling.

Mack added, "Happy wife, happy life, as the old saying goes. Angelica, we should go, and thank you so much for this helpful discussion. I hope you don't mind if we call you if there's something else to ask you. Here's my card—please call anytime."

"If something else comes up, I will."

"Oh, and one more thing...did Bill ever mention who he owed his gambling debts to?" Mack asked.

"I came right out and asked him that once. We were having lunch together downstairs at a place on the concourse. I hoped Bill might confide in me, but all he said was: *'You don't know, and you don't want to know.'* It sounded sinister. I heard fear in his voice, and the way he said it frightened me."

CHAPTER 13

MACK SAT IN HIS vehicle with M in the well-lit parking garage beneath the Selector Tower. He didn't want to leave while he was still thinking about what had occurred on the tenth floor.

"I'd like to hear your first impressions, M. Let's do a quick review of those two interviews before we head out."

"Well, Angelica proved to be a great resource, didn't she? Smart of you to charm her like you did, buddy. I bet most PIs and cops would have walked right by her. They'd assume she's all good looks, no brains, and nothing worthwhile to say. Surprise, right? As for Harris, I don't believe he was involved in Stewart's murder. What was your take?"

"Two things stand out to me. One, something big was going on between Tomlinson and Stewart; and two, it seems heavy-duty people were into Stewart's pockets for more than spare change. We need to know more about the gambling."

"Maybe we'll get something tomorrow from Bill's wife, Maggie. Fingers crossed."

× × ×

A TORRENTIAL DOWNPOUR BEGAN as Mack pulled out of the parking garage and into heavy downtown traffic.

"What happened to the nice day? Everything was rosy when we got here," M said.

Just then, Mack's cell phone rang. Suspecting it was important, he accepted it while speaking hands-free.

"Mack, it's Nik. Where are you?"

"In my SUV trying to get away from the financial district, but it's raining cats, dogs, and even a few of those flying pigs we've heard so much about."

"I'm not too far from your office—I thought I'd swing by. I've got news."

"Okay, but there's no one there right now, so I've been call-forwarding to my cell. M's with me, and Pauline has the day off. Why don't we meet at Benny's for lunch? That way I can pick up a treat for my Wonder-dog."

"Done. See you and M in a half-hour—and I'll pick up the lunch tab for two nice guys like you."

"Aw, Nik, that's so sweet," Mack said. He laughed out loud with M as he ended the call.

× × ×

OF THE RESTAURANTS, BISTROS, and diners Mack visited, he liked Benny's Diner the best—by far. The place had the atmosphere of a classic rock 'n' roll soda-fountain hangout, but everything was clean and shiny. Benny was a portly little man who had continued to work in his place since his wife died. He lived for his business and shuffled around every day, greeting each patron as though they were lifelong friends. Mack never failed to appreciate his warm-hearted and caring nature.

Mack and M had been sitting at a table near the back corner of Benny's for a few minutes drying themselves, when

Nik Lewis came in and shook himself off. He was wearing a long beige trench coat and a brown fedora with a wide hatband. He appeared to have stepped right out of the 1940s.

"Nice hat," Mack said.

"You look like a cop," M said, smirking.

"Thanks, guys. Those are the two nicest comments anyone has said to me today. For a while I figured I'd need a boat to get here. It's a-pissin'—even Noah would be concerned."

Benny spotted Mack, M, and Nik, and hustled over to greet them.

"Crumb of a day out, huh, guys?" Benny said, with a thick Italian accent. "I tella you what. Coffee is ona house jus' for you guys today. Lemme know what else I cana get you. Oh, an'a I got for your dog something, Mack. Take when you leave. You no forget!"

"Benny, you're the best. I wish heaven made more people like you," Mack said, grateful to Benny for being so hospitable, yet again.

Benny sauntered away while smiling and waving to others as they came in from the rain. Lewis waited until he was served coffee, then began talking after a few careful gulps of the hot brew.

"Guys, I'm the bearer of great news you are just gonna love—we've arrested Eddie Venn," Lewis announced with a wide, toothy grin.

Mack responded with a little whoop. "You mean I can go out running with my dog again and not get run over...or have to worry anyone will shoot me? How good is that? I might even see my girlfriend sometime!"

They all started to laugh.

"When did you cage his ass?" M asked.

"We arrested him last night, read him his Miranda rights, and charged him with attempted murder on you, Mack. My guys also arrested two others who were busy taking apart stolen vehicles in their chop-shop. We took no chances—we brought in our SWAT team to be sure no one would get hurt during the arrest. You know what they say about approaching a cornered rat—we were extra careful and prepared to shoot first if necessary."

"I can see why you used SWAT. Man, I wish I had been there!" Mack said.

Lewis grimaced. "Well, I went to the head of our division to see if I could get permission to have you there for the arrest. Hey, you used to be one of us, right? He said no—we had our hands full as it was, and if you got shot or hurt, there'd be hell to pay. He said we didn't need a pile of tough questions."

Mack felt truly moved as he felt his relationship with Lewis had changed. They were working and engaging as friends again, and Serena had been right. "Nik, thank you," he said. "That's super you went to bat for me, and I appreciate the effort."

"Yeah, well, now we've got a heap more work to do," Lewis said, waving off the thanks. "This raises questions: What vehicles did they steal, and how and where did they fence the auto-parts? Also, how deep does this go, and who the hell else is involved?"

They ordered their lunch: corned beef sandwich platters with coleslaw, warm kettle-cooked potato chips, dill pickles, and soft drinks. When Mack said, "It doesn't get any better than this," M and Lewis agreed with big smiles.

"What about the murder charge on Stewart?" Mack asked.

"Well, let me give you a little backstory so this doesn't get confusing. After we spoke in my office last time, we put out a BOLO on Venn's black F-150 pickup. It took a while, but one of our officers spotted it on a country road and followed at a distance. Later, it was seen turning into an old country place that sits on a large piece of land out west of Boston."

"What the heck was he doing out there?" Mack asked. "I

thought Venn was an urban guy—at least that's the mental image I had of slime-boy. Maybe it's because of the crap I've heard concerning his dirty business dealings with the Vitale Mob."

"Our research on the place showed it had belonged to one Lucinda Venn until a few years ago. That was Eddie's mother, who had willed it to her divorced daughter, Penny, before she died. According to our sources on the street and elsewhere, the old gal didn't give a hoot for her son, given he hung out with a rotten bunch of ne'er-do-wells."

"I've always said you can fool most of the people most of the time—but you can't fool your mom," M said.

"Yeah, for sure. We watched his sister Penny's place for a while, and concluded that Eddie was hiding out there while lying low. I suspect he only planned to be there long enough to fix his truck after that *rush and crush* he tried on you, Mack. He didn't want to drive his damaged pickup around and get spotted by police, but fortunately for our 'Be-on-the-lookout,' we got him anyway."

"I should buy tickets to a football game for the cop who spotted him," Mack said.

"I'll let her know—I gotta remember to ask her if she likes football. Good person, good cop. Since Eddie was gonna be stationary for a while, we got a search warrant for his sister's country house and her big ol' barn out back. We got another one for Eddie's condo downtown. The judge granted the warrants right away, since we had Venn nailed for trying to kill you, Mack. We also had his butt seated on a Tartan barstool in the video from the night of Stewart's murder. As I already mentioned, we matched it to your photos, M."

M grinned. "Glad to be of service."

"So, we served an arrest warrant for that attempt on you, Mack, but not for Stewart's death," Lewis continued. "After the arrest, I spent a few minutes speaking to Eddie's sister, Penny.

Man, was she upset! Her precious ugly brother was being charged with a serious crime, and she had a huge problem with the handcuffs we put on him. I mean, can you imagine that, guys? Her skinny rotten brother on his way downtown to be locked up like a common criminal! Just imagine that!"

Mack and M laughed at Lewis's sarcastic comment. Their lunch orders arrived, and Lewis asked to have the check for the lunch given to him when it was ready. Mack and M thanked him.

"I can't wait to hear what Eddie's sister had to say," Mack said.

"Well, listen to this...we found a fully equipped chop-shop in the barn out back. It had the latest and greatest toys for taking stolen vehicles apart so they could sell off the pieces to the highest bidders. It's one place Stewart's car could have ended up if Venn had managed to get it there. Out of the Bentley they'd get at least thirty grand for the motor alone, given it was virtually new and had such low mileage. Add the cash from the other car parts—the tranny, seats, wheels, and more, plus the cash for killing Stewart? That totals a big haul, and they wouldn't care about any blood in the trunk. They'd just pull the carpet out and burn it, then wash down everything else."

"Wouldn't they be concerned the parts they planned to sell were red hot? I mean, they came out of a murdered guy's car," M said.

"Hell, we're not discussing a low-life street gang here. These guys are pros, with well-paid contacts at the Boston waterfront and elsewhere. The stuff would be out of the country and in the hands of buyers within a few days—people who love to take advantage of Americans; foreigners who couldn't give a rat's ass how hot the goods are, or if they even have serial numbers. All they'd care about is the price."

"Did you find any hammers?" M asked.

"Glad you mentioned that! Yes, we sure did! Ever hear of a bag of them?" Lewis asked.

"Only when someone is as dumb as—" Mack answered, laughing.

"We found a few hammers of different types, so we labeled and bagged them for the lab. There was a large ball-peen under the seat of Eddie's truck; the rest were in the chop-shop in his sister's barn. They're being checked out for Stewart's DNA as we speak. There were other metal tools that could smack someone dead too, so we're checking those as well. We're praying for a match."

"Let's hope," Mack said.

"To finish up on the sister thing—I asked her if she owned the farm and buildings, and why she needed the mechanical equipment in the barn out back. I wanted to see what she'd say, so here's the answer I got, and I quote: *'Yes, I own this place, but my brother, Eddie, and his friends play with cars and metal junk in the barn. I never go in there because it's packed full, and it's greasy, smelly, and scary.'* That's not what I expected her to say."

"Sounds like you'd be wasting public dollars charging Eddie's sis with anything," M said.

"Yeah. I was going to charge Penny as an accessory, but I doubt I'll bother. She's innocent and would beat a charge like that anyway."

"I've always said the best place to hide something is right under someone's big nose. That's exactly what Eddie did—Penny's nose is all the proof I need of that," Mack said, smiling.

Lewis nodded. "So true."

"Say, are you gonna finish that dill pickle on your plate, Nik? There's folks starving in other countries, so you shouldn't waste it." M had a twinkle in his eyes as he looked at Nik—he loved dill pickles.

"They never wasted good food in the forces, so why waste

this pickle now? Is that what you're thinking? Okay, help yourself, M. I don't plan to take it back to the office. I mean, if someone asked me what I had in my little brown bag and I said it was a pickle, they'd be laughing at me for at least a week. I can hear them howling now."

Mack laughed and then asked, "I assume Venn called for his hotshot lawyer to come get him released?"

Lewis snorted in indignation. "I told Lupino right to his face that Venn was mine, baby. I said I read Eddie his Miranda rights and told him he won't be going anywhere for a long, long time. I did it with a big smile while saying we were charging Venn with attempted murder and had seized his damaged truck as evidence. We'd be sure to match the scratches and paint patches on the front and side of his pickup to the metal fence at Checkerboard Park. I assured him I'd wrap everything and put a big pink bow on top so he'd feel really special."

Mack chuckled, then finished his coffee and waved to Benny. He asked for more coffee and a toasted cinnamon-raisin bagel with lots of butter for dessert—his favorite. Then he said, "After all the unhindered walks Eddie Venn took out of your station in the past with Lupino, that little chat you had with him must have felt very satisfying."

"You got that right! I'll keep you posted on developments. I'd still be careful when you're out running, though. Venn's got friends."

"Thanks—I will be, Nik. I'm stuck on one more thing though."

"What's that?"

"Is Venn left-handed?" Mack asked.

"Why yes, he is! We took his fingerprints, and I had him sign his name to see whether it matched the ID in his wallet or not. He used his left hand to sign." They high-fived at the mention of that.

"How about you guys?" Lewis asked. "Any news from your end of the field?"

"We interviewed a beautiful young lady on the Stewart matter," M said, sporting a wide smile.

"Okay, so gimme the goods...what young lady?" Lewis rested his arms on the table and leaned in closer.

"We did much-needed research over at the Selector Tower," Mack said, adding, "it was all above-board and strictly in the line-of-duty, as your crew would call it, Nik. First, we interviewed Lorne Harris, Stewart's second-in-command. Quite the spread they have—the office reeks of big bucks. I don't think I'll be leasing any space in *that* building. Anyway, both M's take and mine was that Harris was clean."

"But the central question here is: Did you smell guilt anywhere?" Lewis asked.

"Not with Harris or that receptionist we just mentioned. She has a lovely name that rolls off your tongue—An...gel...i... ca." Mack started to laugh, saying, "She's too damn beautiful to be guilty of anything. And that perfume...wow!"

"Hell, that kind of thinking could lose us a war," Lewis said, sounding disappointed.

"Seriously, a piece of eye candy like her can be as guilty as sin of all kinds of things, but I was glad we interviewed her. There's much more to her than just a pretty face and gorgeous figure—she tipped us off to important leads."

"Yeah, what leads?" Lewis asked, one eyebrow raised.

"I thought you'd never ask," Mack teased.

He took a final bite of his bagel, then described the mysterious discussions Angelica heard between Stewart and Royce Tomlinson in the sales department that she thought concerned secret shipments of some kind. "Billy-boy also told her about big gambling debts she thinks were with heavyweight thugs. My bet is he owed the Vitale Mob big-time."

"You folks gonna interview this Tomlinson guy?" Lewis

asked.

"Sure, but I was thinking of talking with Bill's wife first. I want to see what vibes we get from her. That may tell us something—or not. I'm curious what will pop out given several money issues: the secret offer-to-purchase for the company; the company shares Stewart was holding; the question of insurance; several estate issues; oh yeah, and a will. And lest we forget, the gambling debts Maggie knew about, as confirmed by Angelica. It's enough to make our always suspicious heads explode."

"We're already looking into the will and insurance from our end, but maybe you'll come up with something we don't uncover. Guys, look—I gotta get going. It's been good to see you both looking so alive and healthy. Keep in touch and let me know if you think Bill's wife is straight up or not. See you, and give my best regards to Pauline."

Lewis paid for the meals and walked out into the damp Boston air. It had stopped raining, and it was time for Mack and M to get back to their office. Benny called out as they were leaving.

"Hey, Mack, hey you wait. I gotta dog stuff—you no forget!" With that loud utterance, Benny handed Mack a heavy plastic bag full of dog treats wrapped in waxed brown butcher paper. He had been saving up goodies, large beef bones with a lot of meat on them, for Woof in his fridge for a few days. Benny was always careful to choose thick, hard bones that wouldn't splinter when Woof chewed them.

"You're the best, Benito, and you're going to make my dog the happiest hound in Boston."

Benny beamed. "Jus' for you, biga guy."

CHAPTER 14

THE SKY CLEARED AND the day warmed after a cool, rainy afternoon. Serena was excited Mack had asked her to join him for dinner at the Blue Mermaid—her favorite restaurant. It was Thursday evening, and they hadn't seen each other since Sunday. So much had happened in the last few days. A nice meal was an opportunity to spend quality time together and give each other an update. Mack thought the custom-cut sports jacket he had worn all day would be okay for the upscale restaurant, so didn't swing by his place to change.

He arrived at the restaurant a few minutes early and was seated at his favorite corner table by the large windows overlooking Boston Harbor. Even with the great view, Mack always sat with his back to the windows so he could survey the entire room. He checked out everything and everyone while making mental notes—a habit he had learned while with the police. A few minutes later, he spotted Serena. She looked terrific in a tangerine sundress complemented by large black pearls and black high heels. She had a big smile on her pretty face as they hugged each other.

"I regret it's been so long since I last saw you, but there was a lot of business I had to take care of first," Mack said.

"Are you finally out from under it?"

"No, not yet—we've made good progress, but I'm still concerned about a few things."

"So—fill me in as only you can..." She raised a seductive eyebrow.

"Oh, hurt me, Serena. Here we are in a restaurant where I'm helpless to ravage you."

"Suffer like I have—use your imagination."

"Um, I lost my train of thought—it went huffing and puffing down the tracks somewhere. Oh yeah, I meant to ask, how is Sydney doing?"

"She's having supper with Heather again. Pam invited me to join them, but I told her I had a date with you." Serena smiled. "Sydney wanted to see you too—she misses you."

"I miss her too. Hey, you mean I might have lost the two of you to a calorie-rich home-cooked meal? Whew—close call!"

The waiter came to take their orders. Serena wanted a platter of fresh crab, and agreed to start with spicy shrimp cocktails. Mack ordered a bacon-wrapped filet mignon medium-rare, along with a strawberry watermelon arugula salad. They both ordered a margarita, their preferred cocktail.

"So...now we're back to you filling *me* in," Serena teased.

"Is that a doctor I hear talking naughty?"

"That's not naughty talk—that's your warped male mind doing too much dreaming."

They both chuckled, and after a few minutes discussing their intentions when alone, their margaritas arrived. They toasted to *life, liberty, and the pursuit of happiness,* a favorite of theirs. Then Mack raised his glass and clinked it with Serena's, saying, "Here's another toast, sweetheart. This one's to the police for arresting the snake we figure murdered Bill Stewart—Eddie Venn."

"Did Venn commit the murder on his own, or is someone else involved?

"Wouldn't I love to know the answer to those questions—man, oh man! That's the next important chapter in my case file. I don't believe it was just about stealing a Bentley and selling the parts to shady buyers."

"So, why then?"

"This whole thing smells like it's a part of something bigger, Serena. I suspect there are several people involved, especially after an interview I had with the receptionist at Royal Ransom Collectibles—the company Whiting and Stewart ran together."

"What did you learn there?"

"An important lesson I already knew. Receptionists get to see and hear a lot of stuff, so any investigator who ignores a receptionist is a fool."

When their waiter approached, Mack ordered a second margarita. Serena's first was still evaporating after the two little sips she'd taken for their toasts. Mack was silent for a moment while towering his fingers. Then he took a hard swallow and said, "They charged Venn with attempted murder."

"Why *attempted murder?* I thought you said Stewart was—"

"Dead? Sure, but the police have to see if they can get a DNA match on something. They collected some potential murder weapons. I know it takes time to do DNA tests because they're tricky. If there's a match, they'll charge Venn with the murder of Stewart."

"Yes, DNA results can be dicey. So many things can occur within the process to contaminate a sample. A buccal swab from inside Eddie Venn's cheek would be best. You need a court order for that, but I assume that's what they did. They should have been able to get DNA sample clearance for him, given all the evidence they have."

"Gee, I'd say you have a future as a PI, but I'm not so sure

I could be a doctor."

"Excuse me, but you still aren't making any sense. Bill Stewart is as dead as a doormat. So, where does an *attempted* murder charge fit in this?"

Mack cringed as he confessed the truth. "Venn tried to kill me with his truck on Tuesday night—he tried to run me over."

Serena gasped; then her nostrils flared in fury. "Mackenzie Sampson! If we were anywhere else, I'm sure I'd scream at you! How could you not tell me about this? I should get up right now and leave. Thanks so much for ruining our lovely evening together!" She had been holding her napkin and threw it on the table in disgust.

"I'm sorry, Serena...I've tried and tried to figure out a way to tell you for two days. Please listen!" Mack tried to hold her hand, but she pulled away. "There was no easy way to consider your feelings and tell you what happened at the same time. And I couldn't do it while Venn was still a free man because you'd live in fear he'd try to attack me again. With him in jail, that's not a concern. I was trying to save you and Syd a lot of grief."

Serena's voice was tight as she controlled her anger. "From now on, Mr. Mackenzie Sampson, let me be the judge of what I can handle and what I can't. I'm a big girl—a doctor—a mature adult. I'm not a little fraidy-cat!"

"I deserve to be scolded, I know, but I needed to work up to telling you about it. I still don't understand it. Who'd ever figure a nutcase like Venn would want to run me over? It makes no sense!"

"That doesn't let you off the hook. You deserve more than a scolding; you should be spanked like a foolish child."

"Spank away." Mack felt exhausted and hoped Serena would ease up; he forced a smile.

"This isn't one bit funny, Mackenzie Sampson. I'll find a way to forgive you...but you're going straight home by yourself after this dinner with your tail between your legs. That's far less punishment than you deserve. I'm not in the mood to be romantic or affectionate after what you just told me, that's for damn sure!"

"Can I finish your margarita?"

"Oh, what am I going to do with you? You're such a big kid! You're lucky you're not *wearing* my drink!"

After a long silence between them, Mack saw Serena shrug her shoulders and smile. Good. A moment later she said, "Okay...well, I guess you can have my drink, but please don't have any more. When you get back to your place...you get to go to bed all by yourself!"

Although disappointed about not sharing intimate time with Serena after their meal, Mack considered himself fortunate he'd gotten off as gracefully as he did. He knew she had every right to be upset with him. Still, sometimes she was too matter-of-fact—too damn tough for his liking. He figured now was not the time to dwell on that. Paul McCartney was right...*Let it be,* he thought. *Let it be.*

CHAPTER 15

M LEFT TWO OF HIS drinking buddies at Sharkey's Place after finishing a few games of pool. His cardinal rule was to never drink before playing for money though. Sharkey's was one of his favorite hangouts in Boston's North End where everybody knew him as an excellent player—a well-earned reputation over many years of gaming with challenging opponents.

M carried his handcrafted pool cue in a leather case as he walked home to his condo. The cue was dear to him—a special gift for solving a difficult murder case soon after he started working with Mack. If he had to defend himself, he would never use the cue as a weapon for fear of damaging it—no way.

M had no hesitation walking alone at night and no fear of the streets. He had grown up in a poor neighborhood and had been threatened or attacked for money several times. He referred to those as *close calls* and *no big deal.* He rarely talked about such things because he didn't need to prove anything to anyone. As he had done countless times before, he listened to his footsteps on the dry pavement as he walked in his steel-toed boots.

His mind wandered for a while, but it snapped back in a flash as he focused on movements in the distance. A motley group of four thugs, likely members of a local gang, stepped out into the street from a dark alley ahead and spread out across his path. M didn't turn back, but continued to walk toward them.

"Hey, short-stuff! What you got in that nice little case? Bet it's a custom pool cue. Looks *sooooo* special. You should hand it over," said the second from the left. "What you think, Magnum, look like a pool cue to you? We could get good bucks for that!"

The one who had spoken appeared to be the leader: the alpha male. He was rotating a large Bowie knife in his hands.

The guy farthest to M's right was as wide as he was tall, and he was holding a two-by-four with a spike through the end. He answered, "It sure do, Harley. Mister Mother here should donate it to you right now so he don't get hurt. It'd be a cryin' shame if something bad happened to him. Boo hoo hoooo. I say he should hand his fat wallet over too while he's being so charitable."

M understood hand-to-hand combat better than most men alive. He lived and breathed attack and defense tactics. He didn't see a gun on any of them, his number one concern, and stopped a few feet in front of the four and remained silent. He was sizing up the strike targets on each of them and planning the sequencing and timing of his attack. The furthest to M's left held a small aluminum baseball bat that might have looked innocent under different circumstances. The guy standing between Harley and Magnum, second from M's far right, was holding a length of metal pipe he had probably found discarded somewhere.

Harley nodded to M's left. "Yeah, Hacker says he won't hurt you with his little bat if you give us your wallet. Ain't that right, Hacker?"

"Wouldn't hurt one hair on his puny little pointed head," Hacker said, laughing. "What *you* say, Tattoo? Better still, what's your metal pipe say?" Tattoo didn't respond, just continued to fix M with a menacing stare.

M spoke to them with the intent of easing the tension. "I'll set this cue case behind me along with my wallet. If any one of you can get past me and grab them, they're yours. But the best idea would be for you boys to put your little toys on the pavement and walk away." The four broke into loud hoots and laughter.

"If you set your toys on the pavement, I promise to fight you without even using my hands," M said. "If you don't, well, I'll have to use them. You don't want me to use my hands now, do you?"

Before they could answer, M moved forward to his far right with lightning speed, kicking Magnum between the legs. Screaming in shock and pain, the gangbanger fell to his knees, dropping his two-by-four to clutch at his crotch. Before the three others realized what was happening, M kicked the legs out from under Tattoo, second on his right. Taken by complete surprise, his length of metal pipe went clanking out into the street as M stepped down hard on his windpipe.

Harley swung into action as M was coming down on Tattoo's neck, slashing him across the left arm with his knife. As the knife swung away, M hit Harley with a right uppercut that broke his jaw. As the punk fell back, M hit him again, this time in the sternum with a crushing chop. M had broken many hardwood and concrete blocks with the same chopping move.

Hacker whacked him above the kneecap with the aluminum bat and M felt his left leg go numb. If the blow had been any lower, he might have fallen. M grabbed Hacker's left wrist and, in the blink of an eye, twisted it behind his back. He gave it a driving upward push with enormous force, breaking the wrist and dislocating the shoulder.

M then hit Hacker with a smashing left to his stomach, leaving him on the pavement gasping for air and rolling in pain.

Swiftly, M moved aside and picked up the Bowie knife, knelt on one knee in front of Harley, and grabbed him angrily by the hair. As he watched blood ooze from his own arm, M held the razor-sharp blade to Harley's throat, glaring into the thug's panicked eyes. As his anger subsided, M wiped the blood off the knife blade using Harley's T-shirt. Then he stood and slid the Bowie under his belt and stepped away.

It was over fast. He had hurt his attackers: two staggered off groaning, and two writhed in pain on the pavement. It would take a long time for them to heal. M hadn't used any of his death blows, but he could have killed all of them easily. His hands and feet were his weapons; he needed no others. The four gangbangers had no clue how fortunate they were to still be alive—especially Harley.

M didn't call the police; it was against his credo. Besides, he didn't want to get them involved and have to complete lengthy interviews and statements. Nor did he want to view lineups or finger the culprits, then end up spending time sitting in court. No, he just wanted to be left alone. He knew he had hurt them badly, and that was enough. The four might have died over a pool cue and wallet they never even got to touch. End of story.

M had been fortunate to walk away from the street fight with only a bad cut to his arm and a bruised left leg. He had forgotten what an exhilarating rush it had been as a lone fighter with the power and skill to instill fear in the hearts of several evil men at the same time and win.

CHAPTER 16

Friday

MACK CALLED M EARLY IN the morning and asked him to dress up a notch. He wanted both of them to look good when they met with Maggie Stewart. He joked he wasn't trying to suck up for milk and cookies, but wanted them to look respectful. Considering the recent loss of her husband, he didn't want her to feel threatened or nervous. Pauline had advised Mack many times that given his size and M's physical conditioning, they should be careful not to appear intimidating in front of people they interviewed. He took her advice to heart.

Mack arrived at his office at 8:00 a.m., intending to talk to Whiting again and give him another update. The last time they'd spoken was Wednesday morning, but lots had happened since. The call would be a good way to help ensure Whiting stayed satisfied with their services—business is business.

He made the call, but Angelica told him Whiting wasn't in his office yet. Mack left a message asking Whiting to return his call when possible, saying he planned to update him on his case. He also wanted to mention his upcoming meeting at 10:00 a.m. with Maggie Stewart.

Next, Mack called Lewis to find out if they'd found Stewart's DNA on any of the metal tools they bagged up. Mack was lucky to get through to him on his first try.

"You're getting easier to reach as you get older," Mack said while grinning.

"Still being a smart-ass, Mackenzie? Let me tell you something...we got this Boston Gay Pride Week happening soon. The whole thing's gotta go off without a hitch. We're expected to keep Johnny Q. Public safe. Just imagine *that* if you will. There are a few bad actors out there, as we all know, who would love to damage a public event with guns, bombs, or a few flaming cocktails just to get attention for their unworthy cause."

"I won't keep you," Mack said. "I know it will be tough on you and your force for a while. I just wanted to call and give you a heads-up because we plan to interview Maggie Stewart this morning. Any special requests?"

"I've still got questions on how the money will flow now that Stewart's playin' a harp or wearing a pair of red horns. We're still working on the will and insurance angles. Do what you do, my friend, and we'll compare notes later. I'm assuming Maggie's clean, but she may be a good source of information for us. You tell me if I'm mistaken after you see her. Are you going to meet her at her home?"

"Yes, it's northwest of Boylston, near Hammond somewhere, not too far from where I grew up. Nice area."

"I've heard you were raised with gold coins in your pockets, Mack. I've been by the Stewart place more than once, and it's a beautiful Tudor mansion on a large piece of property. Gotta be worth three million—maybe more. It'll impress even a smart-ass grad from Harvard."

"I'm looking forward to seeing it. Before I forget, though, how's the DNA testing going?"

"There was a small glitch, but nothing serious. We want

rock solid evidence, so I asked our lab wizards to take their sweet-ass time and be sure to get it right. Better to be slow than sorry."

"Okay, over and out...for now. I'll be in touch. Good luck, and keep everyone safe, including yourself. Most of all, don't have too much fun at that Pride Parade!"

Lewis grumbled, "Real hilarious, smart-ass." Then he hung up.

× × ×

"MAGGIE WILL BE WITH you in a moment, so please make yourselves comfortable," said Jessica, the maid, as she led Mack and M into the study. It was furnished with dark brown leather furniture that complemented the honey-toned oak walls. Several expensive woven wool carpets adorned with Scottish countryside scenes covered areas of the floor, adding to the warmth of the room.

Mack assumed Maggie depended on Jessica, and concluded there must be others to help take care of the fine home. He had seen many expensive Boston homes, but this was one of the best for its size and design. Maggie and her late husband, Bill, appeared to have spared no expense in furnishing and maintaining it.

A few minutes later, Jessica introduced Mack and M to Maggie. Bill Stewart's widow was dressed in a dark gray long-sleeve top with a white silk scarf, black skirt, and high-heeled black shoes. She wore large gold earrings, but no other jewelry except for her wedding ring. Her highlighted blond hair was cut fashionably shorter and her face was heavily made up. Mack figured her to be in her late forties, and though attractive, her features suggested someone who had led a tough life, not a pampered one. It was a noticeable visual contradiction. She sat in an armchair opposite them.

"We're very sorry for your loss, Mrs. Stewart," Mack said. "I've heard your husband, Bill, was a fine man."

"Thank you so much for your kind words—and yes, he was."

Mack continued, "This is my associate, M. I believe you know that we were hired by John Whiting to investigate the tragic passing of your husband."

"Please call me Maggie—everyone does. May I get either of you something to drink? I've asked Jessica to brew a fresh pot of coffee."

"You just said the magic word," Mack said, smiling.

"What about you, M? I'm curious—is that your real name?"

M dipped his head politely. "My full name is Emilio, but no one ever uses it anymore. Oh, and no coffee for me, thanks."

In a few minutes, Jessica appeared at the entry to the study with a small rolling cart topped with coffee, cream, milk, sugar, and cookies. She rolled the cart in front of the couch and left, closing the door behind her. While Maggie busied herself pouring Mack a cup of coffee, M winked subtly at Mack and mouthed, "Milk and cookies!"

Mack wanted to start this interview carefully, so he decided to ask broad-brush questions first.

"How did you end up living in such a fine older home?" he asked, accepting the cup of coffee gratefully.

Maggie settled back in her armchair. "Bill wanted to live near John for business reasons. John bought his place for his wife, Joan, and Bill wasn't to be outdone. I paid half of the purchase cost from a previous inheritance, which Bill appreciated because he didn't want to carry a mortgage."

"It's obvious this home has been well maintained—tough job given its size," Mack said.

"The hard work has been worth it, and we were fortunate to find good people at reasonable rates. Bill was always so busy—he never had time to do any work around here. I tend to the plants because I like that sort of thing, but there's always so much more to do with such a large older home."

"Nice room we're in now—I like it," M said with a smile.

"This study was Bill's favorite room in the home. The first owners built this place just before the stock market crash in 1929. In those days, people either listened to the radio or read lots of books to relax. That explains the ample oak shelving in here. Bill filled many of them with books he loved, but you can see several shelves are unused except for a few collectibles, ornaments, and keepsakes from his travels."

"He obviously had an interesting life. May I ask how you and Bill met?"

She shrugged and said, "Bill and John were supporting a candidate for governor in the midterm elections, and Bill came alone to the fundraising dinner. As I recall, it was because John couldn't join him that night. Besides, it was a thousand dollars a plate. A friend and I were there, and Bill ended up seated next to me. The rest is history, as they say."

"Sometimes it's that simple, isn't it?" Mack asked.

Maggie smiled. "Yes, we were both free and so our relationship developed quickly. It seemed only a brief moment in time and then here we were in this lovely older home."

"As with his sales career, Bill knew what he wanted and went after it," said M.

"Yes, that sums it up nicely."

"Were either of you married before?" M asked. M believed history was a great teacher and guide, so wanted to see if anything useful would be revealed.

Maggie paused for a long moment and then said, "Bill and I both were. Bill's first wife couldn't have kids. He claimed that's what ruined their relationship. Apparently, they tried everything, but nothing worked. Her feelings of inadequacy ended their marriage—at least according to the way Bill told it. I guess there's always two sides to every story, though."

"I can't tell you the number of people who think there's only one side to a story," Mack said.

"I'm sure. Anyway, I lost my first husband when he disappeared and was later found dead. It's something I'd prefer not to talk about because it left me desperate for income. My legal rights to the ownership of our assets were held in limbo for a long time—too long. I hoped things would move along more quickly than they did, but I was told the court needed proof he was dead before releasing a penny, or I'd have to wait many years."

"I'm sorry to hear that," Mack said in a sympathetic tone.

"Oh, but I was in good shape once they settled all that nonsense," Maggie added with a nod.

Mack felt her expression looked cunning, and got the strange feeling she wasn't what she appeared to be.

"What did you do for a living before you met Bill?" he asked.

"Various office jobs."

"Did you take any courses or training to do any *specific* job?" M asked her.

"A couple."

She lit a cigarette and glanced around the room nervously. He thought he saw a glare from her after his question, but wasn't sure. He planned to intensify his questioning while looking for something more specific; clearly, she wasn't going to volunteer anything.

"Are you intending to stay in this house, or do you plan to sell it?" Mack asked.

Maggie shook her head sadly. "So many decisions to make, and it's too soon. I have many good memories here, but it's a huge amount of space for only one person, so we'll have to see."

"Do you have any kids from your first marriage who could stay with you?" Mack asked.

"No children and no feelings of inadequacy. I imagine that's why Bill and I got along so well. We liked to socialize and party, and there were no ties holding either of us back."

Maggie took another long draw on her cigarette, but her style of smoking and exhaling seemed suited to a burly man, certainly not a woman of good breeding. M frowned on those who smoked—especially indoors, and he became more suspicious of her as he studied her mannerisms.

"But you said Bill wanted kids, didn't you?" M said.

"With his first wife, yes. As he aged after his divorce, he gave up on the idea. I was too old to consider having a baby, so..." Following a deep drag on her cigarette, she exhaled through her nose.

Mack was devising several questions to ask Maggie, such as her views on Bill's work and his association with Whiting. Did Bill treat her well and were they compatible? Had he provided for her financially beyond the value of their home? Did Maggie suspect foul play from anyone?

M got the feeling that Maggie was a fake—a walking and talking con job. She had a hard demeanor made harder with too much makeup, especially around the eyes. He thought she smoked like a trucker and looked tough as she talked. The clues were in the emphasis of certain words, and the way she pronounced them...and in the way she sat and crossed her legs, showing way too much of them. M had a theory he wanted to test.

"Are you street?" M asked. The question seemed to come from out of nowhere and hang in the air. An uncomfortable silence grew between them. She glared at M, but said nothing.

Mack turned to M with surprise, suspecting he was onto something. He felt he'd better let him run with what he was thinking before asking more of his own questions.

For a person who had lived on the street and knew the street code, saying nothing to a direct question like M's would show a lack of respect. M had asked her if she had lived or had made a living on the street. Any street person would understand those three little words like their own name. If you were aware of the rules of the street, then not responding was something you just didn't do.

As she took another long drag on her cigarette, her eyes never left M's. After a moment, she aggressively crushed her cigarette in the ashtray beside her and stood up. "It's time you gentlemen left my home. We're finished here. Jessica," she called, "see our guests out the front door. Good day." With that, she turned and left.

M was smiling as they walked to Mack's SUV.

Mack was not. He'd had a long list of questions he wanted to ask Maggie; and he was worried their big break of a job with Whiting had just gone up in smoke. He shot M a "What the hell just happened?" look.

"They served us milk and cookies, Mack," M said.

Mack was eager to hear M's real explanation, but wanted to get back to the privacy of their own office to discuss it. He nudged his partner as they reached the SUV. "See...I guess dressing up a little helped us achieve a rare moment filled with nice benefits—even though she threw us out on our asses right after that."

CHAPTER 17

THERE WAS NO ONE assigned to make the coffee at Mackenzie Investigations. M never made any, and Pauline offered frequently only because she figured it helped get her better raises. Mack loved his coffee, so she felt she was scoring brownie points with every pot she brewed. She liked a fresh cup first thing in the morning once in a while too, but said if she had any later in the day, it made her hyper. Mack always teased it wasn't the coffee, it was her brain jammed on high speed.

Mack called the office to say he would appreciate it if she could have a pot ready for him when he got back—he needed one badly after interviewing Maggie. Then he changed his mind and said he'd appreciate it if she brewed two pots for the meeting coming up with the three of them. She knew that meant it would be long and thought-provoking. He also asked her to order lunch for them—and Woof. *Real food,* he specified.

Upon his return with M, Mack spent a few minutes throwing a ball to Woof in the parking lot out back, then returned to fill his mug with steaming hot coffee. He walked into the conference room and sat in his favorite armchair as Pauline and M joined him.

"Has Whiting called me back yet, Paul?" Mack asked anxiously.

"Not yet."

"Damn. I left a message on his machine before M and I headed off to the Stewart home. I wanted to tell him we had a planned meeting with Maggie...but it's too late for that now. If he speaks to her before calling me, he will not be a happy camper."

"What's wrong? Did you get her upset?" Pauline asked, looking back and forth between Mack and M.

"Who, me? Would I do such a thing?" Mack jerked his thumb toward M.

"It's my doing, Paul—Mack's clean on this one," M said.

"Okay, okay...will someone tell me what's going on?" Pauline pleaded.

"M, you're on stage, buddy," Mack said, nodding at him. "Show Paul how well you can sing and dance your way out of *this one*, why don't you?"

Just then their lunch arrived, so Pauline handed it out it and gave Woof his portion. Deli-perfect hot roast beef sandwiches all around, with beefsteak fries on the side. Woof was in heaven.

Pauline kicked off the discussion. "Why not start by telling me how she and Bill Stewart met? That's the first thing I want to know."

Mack shrugged. "Maggie and a girlfriend were at a political fundraising dinner. It was one of those pricey thousand-bucks-a-plate deals, and she and Bill ended up sitting together."

"How did those two get that much cash for that freakin' dinner?" Pauline asked.

"Great question. I'd better start taking a few notes," Mack said, setting his mug down and picking up his pen.

M nodded. "I picked up on that too, and I had my suspicions about how lots of money appeared in her life, but let me get a few of my thoughts out on the table first."

"Sure, M, you've got the stage as I said, so dance away, pal," Mack said.

"Mack, you'll recall you asked Maggie what she did for a living before she met Bill, but she didn't give you a straight answer. All she said was, 'general office duties.' I tried to get to the heart of it, like what training she had or anything along those lines, but that yielded nothing. Maggie was being evasive and stonewalled me. I focused on what was wrong with Maggie as I watched her. She had a hard bearing and wore way too much makeup. No sin in that, but she seemed too insensitive and crude to me. Oh, and her dress was way too short."

"No crime, I agree," Pauline said. "It's fortunate for you guys we women come in a rainbow of sizes, shapes, and shades."

"Yes, but hear me out," M urged. "Whiting told us she was sociable but had a tough side to her."

"I've got a hard side too," Pauline said, responding in jest to M. "Just try me."

"No thanks, Paul. I'm no fool," M said.

Mack grinned. "Me neither."

"But I'm talking *street-hardened* here," M said, sounding frustrated. "There's a big difference between how Maggie looks and how *you* look, Paul. I mean, I watched the way she smoked; her style was as subtle as a barfly. Then there was something in the way she walked, talked, and sat, exposing so much of her legs that you could almost see home plate."

"Home plate, huh? You guys always talk sports?" Pauline said while winking at M.

"Sure–it's how we get by," M said, smiling.

"Competitive sport is the essence of life to us men," Mack added.

"Can I finish this, huh?" M asked, frustrated.

"Well, you're the one talking sports," Pauline said, chuckling.

M raised his voice. "Her language sounded a little off to me too. The real kicker, though, was the way she glared at me when I asked her a little three-word question to test my suspicions. You needed a machete to cut the air between us after that."

"That had to be quite the question," Pauline said.

"All he asked her was, 'Are you street?'" Mack said.

"What?" Pauline asked, puzzled. "That was it?"

"That was it," M said.

Mack continued, "Then Maggie got up and said, 'We're finished here.' She walked straight out of the room, leaving us sitting there with the silver platter of cookies."

"I can see why you upset her," Pauline said. "Your question sounded rude, but I'm not sure why."

"Explain this to us, M," Mack said. "Pauline and I are confused."

"Right. First, notice I only asked her my question once. That's important. If someone has never lived or worked on the streets and you asked them that question, they'd be confused and ask you to repeat it. I've seen that happen more than once because they're not sure they heard you correctly the first time. The normal reaction is to answer it with a question, like *What did you say?* or *What does that mean?* Just like you did, Paul."

"So, because she didn't ask you what you said, she already knew—is that it?" Pauline asked.

"Right. I had a hunch—pure speculation, I admit, but I played it. I put her in a position of being damned if she answered me, and damned if she didn't. See, if she answered me, it would be an admission she understood the term. It could have opened a can of worms for her. If she didn't, it meant disrespect toward the person asking the question—me. She didn't care what I thought, but she realized she lost face when she concluded I was onto her."

"But what were you getting at, M?" asked Mack. "To be honest, I had my concerns with your question when you asked it because I wanted to ask her about Stewart's finances and some other things."

"She wouldn't have told you anything the cops won't find out. It's my considered opinion that who we're dealing with here is a high-class call girl; an experienced female wolf in sheep's clothing. I'm not saying I'm right, but that's my belief. I've got her pegged as a prostitute who services men with big money. I figure she looked for them at expensive venues, like that political dinner. The entry cost of it was pocket change to her—she could make that off a rich client in an hour. I know my little three-word question isn't any proof," M said. "But I'll bet the farm and the cows that Maggie made a living hustling wealthy men. Those women grow old fast because it's a tough business. I figure that's where she got her hard edge—I've seen that many times in the past. Eventually they want to find a wealthy sugar daddy and settle in someplace comfy. That's when they need to be careful and keep their former life a secret, or risk having a big problem."

"Is that what's going on with Maggie?" Pauline asked.

"Well, she probably got out of the business the first time she married," M said. "She ended up in a legal Neverland when her first husband disappeared but wasn't confirmed dead. Later, she received what I assume to be a substantial settlement. In the meantime, though, she returned to her tax-free business as usual out of necessity because they froze his assets. Plus, she needed to hunt for another husband with money."

"Whiting said she first met Bill six or seven years ago, so our story continues with a new twist," Mack said.

"Right, that's when she found a new nest to settle into," M said.

"Another dumb man not thinking with his brain." Pauline chuckled.

Mack added, "Well, that nest of hers may fall apart soon."

"She probably had advance warning," M said. "You can be sure she's still connected to an underworld where news travels fast."

× × ×

LATER THAT FRIDAY AFTERNOON, Pauline poked her head around the corner of Mack's office door with a concerned look.

"John Whiting's on the phone, and he sounds really pissed."

"I know what to expect, Paul—I've got it."

Mack took the call determined to hear what Whiting had to say before getting defensive.

"Hello, John. Glad you called me back," Mack said, trying to sound upbeat.

"I ought to fire you and your muscle-packed M guy right now after the stunt you pulled at Maggie's place this morning! What the hell were you doing? She's bloody upset! You were guests in her home for only a few minutes, and in that short time she felt you disrespected her. You destroyed any desire she had to discuss her husband's death, which was the only reason you were there!"

"And how could we do all that in a few minutes?"

"Are you jousting with me? M asked her a crazy question, suggesting she was a common street hooker in her past. How rude can you get? Geez! Just look at where she lives! She's been my best friend's wife for years, for heaven's sake! I want an explanation and fast! Like I said, she's upset, and I don't need any trouble from her."

"John, listen to me please—this isn't a matter to discuss over the phone. Promise me you'll give me a fair chance to explain. That's all I ask—I deserve that, don't I? I need to do some preliminary work for our meeting and it will take time, so I'll see you in your office on Tuesday morning. Is that okay with you?"

"I guess, but why so long, and why *my* office? I'd rather come to yours."

"When I called you this morning before we left for Maggie's place, I wanted to ask you to set up interviews for me with two of your people—Bethany Williams and Royce Tomlinson. That's why I want to meet in your office. Believe me, I don't like to go downtown unless it's necessary."

"Tomlinson's away on assignment. Bethany's here, so you can talk to her first if you need to, but the Royce meeting won't happen until later."

"That'll be fine. You'll see—everything will work out, but you've got to trust us. I look forward to seeing you on Tuesday."

× × ×

MACK REALIZED HE HAD only three days to prepare for his meeting with Whiting. He convened a short strategy meeting with M and Pauline so they could get their ducks in a row. He emphasized there was no way in hell they could afford to lose this case. Their future together depended on the money, so it had to work out somehow.

"Paul, the main thing Whiting's looking for is our explanation for why we offended Maggie. I can't even suggest to him she's not what she appears to be without having concrete proof—but she sure got upset over M's little question!"

"You want a complete background check and for me to dig up as much dirt as I can—is that it in a nutshell?" Pauline asked.

Mack laughed. "I'm glad we understand each other. Get

right on it, and dig like crazy with that little shovel of yours—access our research databases and call my buddies, Lewis and Drakowski. We're up against a tough one here, so we need any help they'll provide. Failure is not an option!"

With that, Pauline returned to her desk at the front.

"M, can you get us a few photos of Maggie Stewart to show around town? A shot of her getting into her car or walking in a mall?"

"If she was as popular with men as we suspect, someone will recognize her photo. I'll get the goods on her," M said.

"Higher-end hotel managers or their staff may still remember her," Mack said. "Talk to the upscale escort services, and a madam or two hustling expensive call girls. To get their attention, say there are a few influential people such as the Boston Police who won't be too pleased if anyone is uncooperative or refuses to help. It may end up earning them a surprise visit or two."

"Lewis is on the line for you," Pauline shouted to Mack from her desk.

Mack grabbed his phone. "Hey, Nik, I'm calling to tell you we need to complete a quick but thorough background check on Bill Stewart's wife, Maggie. Most likely Maggie stands for Margaret, and I'll need everything I can get my hands on. That's why I called you first. I've put Pauline on the databases and M on the street work."

"Why the urgency? Did you find something juicy when you interviewed her?"

"She asked us to leave her place after we talked to her for just a few minutes. It was a pathetic interview, my worst ever."

"If it was so bad, something juicy must have happened," Lewis said. "Tell me more."

"You like salacious details, don't you, Nik?"

"No apologies. In this job, you always want to hear something interesting and different."

"Well, M had her pegged as a high-class lady of the evening in her not-too-distant past. My guess is she started out as a common street hooker. M's got a better nose for that stuff than me, so I trust his judgment. All he asked her was, 'Are you street?' and she shut us down. You'd have thought one of us had cut a nasty fart."

"Man, is this my professional friend talking?"

"I'm just disappointed I didn't get time to ask her the rest of my questions."

"She's that touchy?"

"Way too touchy—like a hair trigger on a pistol. There are pieces of this large puzzle that don't fit together, but when I put myself in M's shoes, I begin to see the light. There are many mysteries about Maggie, so it's important to nail a few down. On top of that, Whiting's upset at us for offending her—he's threatening to fire us."

"No fun losing your meal ticket when times have been so tough for you financially. Word has it your skill at jumping over fences has improved, Mack, but trust me, there's no future in it. Next thing I know, you'll be entering the high-jump competition in the next Olympics."

"Now who's the smart-ass? You know I'm too old for the Olympics," Mack said, laughing.

"Well, my friend...you've finally gained some ground. I've got to get back to the stack of files on my desk, so take care and keep me posted."

CHAPTER 18

Monday, Mid-June

BY MONDAY MORNING, THINGS were coming together. Mack had worked the weekend at the office with M and Pauline, and it highlighted to him that computers were both a blessing and a curse. In the past he could have left his work at the office, but not anymore. Now it went with him wherever he went. He even had work calling him on his cell phone.

Mack had spoken with Serena the night before, assuring her everything was okay—it was just his massive workload keeping them apart. He told her he'd come over after work Monday to spend time with her and Syd, and reminded her of their upcoming dinner-theater show.

Now Mack was seated in front of papers, photos, and files in the conference room, staring at them while thinking about Serena. He was committed to seeing her, but the stress of knowing he had to finish everything in readiness for Whiting was bugging him. He wanted a summary of all the work completed on Maggie to be sure he had the facts straight and to understand what follow-ups were outstanding for his meeting.

"M, what did you find for us as you pounded the pavement

downtown?" Mack asked.

"Let Paul go first, Mack. She's the one with the news that matters—she's got the names Maggie used to call herself in her former life."

Pauline waved him off. "Go ahead, M. You got great stuff too."

"Well, okay, I got two close-up shots of Maggie getting out of her sporty little Mercedes at the Picton Mall. Then I headed downtown to some of the better hotels." M showed Mack the photos.

"Good thing she posed for those photos," Mack said, smiling his approval.

"She had no clue I was even taking them. It didn't take long after that to find someone who recognized her. I hit pay dirt at the third hotel I visited—the Grand Regal, where Maggie, aka Alley, was remembered by a doorman named Brian. He told me she could be seen in the lobby with a different male hotel guest at least twice a week. There was no doubt it was her—he was one hundred percent positive."

"Great work," Mack said. "Your determination paid off."

"This Brian guy said he tried to shoo her away many times since the Regal is a classy place," M added. "According to him, she hung out at Sylvester's as well, that *private gentlemen* only club where you'd better have lots of money. I tipped him a Franklin as a thank you."

"Good work got you a lucky find, and it was well worth a hundred bucks to confirm what we suspected." Mack sat back, pleased with M's news. "Okay, Paul, your turn."

"This Maggie is quite a gal—M was soooo right. It's been difficult to piece together her life over the last twenty-five years. The main reason is she changed her name so many times."

M smiled at Pauline's compliment. Pauline took a sip of her hot chocolate and continued, "She was born Margaret

Mitchell in Hartford, Connecticut. When she was small her family moved to western Massachusetts, likely so her father could find work. Her mother has no work history, so probably was a stay-at-home mom who cared for Margaret and her older brother, Lenny. From what I could find out about Lenny Mitchell, he finished high school, but a few years later he ended up getting five-to-ten for armed robbery."

"Good to know. How did Margaret come to our city, and when?" Mack asked.

"She surfaced on police records here several years ago when she was booked and fingerprinted. The police files show she was working under the name Allison Katters back then. She got a legal name change to Katters, but later used the street name Alley Katt to hide her real last name from her johns."

"That's quite a pair of kids old Mom and Dad Mitchell raised, now isn't it?" Mack said.

Pauline nodded. "A stellar pair. Maggie became well-known as Alley in the shady areas of town, so her police file says. Alley in the alley—clever, huh? She also used the street name Katt Nipp, another winner to write home about. If you're talking to Drakowski, be sure to thank him for the help he gave me on this."

"I will, Paul," Mack said. "Good thing he likes you so much."

"Yeah, I guess. Anyway, what a creative person our Maggie was, clearly displayed by selecting such unique names for herself," Pauline said.

"The names sound cheap, but she wasn't, if you catch my meaning," commented Mack. "Those names must have made her easier to remember and playful-sounding to her johns. Hey, like any business, self-promotion is everything."

"Guess it paid off," said Pauline. "Notes in her file show she met her first rich husband, Jack Schroeder, at a political fundraiser, and took his name when they married. He was the head of one of the largest banks in Massachusetts at the time, and several years ago, about three years after they were married, he just vanished."

Mack gave a low whistle. "I remember that only too well, and not fondly. There was a media frenzy about it at the time, and I was at the scene when they pulled him out of the river still sitting in his Porsche. That was a horrible memory for me in more ways than one! I checked after our meeting with Maggie, and sure enough, the guy she married and the one in the Porsche are one and the same."

"I guess we all remember; it was a big deal," Paul said. "When Schroeder disappeared, they suspected foul play with the bank finances and a huge audit was conducted, but no irregularities were found. As unbelievable as it sounds, Maggie had been booked a few weeks before her marriage to Schroeder for solicitation under the Allison Katters name. They gave her ninety days probation and no jail time. Take a wild guess who her lawyer was. The initials G and L would be a big hint."

"You can't mean our old pal, Gucci Lupino, of Marino, Hawthorne & Sharp—that Lupino?" Mack asked. "The same Lupino who represents the Vitale Mob on their criminal matters—that Lupino?"

"You can't be serious!" M said.

"The very same," Pauline assured them. "It's confirmed in the court records."

"Man! That's a find and a half, Paul!" Mack said, beaming. "You're at least a few hundred miles closer to Hawaii this very minute!" He high-fived Pauline and M.

"I suppose she could afford Lupino by then," Pauline added. "Do you think Maggie was connected to the Mob?"

"I have no idea. She probably did favors in exchange for his legal work," said M. "Even sleazy lawyers want to get laid occasionally."

"I won't bother to comment on that," Pauline said, crossing her arms.

"Nor I," Mack said, grinning.

"Anyway, I'm sure she couldn't wait to drop the Allison Katters name in favor of her new married one," Pauline went on. "That gave her another chance to appear respectable—this time as Mrs. Margaret Schroeder. Sometimes intelligent men can be so dumb! You'd think Jack would have checked out who he was marrying, but noooo! He wasn't thinking with his brain...if you know what I mean. Anyway, the reason for his disappearance was inconclusive, but we now know he turned up several months later when the Boston PD fished his white Porsche out of a river west of here."

Mack and Pauline exchanged wry smiles over M's sorrow at the thought of the ruined car.

"Jack had been decomposing for long enough that it destroyed any chance the police had to gather any meaningful evidence on his killer," Mack said. "I wouldn't have wanted to be the Medical Examiner on that corpse, I can tell you! I was on-site when they found the car...and what was left of Jack. It turned out to be a bad day for the both of us."

"Leave those awful thoughts behind you, Mack. To sum up," said Pauline, "when I look at Maggie, or whatever her name is today, I see a woman who has a vile past and two dead husbands. Both died under horrible circumstances and were found in luxury cars. Maggie stood to inherit loads of money from each. The way you told me Whiting spoke about her at first, I thought she'd be a sweet girl—so much for first impressions. It goes to show there's no accounting for the preferences men have for women."

"Paul, if you're this good at criminal research now," Mack said, "imagine how good you'll be after returning from a sun-filled vacation. Thanks to you and M for coming up with a heap of great stuff for our meeting with Whiting tomorrow. There's no way he'll fire us now. You both deserve a lot of credit, so after we get to the end of the dirty trail on this case, you're each getting an extra week of holidays as a bonus. Congratulations!"

"Hey thanks, and nice try giving us the credit, but you deserve a lot of credit too, Mack. It wasn't me who Venn tried to kill with his truck," Pauline pointed out.

"I agree," said M. "It's generous of you to give us an extra week, but why don't *you* take some time off—you could use it."

"Um...I'll see," Mack said, towering his fingers.

Pauline jumped to her feet. "Oh, and I saved the best for last! Drakowski said he got this straight from Lewis on the weekend. The DNA tests the lab people did on those hammers and the other stuff from Venn's sister's place resulted in a match. Stewart's DNA was on one of the hammers—the big one they found under the seat of his pickup."

"Just like the Medical Examiner figured," Mack said. "Damn! I knew Venn killed Stewart. Now it's conclusive. I assume they're preparing the paperwork to charge him with murder?"

"Yes, Drakowski assured me it's in process. I don't think I ever heard him so happy," Pauline said.

Mack got up and headed for the conference room door. "Don't move," he said. "This calls for a special toast! I'll grab three glasses and the best bottle of well-aged Kentucky bourbon I have. I also have another something to tell you."

Mack returned with the bourbon and glasses, then poured a round and proposed his toast: "To our continued success against crime and oppression wherever we may find it!"

With that they touched glasses, and had a taste of the fine old bourbon. Mack smiled as Pauline coughed after her first sip. M's bourbon vanished without a sound.

"The last thing before I forget. Independence Day is coming up fast—only two-and-a-half weeks away. On July Fourth, which falls on a Saturday this year, I want to treat everyone to a barbeque dinner at my place. I hope you'll join me for the best steaks and ribs in the universe, all prepared by yours truly."

"What a great idea, Mack," said Pauline. "Keith and I were wondering what we'd do on the Fourth, but spending it with you guys would be super!"

"Nice," M said. "The beer at your place is always very cold!"

"Just for you, buddy. Then we'll go together to watch that huge fireworks display to music they hold every year by the Charles River. The crowds are always ridiculous, but I've asked Mr. Lewis to arrange a police escort for us since we helped to nail Venn the way we did."

Pauline and M looked at him with surprise.

"Well...okay, I lied—no escort. But it was a nice thought, wasn't it?" They all laughed.

× × ×

Tuesday

MACK AND M ARRIVED AT the Selector Tower dressed upscale for their meeting. They were cleared immediately by security to go up to the tenth floor. When the elevator doors opened at the Royal Ransom floor, an impeccable Angelica greeted them with her beautiful smile.

"Gentlemen, nice to see you again. Mr. Whiting is expecting you, so please follow me."

John Whiting greeted them as they entered his palatial office. Whiting was wearing a dark gray pinstripe suit and black silk tie. Mack admired the suit, guessing it was from Savile Row in Mayfair, central London, or a high-end Italian tailor. There was no doubt it cost several thousand dollars. It seemed designed to harmonize with the floor-to-ceiling smoked glass windows and concealed his ample belly.

"Glad you could make it—you're right on time. Can I get you any refreshments before we start?" Whiting said while touching elbows with both Mack and M.

"Thanks for asking, but I don't need a thing," Mack said.

"Me neither," M confirmed.

"Before I get started, I've asked Bethany to stand by to speak with you."

"Kind of you to remember, John. We'll see how our time goes," Mack said.

"No problem. By the way, I didn't mean to be so rough on you when we last met. It was just my raw nerves. You see, I've been under pressure from Maggie," Whiting explained, "and the last thing I needed was her scolding me again. But I'm still convinced I made the right decision hiring you two."

"We three," Mack said, smiling.

"Three? Oh, of course. I'd better not forget Pauline—the real boss."

"Better not—the consequences could be dire," M added.

"Why the pressure from Maggie now?" Mack asked as they settled into chairs. "Doesn't she realize the large void Bill's death has left in your business and for you? If I were her, I'd want to make sure the company can still function, and I'd want assurances the investments are stable."

"She's fortunate you care about Bill enough to want to find the reason for his murder," M added.

Whiting grimaced. "That's nice and sensible, but what Maggie wants from me most is the payout for Bill's shares in this company. I don't understand the urgency, but she hired a hotshot lawyer and says she wants forty-nine percent of the fifty-five-million-dollar purchase offer—and soon. I recall I mentioned that to you. That would put her shares at a value of more than twenty-seven million."

"Is that *all* she wants? How could we possibly forget?" Mack said. "Are you planning to accept that offer?"

Whiting shook his head. "Here's the problem in a nutshell. That offer is over-inflated—period. Our company is worth thirty-nine to forty-two million tops, and that's on a great day. We're a sales clearing house and maintain little inventory. The main assets we have are our properties. A market value of around forty million is nice, but it's not fifty-five, which is almost twenty-five percent inflated. So...does Bill's death deflate the value or not? In my opinion it does, and by quite a bit. How the hell do I figure *that* into the equation given everything that's happened?"

"It's overwhelming," M said.

"Sure is! Why any individual or group of investors would want to offer so much for the company makes no sense. If I were a potential buyer and found out super-salesman Wild Bill Stewart was dead, I'd retract it in a heartbeat. So much of our business flowed through Bill that anyone who made a high offer like that would crap themselves."

"I see your point," Mack said.

Whiting heaved a sigh. "There's something rotten here. I can't be *that* far off in my thinking about the total value—I can't be. No one knows this company better than I do. Besides, it's one thing to get a great offer, but it's entirely another to collect all the money!"

"Do you mind if I ask you who made the offer?" Mack asked. "I hope you'll share the details of that with us, because it may have something to do with Bill's death."

"The offer came through a high-powered Boston law firm by the name of Marino, Hawthorne & Sharp. Everyone calls it MHS for short. They take up six floors and the basement of their own office building in Cambridge. If you want to pay huge bucks for a top lawyer, you'll certainly do it there. They specialize in corporate tax law. I have no reason to think it's a bogus offer, except for the amount. Others would tell me to shut up and take the money, but I'm no fool. As the old saying goes, *If it sounds too good to be true, you can bet it is.*"

"And how does Bill's death figure into this?" M asked.

"I guess I'm always suspicious when it comes to coincidences. My wife, Joan, and I don't want to sell our private company. I'm the majority shareholder, so it's my decision. No one can force me to sell if I don't want to—at any price!"

"I can understand your thinking," Mack assured him. "I wouldn't sell *our* little company for a big offer either, and I assume my reasons are much the same as yours—right, M?"

"I know there's no way you'd sell," M confirmed while smiling. "You and I are having way too much fun."

"I'm not sure I'd use the word *fun*, but Royal Ransom is in my soul," said Whiting, "and it's at the heart of who I am. It's what I live for and work at every single day. Sell a single share? No damn way! This company was built from scratch. I feel it still has a long way to go while I'm at the helm. I believe I have many good years left in me to continue to build, and I've felt fulfilled every day I've spent as the CEO. I'm an optimist, Mack—I can do this! There's a way to push ahead...even without the sales magic of Bill Stewart."

"It's encouraging to see your passion and determination. Part of my dad's mantra was that *persistence wins* in all things. Based on what you've told me and what I've seen of your company so far, you have what it takes to continue to succeed," Mack said.

M nodded. "Given my experiences in the U.S. Special Forces as a close-quarters combat trainer, what Mack says is true. Perseverance and constancy of purpose are the keys to all great achievements."

"Thanks to both of you for your confidence in me—I needed that!"

"Both of us mean it," Mack added.

"It's important for you to know that Bill and Maggie wanted to accept the offer as soon as possible," John said. "They're pessimists. They always felt if something could go wrong it would, so they wanted to take the money and run. That was their way of thinking, and they wouldn't hear otherwise. I kept saying they should take their time and be careful, but they weren't listening."

"We're curious how you'll proceed without Bill. Do you have a plan?" asked Mack.

"Well, I had to start somewhere, so I hired people to help me," Whiting said. "I wanted to be proactive and take this entire matter step-by-step. Step one was to get the real market value for my company nailed down. We have a shareholder buy-sell agreement with ten main clauses. I don't want to get too immersed in legal-speak with you, but suffice it to say that clause number three is important. It is: 'Fair market value shall be determined by using the average of three market value appraisals, which shall include an estimate of the goodwill of the company.'"

"Makes sense," Mack said.

Whiting continued, "I examined this issue weeks ago. In fact, it was right after that pie-in-the-sky offer arrived from MHS. I've always been suspicious about things that don't make good common sense. Unless I can understand it in simple terms, no way I'll get involved. There are so many corrupt people out there expecting a piece of something they have no right to."

"Yes, find out what your true market value is so you can move ahead by making better, more informed decisions," Mack confirmed.

"Hey, before I go any further, you two have some explaining to do for me, don't you? I don't mean to get off track, M, but I'm curious why you asked Maggie such a rude question.

I've only heard her side of the story—there are always two sides."

Mack knit his brows in concern. "John, we've got a lot to tell you, so it's a damn good thing you're sitting down!"

CHAPTER 19

"THE MOST IMPORTANT THING I have to tell you is that Bill's killer is sitting in jail at this very moment," Mack said.

"What? How can you be so sure you've got the right person so fast?" Whiting asked, sounding somewhat apprehensive.

"It's simple. The police have your friend Bill's DNA on a hammer owned by Eddie Venn, a known Mob hitman. The police arrested him along with two others at Venn's auto chop-shop."

"How'd they manage to find him?"

"It was all thanks to M's photos. A cop spotted the license plate number that M captured the night Venn tried to run me over at Checkerboard Park. And they ID'd Venn as the guy who followed your friend, Bill, out of the Tartan pub the night he was killed. They matched the Tartan video to other photos M took at the park."

"Sounds like pretty solid evidence," Whiting said.

"Elementary, dear Watson," said M.

Mack continued, "Well yes, it *is* elementary, but the police analysis guys used some high-grade facial-recognition programs old Sherlock never had access to just to be sure."

"So, it's pretty good odds you've got the right guy,"

Whiting said.

"Unless Eddie has a twin brother we don't know about—which I can assure you he doesn't," said Mack. "And Eddie Venn's pickup had paint scrapes on it that matched the fence at Checkerboard Park. Plus, given the fact that Bill's killer was left-handed: Venn's a lefty, and he had a hammer in his possession with Bill's DNA on it, and bingo, you've got your man close to being convicted."

"His goose appears to be cooked, even with Loophole Lupino as his lawyer," M said, smiling. "I think we should break out the cranberry sauce. It's so good with cooked goose."

"Of course, Venn isn't talking, claiming his Fifth Amendment Rights. And the police are being careful to follow due process so as not to open any loopholes for his testy lawyer, Lupino," Mack added.

"It's obvious I hired the right people for this," Whiting said while smiling at Mack and M. "You fellows work at warp speed, for sure. How you got to this Eddie Venn character so quickly is really amazing to me!"

"Well, the fact that Venn tried to kill me sped up the process," Mack said. "But thanks for the compliment, John. It's most appreciated."

Whiting continued, "It sure would be nice if we could find out who put Venn up to this and why. I mean, why would a Mob enforcer want to kill Bill anyway—or you, for that matter? Someone would have had to contract Venn to do it, am I right?"

"All good questions to which there are no easy answers. Rest assured, though, find them we will," Mack said.

"Okay, so we agree we need to know who hired Venn, but he's not talking. That's why we torture him—is that our plan? I sure hope so," M said with a fiendish grin.

Though Whiting remained expressionless at M's off-color comment, Mack decided he should clarify. "I know you'd love to get your pair of vise-grip hands around Fast Eddie's throat for what he tried to do to me, M, but the law doesn't allow that. We'll just have to find another way to get the answers we need."

"Darn," M replied, as if serious.

"Let's move on and turn our attention to Maggie Stewart," Mack said.

"That's what I want to get at as well," Whiting affirmed.

"John, I'm going to tell you straight out that Maggie was a high-class prostitute before she married your friend, Bill. I have solid proof behind every word that just came out of my mouth."

Whiting's eyes glowed with rage. "What the hell are you talking about? Are we talking about the same person here? Maggie Stewart—my friend? Bill's wife?"

"The same," M said, firmly. "She was born Margaret Mitchell, and as far as I'm concerned, that turned out to be two bad uses of the letter M."

Mack then told Whiting about Maggie's sordid past.

"I'm speechless! I don't know what the hell to say." Whiting pushed back into his leather chair and gripped the armrests to hold himself steady.

Mack spoke sympathetically. "I know this is all a shock to you. I asked Pauline to dig into Maggie's background and police records. I can assure you that you're not going to like the rest of what the three of us have to tell you any better than what I just revealed—the woman is quite a piece of work."

"My Lord, I feel like I can't even breathe," Whiting said. He picked up his phone and asked Angelica to bring some glasses and a pitcher of sparkling ice water with slices of lemon to his office.

"Do you feel up to continuing to talk with us? We can always pick this up another time if you like," Mack assured him.

"I'll be fine—it just seemed for a moment there that life was starting to spin out of control. You think you know someone and then *poof*, it's gone—vaporized right before you. I mean, I suspected Maggie was no angel in her past, and I don't claim to know much about the secret lives of women, but I had no idea about this horrible revelation."

"Let me assure you that in our business of catch-the-criminals, when you think you see light at the end of the tunnel, be bloody careful. It's most likely the headlight on the engine of a train coming right at you. One minute you think you've got it all figured out and the next, you realize how stupid you've been to think you've got it all figured out."

"I'm starting to see what you mean," Whiting said, sounding slightly less stunned—but only slightly. He removed his glasses and cleaned them with a small cloth, then replaced them on his face as if they would permit a clearer view of the situation.

"Look at it this way, you've already started to define a great new approach; a new plan to get to the bottom of this mess. You probably don't even realize that yet," Mack said.

"I have? How?"

"By starting at step one in the process, which was determining an actual market value for your company. You chose a factual basis for your approach right from the outset. We must use only reliable information on every aspect of this case as we examine it. We build a solid foundation together, one solid block at a time."

Angelica arrived with a big, friendly smile, carrying a golden tray with a pitcher of carbonated ice water, sliced lemons, and three crystal glasses. Mack breathed a sigh as he watched her heavenly form exit from the room. She had brought a ray of sunshine into a gloomy conversation. The faint scent of her pleasant flowery perfume lingered behind her as she closed the office door. Whiting poured himself a glass of the cold water and squeezed some lemon into it. His hands shaking slightly, he took a sip, then asked Mack and M to please help themselves.

"The next step in our plan is to find out who hired Venn to murder Bill," Mack said. "I think Maggie knows a lot more about Bill's death than anyone suspects, but I need to verify if it's true."

"And just how do you intend to do that?" Whiting asked.

Mack noticed Whiting's somewhat challenging tone, which he chalked up to defensiveness: His client still hadn't accepted the truth about his friend, Maggie.

"I'm not sure," he answered gently. "Just because Maggie was a pricey prostitute in a previous secret life doesn't make her a murder suspect. It certainly doesn't help her to look innocent, though. From now on, John, you'll need to begin to be careful about where you go, whom you talk to, and what you do, especially when it comes to Maggie."

"How the hell can I do that?" Whiting burst out angrily. "As I understand things, she just inherited forty-nine percent of Royal Ransom and she wants to be paid out! Right now, she's my only business partner, whether I like the situation or not. Given what you just told me, I have every right to be *extremely* concerned. It's the unknown aspects of a new situation I always worry about."

Whiting ran a tissue over his balding scalp, which was beaded with sweat, then paused for another sip of water. Mack thought he was starting to look and sound more frightened as he considered his situation.

"There's something else, too," the portly man said. "Just to mention another of her wants and needs, Maggie has talked to me more than once about her brother, Lenny Mitchell. She wants me to give him a job in our sales department. Bill said he thought the idea was a good one, but he was as biased as hell. I knew darn well Maggie was pushing him hard. I held off making any decision about her brother because I didn't think he was needed at the time. Now that Bill is gone, it's going to be harder for me to say no."

Frowning, Mack told Whiting about Lenny's prison record for armed robbery. "Maybe as part of our plan to prove who Bill's killer is, we use Lenny as one of our pawns in this 3D chess game," he suggested. He held up a hand at Whiting's appalled expression. "I need you to hear me out for a minute please, because I'm just thinking out loud. It'll cost you some money to hire Maggie's brother, but for the moment let's say you do. For one thing, it'll help to settle her down and get her to ease back a bit. You bring Lenny in as a new salesman to appease her, and you give him an office. Not just *any* office, mind you, but a *special one* that M and I will set up."

"What's going to be so special about it?" Whiting asked, looking from one to the other.

"We'll put a tap on his phone line, and install video and sound surveillance," said Mack. "It might be a good idea to think about Royce Tomlinson's office as well. I'm told there was some secretive stuff going on between Bill and Royce I need to look into. I meant to ask you earlier if you knew anything about that."

"No, I didn't even know something was happening I should be aware of. Are you planning to involve the police in this, Mack? I control the rights to this space given I'm the majority owner of the company," Whiting stated, obviously concerned.

"We have to be careful that the evidence we collect will be admissible in a court of law—I'm talking about out in front of a judge or jury," Mack clarified. "It would be a smart idea to consult with the police to obtain the proper warrant or warrants if and when they believe they're needed. Anyway, we should leave that for them to decide."

"Okay, I follow that logic and it makes sense, but it worries the hell out of me!" Whiting said.

"I don't see why it should," Mack said. "It's a good idea to have the police here to make sure the office gets wired properly with the best available high-tech monitoring equipment. M and I could set it up because we have the experience, but I think it's still best to have their expertise on this. Everything that goes on in Lenny Mitchell's new office and in Royce Tomlinson's will be recorded. At the very least, it will be for our private use, so we'll know what's *really* going on."

"I'm listening to you, Mack, and I trust you, but I'm not sure where this will get us. I mean, what if Lenny is just a regular guy and nothing happens except our normal business?" Whiting asked.

"Then you appease Maggie and get some value for the money you pay Lenny. My guess is you'll probably need at least two people to replace Bill. He was so good at what he did for this company he must have left quite an empty space to fill."

"That's true," Whiting acknowledged, nodding. "It hurts me to think about that."

Mack added, "More importantly, though, there's likely no way to get crafty Maggie to reveal herself unless we catch her unaware. This may be a good way to do that."

"She'll be hypersensitive after our meeting with her," M said. "She probably won't say much to anyone, so we won't hear anything unless we're proactive."

"Thanks, M, and that's exactly my point, John. Here's our chance to try to collect some additional information on Maggie since we all know she's not what she appears to be. This may be a good way to do that."

"You have both completely and utterly destroyed my image of her." Whiting sounded utterly dejected.

"Life has lots of surprises, and many of them aren't nice ones," said M. "I'm speaking from a wealth of experience, by the way. It's never fun to discover that someone you thought sang with angels turns out to be serenading the devil instead."

"Okay," Whiting said. "I'll consider your proposal, but I can't say yes or no right now on the spur of the moment. Let me think about it and I'll let you know soon. How does that sound?"

"Fine with us, and we'll respect any decision you make. The more I think about what I just said, though, the more I like the idea," Mack said.

M nodded firmly. "I second that."

CHAPTER 20

"LET'S GET BACK TO the concern you have about paying Maggie out at some point. Let's talk about that for a few minutes," Mack suggested.

"A few minutes? Damn it, it'll take hours," Whiting responded while leaning forward.

"Yes, it might. But I need to get a few operating principles settled between us first. It's always best to understand what options are open to us at the outset. For example, is there any partnership insurance on Bill? That's insurance that pays out to Royal Ransom in the event one partner or the other dies."

"I don't know much about insurance, and Bill wasn't a fan. He always said insurance companies want your premiums flowing into their coffers with no hassles. They shelter themselves with pages of legalese fine print, and the minute you make a claim, your bloody premiums go through the roof. We didn't have a board of directors to answer to, and Bill insisted that the only people getting rich on insurance were the big-shot executives at the insurance companies. Other than our employees' health plans and liability coverage, Bill wanted nothing to do with insurance."

"Okay, so no money coming your way from a company insurance policy. Are you aware if he had any personal insurance?" Mack asked.

"Same answer. He felt his shareholding with the company was all the insurance he needed to protect his wife, and he trusted me to run our company efficiently. Besides, she got a huge chunk of money from her first husband and they had no kids to worry about, so I had to admit Bill had a point. Why pay extra money when there's no need?"

"So...outline your shareholder buy-sell agreement for me please," Mack said. "Maggie wants her money, so how's that going to work? What laws apply to protect *your* rights *and* hers?"

"Our shareholder buy-sell agreement is simple and has ample latitude. That's because it's the way Bill and I liked to keep things. I'm familiar with it because I wrote it—I just had our lawyers confirm it because that was all we needed. As I already mentioned, our agreement requires appraisals to prove a fair market value for the shares."

"It's my understanding that Maggie is Bill's only heir. He has no money or shares going to anyone else. That might be good or bad depending on how you look at it."

"If shares were to go to someone who wanted to hold them, that could be good," M said.

"Right," answered Whiting. "If someone other than Maggie got them and wanted to hold them, I wouldn't need to release the money to buy them back. But if Maggie wants to sell her entire block of shares, that's a big problem. Twenty million or so is a huge amount of money to raise. The company has to pay fair market value for any shares it purchases from a shareholder, or it can offer more. Offering more may be necessary, but only in a special circumstance. The company can't offer less, though, because that would be unfair by devaluing the shares."

"How do you figure you could structure a payout?" Mack asked.

John sighed. "I don't want to get into too much detail because it can get complicated. I'll ignore tax issues, and just assume a rough company true market value for my example. Let's say it's forty million for the sake of this discussion, then I'd have to pay just over six and a half million per year over three years. There are other costs involved, but that's close enough."

"Why three years?" Mack asked.

"To simplify things once again for this discussion, the company has three years to pay on shares upon the death of a shareholder with twenty-five percent or greater of the company."

Whiting sipped his sparkling water, then continued. "Maggie can sell her shares to the company at one-third of them each year. There's no strict right-of-first-refusal clause like many private companies have, so she's not forced to sell them back to the company first. Bill and I wanted to let the shareholders—the two of us in effect—have maximum latitude on that."

"That sounds very fair to me," Mack said.

"Yes; in fact, if Maggie offers them to the company first, then so be it. The company can buy them at fair market value or even more, but only if it makes economic sense to do so. Artificially inflating the value is against the law. If the company decides not to buy them for any reason, then she can continue to hold them as an investment. She can even transfer ownership to someone else at her sole discretion, or sell them to a third party—*if* she can find a buyer. Those are the basic rules."

"What if she wants to sell them for less than fair market value for an unknown reason? Can she do that?" M asked. "I want to be clear, since this stuff isn't my thing."

"Sure. She can even donate them to charity if she wants. Our agreement states that our shares shall not be sold *by the company* to anyone for less than fair market value. As I said, that's to protect against share devaluation. If Maggie wants to sell her shares for less money after receiving a fair offer from us, then she'd do best to keep that arrangement to herself. It makes no economic sense for her to do that, but sometimes people do strange things for strange reasons."

"Okay, but she didn't sign your agreement—Bill did, so I'm just wondering how things work in that case."

"Duly noted, M—and a good point," Whiting said. "The buy-sell agreement carries forward and applies to anyone who acquires and holds any of our company shares. That applies as long as they were acquired legally."

"There has to be a catch somewhere in the fine print," M said. "I'm listening."

"Where would the money come from to buy Maggie's shares?" Mack asked.

"Let's be clear—she wants to sell all her shares for a piece of a fifty-five million dollar offer that hasn't even been accepted yet," Whiting said. "I'm not comfortable with the offer because it makes no sense, as I've said. I haven't given you all of my reasons for thinking that way, but I suspect there's something strange going on I don't understand. I'll be asking more questions before I turn it down, but it will likely be filed under *capital G* with the rest of the garbage I throw out. Hey, when push comes to shove, you trust in yourself and your own judgment. That's exactly what I'm doing."

He patted his scalp with a tissue from his pocket once again. "The question becomes, will Maggie be willing to sell to me at fair market value? That estimated value is a damn-sight less than fifty-five-million, so there's no answer at this point. Maybe she'll keep some or all of her shares. No way to tell now."

"So, let's assume you'll pay out six and a half million this year. Where are you going to get that money? From revenue?"

Mack asked. "Just curious..."

"That's not too difficult to answer. Of course, we have cash from profit, but I'm protective of that money. That's because when you run a company that's growing, you must plan to cover your short-side and be able to pay all your bills. It never ceases to amaze me how poorly managed companies can burn through cash so fast. They end up in a serious pickle before they even realize how terrible things have become. By that time, it's most often too late, and a company that can't cover its liabilities, well..."

"That's when executives get desperate to try a last-ditch effort. Desperate people can do very desperate things—like talking to a loan shark," said Mack.

"Money isn't everything as long as you have enough," Whiting said. "The moment you don't, well, you know what hits the fan, don't you?"

"Seen lots of poo on fan blades in my day," M said, smiling.

"Right, and it's mighty ugly—so that's why we supplemented and strengthened our financial position. We did a smart thing and started buying properties for our future expansion in many locations right after we incorporated Royal Ransom. We took out a few low-interest loans and acquired one property at a time. We were careful what we bought and where. If a location didn't work out, we would sell it for a better one—that happened more than once."

"It was good you started buying so many years ago," Mack said.

Whiting smiled grimly. "Yes, we've got a valuable property portfolio now, and that gives us options—though I never dreamed I might have to use them this way. I can sell a property or two and use the proceeds toward Maggie's shares, or lease those same properties back if the purchaser or purchasers are agreeable. I could also look for another good opportunity somewhere and lease or buy that."

"I'm getting more impressed as I hear you describe your company, John," Mack told him. "It sounds like you've been building it with safety and security in mind, step-by-step."

"Slow and steady...as they say. As to our debt, we owe just over nine million. That's the money we still owe on mortgages. I consider that *good debt* because, as we pay it off, it enriches our coffers as the value of the property investment portfolio grows. A few holdings are in choice locations where values are soaring."

"The main thing is that *you* know what *you're* doing, John. As a result, we now understand more about that questionable offer you received," Mack said.

John brightened. "Gentlemen, enough. What say we break for lunch now? There's a nice little restaurant downstairs on the concourse. We can relax and munch, then come back here and spend a few minutes with Bethany. I'll ask her to be on standby in about an hour."

× × ×

FOLLOWING A LIGHT LUNCH, Mack and M met with Bethany Williams, second-in-command to Lorne Harris in the sales department. Bethany had mid-length auburn hair, wore little makeup, and was dressed in a tailored navy-blue jacket over a white blouse with a black skirt. She was of average height and weight, and appeared to be businesslike, just as Whiting had told them to expect.

"Thank you so much for taking time out of your busy day to speak with us, Bethany," Mack said. "John Whiting hired us to look into Bill Stewart's death, so we'd appreciate any help you can give us."

Bethany looked pained. "I'll try. Why would someone want to murder Bill?"

"That's what we are trying to find out. Can you describe

your working relationship with him?" Mack asked.

"Bill and I worked well together, and I respected his sales ability," said Bethany. "He was a wizard—the best role model for closing sales anyone could ever hope for. I learned so many things from him—self-confidence foremost among them—and I'm really sorry he's gone. This is a terrible tragedy that's hard for me to put into words, and a crushing blow for John, who grew up with him."

"Yes, John is hurting bad. In our talks, he told us about Bill's skills as a master salesman—impressive indeed. What's your role with the company, Bethany?"

"Did John explain the structure of our office to you?"

"No," Mack said. "I must admit we've only got a rough idea."

"Well, I should start at the beginning. Boston is the head office for the entire Royal Ransom company, so it's the largest. We are in charge of the other offices in the U.S., Canada, and the five overseas. Most Canadians think Toronto is our main office, but that's window dressing; the majority of corporate decisions are made here in Boston. Now that Bill's gone, Lorne Harris is in charge of sales company-wide. He already had that position before Bill died, but in practice it was Bill who ran things. I report to Lorne, and Royce Tomlinson works for me."

"Then I need your approval to interview Royce when he returns," said Mack. "I've been told he's away on assignment."

"Yes, he's in Dallas. He should be back Friday morning. You're welcome to speak with him if you think it might be fruitful."

"Thanks so much. May I ask if Bill and Royce were close?"

"To be frank with you, I felt I was excluded from many of their conversations. At first, I thought it was because I was a woman and it was just a chauvinistic thing. I don't mean to be unfair, but it got to me sometimes. Do me a favor? I'd prefer you don't repeat that."

“Please don’t worry; M and I have at least a thousand secrets we can’t mention to anyone,” Mack said with a smile. “It’s the nature of what we do as investigators. I want to thank you for your frankness, Bethany.”

“Did Bill have any enemies? Anyone who had a reason to hurt him?” M asked.

“Enemies? That’s a strong word. I can’t think of anyone who would want to hurt Bill. He was a likable man, overflowing with energy. He insisted on having a say in everything going on here, but that was Bill’s personal style. Sure, it was frustrating sometimes, but we always talked out the issues between us until we reached a *best-we-could-get* conclusion. One thing was clear to all: Bill’s management style was the rule of law in here—come hell or high water.”

“Well, Bethany, we should be going,” said Mack. “It’s been a pleasure to meet you, and thanks so much for your comments and honesty. You added to, clarified, and reaffirmed what we knew. Here’s our business card, so please contact either one of us if you can think of anything to add.”

A few minutes later, Mack and M were approaching Mack’s SUV. “I wish we had learned more stuff from Bethany than just the Bill and Royce huddles, damn it—maybe a juicy tidbit or two, but we can’t hit a home run with every interview.”

“I could mention Maggie here, but I won’t,” M said.

“Better not,” Mack said, shaking his head. “It’s time we head back to Fort Mackenzie. It would be good to know Pauline hasn’t sold the place out from under us.”

“You never know with Paul,” M said.

CHAPTER 21

BACK AT THE OFFICE early Tuesday afternoon, Mack filled Pauline in on the meeting he and M had just come from with Whiting. "It was successful in no small part thanks to your terrific research, Paul," he said. He then told them both that he planned to take a little time off to see an old friend and relax. He planned to be back in the office again Friday morning for a meeting with Royce Tomlinson, to include M.

Though he was not someone who ever wanted to show weakness or that he was feeling anxious, Mack explained that stress exacerbated his fight to stay away from his demons—alcohol and drugs. Better to take a break than surrender.

The weather forecast looked favorable, and Pauline and M knew of his great love for the outdoors, so it was no big surprise he wanted to spend some time off under a few pines on a lake. They had heard him speak of someone named Jake many times and knew he was a trusted friend Mack liked to be with.

Mack placed a call to Serena to tell her his plans, but she was unavailable. He left a message for her to call him when she was free, then headed straight out the door to get home and pack. On his way home, Mack placed a call to his friend,

Jake, the owner of North Star Cabins, to say how much he missed his companionship and being at North Star. Jake's place was a group of six log cabins out on a private peninsula jutting into a beautiful, small sand-bottomed lake full of fish.

But Mack's getaway was more than just a short holiday to clear his mind by throwing a line in the water—Mack respected Jake's honesty and down-to-earth basic logic. He felt he needed Jake's insights into some of the things that were troubling him.

Once Jake confirmed cabin number four was vacant, Mack felt an adrenaline rush as he reserved it for that night, the next day, and into early Thursday afternoon. Number four was on the point of the peninsula, and Jake knew it was Mack's favorite.

Just two-and-a-half hours later, Mack pulled off the highway and into the driveway of North Star Cabins.

"You been keeping well?" Mack said as Jake came out to greet him.

Jake smiled. "Sure, no complaints considering I live alone, but I get lots of company from the folks who come up here. Sure beats city livin' as they keep remindin' me."

"It's great to see you looking so fit, Jake. The fresh air up here is working wonders for you. You haven't aged a day since I last saw you."

"Your nose is growing longer as I'm standing here, Mack."

As soon as he got to the cabin, Mack changed into khaki shorts, a white T-shirt, and his well-worn brown leather deck shoes. It wasn't long before he and Woof were out on the water. Mack enjoyed breathing in the warm air, so laden with the scent of pine on a beautiful sunny day. He smiled with each stroke of his paddle, energized by his presence in God's country. Time seemed to have no meaning.

"Hey, Woof, it's almost time to eat, pal," Mack said. He brought the canoe back to shore in front of his cabin. Woof was always eager to jump into the water before the canoe touched the sandy shore. Mack didn't object; he knew Labs loved water, and swimming was as natural to them as breathing.

Mack was never more content than when cooking over an open fire. Each of Jake's cabins came supplied with a large tractor tire rim for a campfire and a stack of split firewood. The rim was placed near shore where water was handy to fetch with a pail Jake supplied.

"We're having steak chunks with my secret sauce on a stick tonight, pal. A special treat done to perfection over a wood-burning fire.

A while later, Mack let his meal settle while listening to Woof chomp on his piece of rawhide. Then he took a short run to Jake's house with Woof.

Mack made a call, chuckling at the bobblehead of Elvis in Jake's kitchen. There was also a picture of The King in a golden frame on the wall.

"Oh, Mack, I'm so disappointed I missed your call," Serena said the moment she picked up. "Are you okay? I called you an hour after you left me a message, but Pauline said you'd already left. She told me she has news for you—please make sure you call her as soon as you can."

"Did she say why? How important is it?"

"Not important enough to come back to Boston. It sounded like she wanted to make sure you knew about something she discovered."

"Okay. I'll call her first thing in the morning."

"Oh gee, before I forget, she said she had *two* important things to tell you, not just one. She wanted me to be sure to say that. I think she wanted to deepen the suspense and make you suffer."

"Nobody can make me suffer like you, Serena, my love. You have no competition on that score."

"Oh goody. Maybe my magic spell is working on you."

"I can assure you I'm entranced. To be away from you is harder on me than I figured."

"Oh, Mack, I love when you say things like that. I can't get enough."

"I'd say more, but I have Jake competing with me here. He's singing, *'...burnin' love...a hunka hunka,'* so I can't hear you too well. Passionate words from Elvis."

"Oh, that's what that is—ha, I was wondering. Okay, I understand; it's always tough when you're not on your own phone."

"You've got the picture. Anyway, getting back to Pauline's message, it's got me concerned."

"Try not to worry; I could tell by her voice she wasn't in panic mode."

"One thing's for sure: even bad news won't keep me from sleeping like a log up here. The fresh air does that to me every time. It's a natural sleeping pill. I don't need any fancy-schmancy prescriptions to get a good night's sleep when I hit the sack here at Jake's place."

"The fewer unnecessary drugs you take, the better. We talked about that."

"Yes, Doc. I miss your smiling face and your companionship, not to mention your natural sleep medicine, so I'm looking forward to seeing you and Sydney on Saturday. I smile thinking about how great you'll look. Watching good comedians on stage pales in comparison to seeing you and Syd dressed up for a date with me."

"Well, have a much-needed rest. You'll see us soon enough. I also have a fancy-schmancy treat for *you* when we're alone together again—I bet you can't guess what it is..."

"And here I thought I'd get a good night's sleep tonight. How foolish of me."

CHAPTER 22

Wednesday

AFTER A SHORT RUN in the morning, Mack was back at Jake's place. "I hope I can use your phone again, Jake. My girlfriend told me to call the office as soon as possible this morning, so here I am."

"Sure, help yourself. I hope you don't mind if I wash my dishes and stumble around while you're talking. Is it okay to give your dog a scrap or two?"

"Okay, I'll make an exception and say yes since he's on a vacation too. Like me, he has no set schedule up here." Mack placed his call and Pauline answered.

"Hey, Paul, how's it going?" Mack suspected Jake was paying attention to every word he said, but didn't care because he knew Jake could only listen to one side of the conversation. He guessed he didn't get much news, so he made sure not to miss a thing.

"Glad to hear your voice, Mack," Pauline said. "How's life in the backwoods? You sure as heck lucked out with the weather!"

"Sure did. Heaven's been kind to me every time I've come here. Hope I can stay a while—apparently you have two messages for me?"

"I took calls from Nik Lewis and John Whiting. They called with news and left messages, so now I have four things to tell you."

"Every time I go off somewhere it gets busy there!"

"Always the way, isn't it?"

"And it's just like you to keep me in suspense, Paul. Please tell me what Lewis said."

"Okay. Nik said he attended a police divisional meeting where they cross-reference cases they're working on between departments. He mentioned something relating to that case of yours where a gang was stealing the stuff out of homes on large properties owned by older wealthy couples. He said on a few of those heists they were giving out free tickets to expensive shows. It was a slick ruse so the crooks could get people out of their homes for the evening. That way, they could ransack their places free of interference."

"Wow, what an amazing coincidence! Just a few days ago, I told Serena about that case as a bedtime story."

"Were you trying to be romantic? Crime stories aren't love stories, Mack. Just mentioning it so you're aware."

"You're so cruel, Pauline," Mack said, smiling.

"Lewis told me to tell you that after the gang got jailed, the police continued to look for how the stolen items were fenced."

"I was wondering how that happened. What else did he say?"

"Several names of suspects came up. Charges against them are pending further evidence; however, two names were mentioned he figured you'd recognize—Bill Stewart and Royce Tomlinson!"

"What? Are you serious? That's unbelievable! You mean those two bastards had a side-scam running? Bill was making a ton of money with Royal Ransom. Why the hell would he even consider being involved in stealing stuff from homes? It's unbelievable!"

"That's two *unbelievables*, Mack. Want to try for three?"

"No, I'll stop there. But hey, I'm floored! Lorne Harris and Bethany Williams mentioned that Stewart and Tomlinson had a secret thing going on between them. I never would have guessed it was the theft-ring scam—not in a million years!"

"When you least expect it, it hits you right between the eyes every time, doesn't it, Mack?"

"You're so right! I'd better cancel my Friday interview with Tomlinson. Be sure to call Bethany Williams for me and tell her something important came up...but please don't mention I went fishing with my dog."

"Guess that wouldn't go over too well."

"No, but I've got to give serious consideration to what you just told me before charging in there like an angry bull smashing china."

"We need to play our cards right on this thing. It's getting crazy, isn't it? Oh, and please let M know I've canceled our meeting Friday, will you? I should be back in Boston by Friday evening, then, since I've got no reason to leave earlier. I want to get a good sleep in my own bed Friday night, because Serena, Syd, and I are going out Saturday and won't get home until late. Let me check with Jake before I open my big mouth any further, though."

Mack covered the phone with his hand and asked Jake if staying until Friday at suppertime was okay. Jake said he needed Mack's cabin for an 11:00 a.m. check-in Saturday, but until then he was fine.

"Yeah, it's okay with Jake. Might as well take extra time to veg. Hey...please don't forget to call Bethany for me."

"I'll do that. What else do you need?"

"How 'bout an update on Whiting?"

"Oh yeah, John called and said I should tell you he got the report back from the consultants on the value of the company shares he mentioned to you and M. The average value came out at forty-two five. He said you'd understand what that meant."

"That's about what he figured it would be at the high end, so he was right after all—fifty-five million was way too high."

"The second thing he wanted you to know is he told Maggie Stewart he won't accept the fifty-five million, and she was pissed. It was an all-or-nothing deal, so she can't take her slice if she goes it alone and sells her shares. The people who made the offer wanted the entire company."

"Whiting made the right move by trusting his instincts. It's not only about the money for him. He loves the company he built and wants to stay and see it flourish. If he loses control, he may not be there for much longer. The new owners might shove him straight out the door."

"I hadn't thought of that."

"Business can be brutal, Paul. There are lots of people with loads of money and no love of life. Whiting doesn't want to end up being one of them. Besides...if he sells, who will guarantee he'll collect all the money?"

"Being out on the street with only a portion of your money isn't what you'd want to end up with after so many years of hard work, is it?"

"No, and he told us there's no other business for him. He figures he's getting too old to start over from scratch, even with a big pile of dough.

"He said Maggie was furious with him to an extent he's never experienced before. He said she'd have scratched his eyes out if she could. She shocked and scared him, not to mention the vicious four-letter words that came pouring out of her mouth."

"We warned him he's dealing with a wildcat! He'd better be damn careful—I think we can guess what she's capable of while enraged."

"I'll say! I sure hope he listens to you, oh wise one." Mack could tell Pauline had a big smile on her face when she said that.

"Oh, I almost forgot!" Pauline added. "The last thing he told me was he hired Maggie's brother, Lenny Mitchell. He said it was against his better judgment, but he did it as a big concession to calm her. It was also because you said it was a good idea. He told me you wanted to work on a revised plan, so do you have one?"

"Yes, I do, and it might even work—who knows? Did he say when Lenny starts at Royal Ransom?"

"He mentioned early next week."

"Thanks, Paul," Mack said. "Be sure to fill in M on any of this he doesn't already know. See you soon." He thanked Jake as well and reminded him to add the long-distance charges to his cabin bill. After confirming their campfire get-together at dusk, he headed out with Woof for a long run through the woods.

The day flew by quickly, and Mack tried hard not to over-analyze everything Pauline had told him. So much had happened in a short time. It was a good thing he was away from his office because it gave him an improved opportunity to think. But his thoughts became troubled with the fear of impending evil after talking to Pauline.

CHAPTER 23

AFTER A FULL DAY OF running, canoeing, and swimming with Woof, Mack watched the big red sun sink low on the horizon as a cool breeze swept North Star. He was ready to kick back and enjoy a cold one. He used his camp axe to split dry firewood from the stack Jake had provided. Then he kindled the campfire by making a small teepee in the tractor ring out of the split wood pieces. Not long after, he was pleased to smell the sweet scent of wood smoke he had missed for so long.

"Hey, Mack, nice to see you've got the fire started—you must have been in the Boy Scouts," Jake said, chuckling. He sat nearby and hummed "Blue Suede Shoes," as Mack worked on the fire.

"You're so right," Mack said, as he listened to Jake. "Yeah, I advanced to an Eagle Scout. A few kids had a hard time getting used to being in the woods, but I took to it like a duck to water. My dad was a busy guy, but I'm glad he was never too busy to spend time with me camping. Jake, how's *your* son doing?"

"Ronny's fine; still working at the local power company and doing okay. Found himself a nice lady by the name of

Cheryl who likes the same country life he does. They get along good and from what I hear that's something special 'cause so many couples split up these days. Ronny and Cheryl drop by every now and again. It's good they never forget about me."

"Jake, you keep up these cabins so well that I might bring my girlfriend and her daughter up here next summer for a visit. I'm sure they'd enjoy it here."

"Good. I figure you could use more time around this place—you should work on that."

"By the way, I don't mind if you hear a thing or two when I'm talking on your phone—I know it's not going any further. My latest case has been a real stumper and nearly got me killed—way too close for comfort. I needed a short break from the madness to clear my head. It felt like I was drinking from a fire hose for a while there."

"Sometimes just talkin' somethin' out can change your viewpoint and help ease the stress."

Mack was always careful not to discuss his active cases when away from his office, though he did like to give Serena a peek into his cases every once in a while—nothing too detailed though. Sitting as he was in the woods by a campfire, however, he felt it was time to get some weight off his chest. He filled Jake in on the highlights of his current case, but left out names, locations, and dates. By the time he finished, he was ready for another beer from the cooler. He also handed one to Jake.

"That's quite a story, Mack. It's damn serious when you realize someone is trying to kill you. That's a bone-chilling wake-up call no one ever wants to experience. People who haven't been in that situation can't imagine what it's like. I remember being in the army way back. I got startled as hell the first time a few bullets went flying by my head—it was terrifying!"

Mack nodded with understanding as his face glowed from the fire. "This latest close call hit-and-run rattled me to my core."

"I've never met a man who wouldn't be. Even from the little you've told me; a few things seem certain."

"What things?"

"Well, Mack, it'll cost you more beer, and you gotta understand I'm just speculatin'. I'm no big important private eye like you, but I'm *backwoods smart* as they say up here. Those smarts are telling me you should be watchin' your backside."

"Speak your mind and don't hold back, my friend," Mack told his friend, knowing he was right.

"The first and most important thing about your predicament is to realize there's a *force* at work behind the scenes."

"A force?"

"Yes, but not like a *Star Wars* force. More like someone is behind the stage pulling strings while the uninformed puppets are out front performing a show that the force is controlling."

"Who are the puppets on stage?"

"To my mind, it's your client–the owner of the company with that big fancy offer; you and your staff; and the cops. You're all running around doing stuff, but there's something big going on backstage, and it's out of the view of all of you. The force is controlling everything."

"This case smelled bad from the start...I couldn't put it into words. You may have just done that for me."

"Well, let's call this force the Puppet Master. This character may be a woman, but odds are it's some male mobster–the same one who I'm guessing made that big offer for the import company. If it turns out to be a group of people or another company, there's always someone in charge at the center of things. That someone is the *Puppet Master*."

"Why would he offer much more than the company is worth?"

"It must be worth it to him. Maybe he wants total control and knows it won't come easy, or he wants to shut down any potential competitors. Maybe he figures the owner doesn't really want to sell, so it's a big carrot on a stick. This Puppet Master guy was probably aware of that already. Think like a fisherman, Mack—if they're not biting, you've got to offer a bigger juicier bait—plain and simple. What business is the company in?"

"Importing valuable antiques, jewelry, and other pricey stuff like art and rare wines."

"So, this Puppet Master needs an importing company—it's simple."

"Hey, if this is what two beers get me, what will the rest of them yield?" Mack said, laughing.

"The thing you have to watch out for is this Puppet Master. You can bet he won't take no for an answer. He's likely someone who's used to getting what he wants. I heard Al Capone once said something like: *'You can get more done with a kind word and a gun than with a kind word alone.'* Be careful, Mack—that's how most of the tough hoodlums think."

"You mean if he can't get the company one way, he'll try another way that's nastier?"

"Wouldn't *you* if you were him?"

"Sure, I guess—if I were a Mob boss and that was the only way I could get what I wanted."

"So, the guy who tried to kill you with his truck is probably a hired thug—a 'yes man' acting on orders from the Puppet Master or an accomplice. And this Puppet Master thought you would be a problem for him right from early on; maybe he knows your reputation. I'm just guessing but..."

"But you might be right. I don't have a better alternative."

"Tell me more about the driver of that pickup truck?"

"He's well-known to the police. So far they haven't charged him with anything."

"And the dead guy's wife? You can bet she's a player—she's in this somewhere, somehow. That woman's downright conniving from what you've told me, Mack."

After Jake finished with his revelations, he and Mack continued to talk about sports, politics, and the love of life. The hours passed until only burning embers remained in the firepit. At that point the beer was gone, so they said goodnight and staggered off to bed.

× × ×

Thursday

MACK SLEPT UNTIL LATE morning. He was grateful for no headache or hangover, and felt refreshed, energized, and contented he was now on the right track to solving his case. *Thanks, Jake.* He smiled as he gazed out the front window of the cabin at the lake. It was glittering like a million diamonds in the sun—so beautiful.

The predictions Jake had made beside the campfire the night before had gotten Mack thinking. He now suspected it was the Vitale Mob behind the offer for Whiting's company, and they likely needed full control of Royal Ransom, though he wasn't sure why.

Mack had learned a lot about the Vitales from the police. The crime lord of the family was known as *The Feared One*, a term spoken in hushed whispers. His real name was Drago, and Mack presumed he was the Puppet Master who was pulling the strings behind the curtain. Drago Vitale was ruthless—feared for both his brawn and his brains. Mack had learned from his father that behind every highly profitable endeavor is a brilliant mind, a corrupt one, or both. In the Stewart murder case, it might be Drago's.

No wonder the offer to buy Royal Ransom had come through Marino, Hawthorne & Sharp, a large and powerful law firm. There was no identifiable CEO out front to represent the prospective purchaser. Drago had probably told Lupino to set up an anonymous offer through his firm. That way Drago's identity and intentions could remain secret.

Drago had only one child as far as Mack knew—a son named Marco. Lewis had told Mack it was Marco's role to help run the family business with an iron fist. Cruelty was no stranger to these folks; Mack had learned that from the many warnings Lewis had given him. Samples of their handiwork had turned up in Boston's harbor, the Charles River, and in back lots and warehouses across the city—even trash bins.

Mack wondered why Drago wanted control of an importing business. Maybe it was a way to gain more power over his adversaries—rival Mob families, gangs, and rogue contractors. Royal Ransom would give the Vitales an instant base of operations in the major cities of America, Canada, and Europe.

Wherever Royal Ransom had an office, Drago and his henchmen could take advantage of a trusted name. Cross-border smuggling would become much easier and less conspicuous because they would lean on a sterling company reputation built over several decades. If this was the plan Drago was working on, it was unfolding as deceptive and well planned.

But if Drago wanted control of Royal Ransom, why kill Bill Stewart? That was the part gnawing at him. Wouldn't anyone taking over an importing business want to keep an incredible and trusted salesperson like Stewart right where he was? Why wasn't Whiting eliminated instead? The Mob would use their own CEO, wouldn't they?

Thanks to Jake, Mack believed he was much closer to getting the answers he needed to solve this strange case. To get at those answers though, he needed at least two things: one—another serving of his bull-headed persistence; and two—lots of good old Lady Luck.

CHAPTER 24

Friday

WHEN MACK AWOKE FROM another good night's sleep, he had changed his mind and wanted to leave early, so he packed up after showering, shaving, and a quick breakfast of granola cereal with fresh blueberries he had picked the day before. He tied the canoe on the roof of his SUV and drove up to the front door of North Star. On the way, Woof hung out of an open back window, sniffing at the fresh morning air.

"I'm surprised you're leaving already. Are you done, buddy?" Jake asked.

"Yes, I've decided to do a hike on my way back to Cleaver Brissom's cabin. I plan to run the trail with Woof."

"How'd you find out about Brissom's place? That's some real backwoods stompin' you're talkin' 'bout."

"My old Scout troop staked and cleared parts of that trail many years ago as a merit badge project. I recall it's twelve miles to the cabin and the only way out is the way you hike in. I'm sure it will bring back fond memories for me. I'm getting psyched up for the Boston Marathon run next April, and this Brissom run is what I need to start getting into better condition. Besides, it'll be good for Woof too. Once my mind accepts the marathon idea, the rest of me should follow along."

"You hope, huh?"

"Well, that's the general idea—fingers crossed."

"Run the marathon before?"

"Once. No problems with psychos with bombs that year, thank heaven. I surprised myself by finishing in the top one hundred."

"Good luck with that, Mack. Be sure to call me and let me know how you make out. I'll tell Ronny and Cheryl we'll know one of the top runners in the race come next April."

"Who will that be?" Mack said, laughing. "Well, I'd best be on my way. Had a great little break away from the craziness thanks to your friendship. I feel energized enough to face my office again. And thanks for your great ideas—you gave me a few things to consider and all it cost me was about a hundred beers. Now that's a good deal! Oh, and be sure and say hi to Ronny and his wife for me."

Mack paid Jake for his stay plus a generous tip, gave him a solid handshake, and wished him a fond farewell. As he left, Jake made him promise to return soon.

× × ×

A SHORT TIME LATER, Mack was in a small, graveled parking area, holding the door of his vehicle open so Woof could jump out. They were at the Brissom rest stop, three hundred feet off the side of the highway. A few picnic tables, located beneath shade trees, and two big stone firepits with dry split firewood were available to travelers. At one end of the rest area was a large, bold sign that read:

The Brissom Trail & Log Cabin

Trail length is 24 miles total
12 miles to the cabin and 12 miles return

Hike at your own risk!
Allow enough time to return during daylight!
Please leave no refuse behind
Have a safe journey
Be sure to lock your vehicle!

"Let's get going, Woofster—it's a long way to the cabin." The air was fresh, humid, and cooler in the forest than at the more exposed rest area. Mack noticed the trail was in excellent condition. He couldn't wait to see the scenic jagged ravine as he made his way to the Brissom place.

The first part of the trail presented no challenge, but halfway along it got rocky and steep. Mack slowed to a fast-paced walk to avoid the chance of spraining or breaking an ankle. *Safety always comes first,* he thought. But slowing his pace made him feel more vulnerable, even with his dog beside him. The sound of a branch breaking sent a chill up his spine. He whipped around. Woof had heard it too, and took a few steps toward where the sound had come from, his ears straight up. Mack's fear was alleviated when his buddy didn't bark; and later Woof relaxed and returned to his side, ready to continue on their way.

As he climbed, Mack forcefully shook off negative feelings. He remembered a point where the steepness of the trail lessened and the ground cover changed to tall grasses and moss patches. Smiling, Mack recalled staking this part of the trail as a Scout many years before. His fears melted away while hiking further with Woof—it was the right thing to do on such a fine day. What a great way to celebrate his freedom, and appreciate nature and Woof's companionship. Mack's mind was finally clear, and he felt much more energetic than he'd expected. It was great to be able to sweep aside his fears, the stresses and strains of business, and think of nothing in particular for a change.

Moments later, he saw the ravine on his left open into a beautiful valley. Facing it, the Brissom cabin soon came into view. At the front of the cabin, Mack stopped to pay attention to Woof. "Good boy. Here's water—you must be thirsty." He poured water into his large, cupped hand and held it low for Woof. In a few quick licks it was gone and then he gave Woof a treat from his bag. He planned to save the rest of the bottled water for himself. Then he recalled a small stream and duck pond behind the cabin where he could get more water for Woof. It had been so long since the last time he had been in this quiet place. He anticipated splashing cool water on his sweaty face, head, and neck. He knew Woof would jump in as soon as he saw the stream.

As he rounded the back of the cabin, a wave of emotion came surging over him as he recalled a wondrous, breathtaking experience. It was in this very spot behind this cabin many years before that he and Jamie Lee had made love for the first time.

It was in the cool autumn while they were hiking. This place was glorious then, filled with an array of bright fall colors as the sun came streaming through the trees. The warm earthy colors surrounded them, seeming to celebrate the tender moments spent in each other's embrace. He began to hear the sounds of the forest: the heavenly songs of the birds in the trees and the rustling of the leaves—nature's orchestra.

He stood mesmerized as he recalled that magical day with Jamie Lee as if it were yesterday. The birds sang then too. He remembered her lovely smile, the intoxicating sweet scent of her hair and skin, and the soft, smooth warmth of her. Now transfixed with awe and completely spellbound, those memories left him breathless. They had made love that day with an intensity he had never experienced with anyone—and may never again.

Today again, Mack's experience was wonderful beyond words. He stood there convinced his beloved Jamie's presence was with him in this precious place...at this precise moment... as surely as he was alive. He bathed in the glow of Jamie's spirit, certain this was predestined, not a coincidence. She had called to him from beyond the valley of death so he could be standing in this sacred place at this very moment to meet her.

Mack fell to his knees and wept tears of joy. Jamie whispered to him: Please go on without me. I promise to be your guardian angel—a spiritual friend who will love you forever.

× × ×

AFTER RETURNING TO THE parking area without incident, Mack couldn't believe his eyes—his SUV was gone! Someone *had* been tracking him! It wasn't his imagination after all. He stood motionless in disbelief for a moment while he gathered his thoughts. The words on the rest area sign glared at him: *'Be sure to lock your vehicle!'* He felt sick as he realized that in his excitement to set out on the trail, he must have forgotten. Did he lock it? He couldn't be sure. Even if he had, it would have been easy enough to break in and hot-wire it while he was gone for so long.

Luckily, his cell phone was the last thing he grabbed before he went on his hike. He almost left it behind because a cell signal was tough to get in the woods—thank goodness he didn't. He knew he could get a signal at this rest stop, so placed a call to M at the office.

"I need you to come and get me, partner," he said. "I've been robbed—my SUV, wallet, everything. Even my precious cedar canoe!"

"What? How the hell...?"

"Woof and I are fine—that's what matters. Details later, buddy. Right now, I'm at the Brissom rest area and my next call will be to the police to report the theft. I'm damn glad I got through to you—I'm in the middle of nowhere out here." Mack gave M the details on how to find him. Then he called the police to report the theft.

When the highway patrol arrived, Mack gave them a full report on what had happened. He told them he knew Lieutenant Detective Nik Lewis and others in the Boston Homicide Department where he used to work. They would vouch for his character and credentials, since he had no ID on him. The state troopers told him this wasn't the first time a vehicle had vanished from a pull-off rest area in the region. They said whoever took Mack's vehicle knew it would be unattended for many hours while he was on his hike and assured him they would issue a BOLO. After asking Mack if he needed a lift, the troopers left.

After their departure, Mack wanted something to do to help him feel better, so he walked into the surrounding area to pick wildflowers. In just fifteen minutes, he had picked a nice multicolored bouquet. Woof sniffed his way across the entire site, marking his territory as he went. Mack refilled a water bottle from a tap and wet the paper towels from his pack. He used towels to wrap the stems of the flowers to keep them moist and prevent them from wilting.

Several people stopped at the Brissom site, so Mack made an effort to talk with each of them. After hearing his tale of woe, a few decided to hike elsewhere. In another hour, M arrived sporting a big smile as he braked his shiny souped-up street machine to stop right where Mack was standing. Mack explained what had happened, but to M it sounded like Mack was ashamed and disappointed in himself.

"This wasn't your fault, pal," M said. "Could happen to anyone. Besides, what you lost is just stuff that can be replaced. The main thing is that you and your big fur ball are okay. If this wasn't an emergency, no way Woof could hitch a ride with me given how Labs shed. It's a good thing I remembered to grab an old blanket before I left. He can rest his hairy butt on that."

"What's a dog hair or two between friends, M...or even quite a few in a situation like this. I'll make it up to you, I promise—buy you a new auto hand-vac or something. Right now, all I can think of is how stupid I am and what I lost—including everything in my wallet. I can't believe I was so damned dumb. Just the thought of calling all those companies to cancel and replace all the cards in my wallet pisses me off! Bloody hell."

On their way back to Boston, Mack asked M to stop at a small country store. It was the kind of store found in most remote rural areas that stock at least one of everything. He borrowed money from M to purchase bottled water and a sturdy white plastic vase with a good-sized base. In the bottom he put a few handfuls of small pea gravel from the side of the road, then added water and the flowers. A while later, they stopped at his father's gravesite, and Mack said a prayer. He left the flowers in front of the large granite gravestone. Then, with a lump in his throat, he waved goodbye.

When Mack arrived home, he felt contented. Despite his stolen SUV, a few positive and important things had happened to be thankful for. He had touched both Jamie Lee and his dad meaningfully; and he'd been presented with unexpected new insights into the Whiting case—thanks to Jake. Not only was he pleased to see his old friend again, but he'd gotten a lot of refreshing exercise in those forested areas dear to him. All this was due to a last-minute decision to get out of Boston and spend quality time with his best friend, Woof.

What he needed to do now was kick back and rest. The tensions and strains of the SUV theft and the long drive back had taken their toll. Mack decided not to call Serena, but sent her a text: *Back safe, great trip, very tired. Will call you in a.m. Love, Mack.* He decided not to worry her, preferring to tell her the bad news about his stolen vehicle later. After checking the TV schedule, he walked to the fridge and took out a large meaty bone for Woof and two cans of strong Canadian beer. A moment later, he was sitting in his favorite recliner in the den, pleased he had only missed the first few minutes of an NFL double-header.

CHAPTER 25

Saturday

MACK DECIDED TO CALL Serena after 10:00 because he knew better than to wake her up early. He had been scolded more than once for not giving her lots of time to sleep in on Saturdays and Sundays. It was Sydney who answered the phone.

"Hello, Mack."

"How did you know it was me, Syd?"

"Simple: Caller ID."

"Oh, I thought you were psychic or something."

"Well, sometimes I can read minds. Scary, huh? Yours is telling me you want to talk to my mom."

"You're right! You're smart like she is."

"She keeps telling me I'm too smart for my own good—whatever that means. Hang on and I'll get her to pick up the phone. She probably thought it was for me 'cause I get way more calls than her."

A moment later, Serena came to the phone.

"Sorry, Mack, I just finished toweling off after a long, hot shower."

"Sorry for what? Hold that pose and I'll be right there!"

"Too bad, so sad—I'm all dressed now, so you're too late. I

saw your text—I'm glad you had a good trip. You needed a break from that crazy job of yours, but you should have stayed longer."

Mack took a hard swallow, then told Serena what had happened when he returned to the Brissom rest area. He explained he hadn't wanted to ruin a good night's sleep for her, so held off until now; he'd spent the morning canceling his credit, bank, and membership cards, and replacing his driver's license and auto insurance documents.

"I'm so sorry that happened to you. What are you going to do for a vehicle?"

"I'm thinking an adult tricycle with an umbrella so I don't get wet when it rains—that way no one will want to steal it."

"A few people out there will steal anything," Serena said, laughing.

"So true, but I'll make sure to buy a good lock." Then Mack told her he was planning to rent an SUV from a friend of his dad's until he learned more about his stolen one. He added, "Mine may show up, but it's likely a long shot."

"Well, what matters is you got away for a rest and came back safe."

"I'm not negative on my trip—it was great! I know I should take more breaks, but the moment I leave town something important comes up at the last minute. At least the SUV theft happened right at the end."

"You'll have to work harder to free up time for yourself. Did you get lots of exercise while you were away?"

"More than enough. Those other entrants in the Boston Marathon will call me *the streak*. They'll ask, *Who the heck was that guy?* as I run by them at high speed."

"So, physically you're fine. What about mentally?"

"How can I tell you're a doctor? Let me count the ways..."

"Really...how do you feel? You *sound* good."

"Despite the theft, I'm better than I've been in a long time,

Serena. Honest. It was great to see Jake again. We got to hang out for a few hours, enjoying an evening campfire and discussing the tough case I'm working on. It felt good to get a few things off my chest, but I never discuss things in enough detail to affect my case if they were revealed by Jake accidentally or unexpectedly to a third party."

"That's great. Hey, I know you need to go rent a vehicle. Do we still have a date for tonight?"

"Oh, for sure! I'm looking forward to it, and I just spoke to Hailey. She confirmed she'll dog-sit Woof for me."

"I've never been to a dinner-theater. What should I expect?"

"The doors open at six and there's a standard four-course dinner plus a late-evening dessert built into the price of each ticket."

"How nice. I bet that's why they call it a dinner-theater."

"Ha ha, okay, so I guess I'm over explaining. Anyway, they have a famous guest chef from France by the name of Louis Provale. I was surprised to find one of his recipe books in my bookcase. I checked because his name sounded familiar, so now he's another important reason I want to go. They told me he'll be cooking up something special."

"Don't tell me what he's preparing—I want it to be a surprise."

"Okay, it's better that way, so you won't concern yourself with calories until it's too late."

"Are you teasing me?"

"We haven't discussed the dessert dishes in detail yet, Serena. That's when I'll *really* tease you."

"Okay, so go on with your adventure story..."

"Dinner will be served at six forty-five in a huge dining room. Then, when we finish our meal, we head into the adjacent theater. The comedy show starts at eight sharp, so everyone must be seated by then."

"Did you ask who is in the show?"

"Yes, three top comedians are scheduled for about a half-hour each. At nine thirty, we head back into the dining room for the chef's awesome calorie-laden desserts and beverages. After that, we head for the exits."

"Margaritas?"

"That's a real possibility!"

"Mm, so delicious. It sounds like so much fun. It'll be great to have laughs with you and Syd. She's looking forward to seeing you so much, Mack—maybe as much as I am. How will you stay busy 'til then?"

"When I get back from the rental place, I was thinking of working on my other cars. I run each one every two weeks or so to keep them charged up and lubricated. They need that because they're like us: no regular exercise and they begin to creak and moan."

"Charged up and lubricated sounds good to me, handsome."

"You're so naughty, Serena—"

"I know you love to be teased. So, go and play with your cars while I make myself beautiful. I'm getting my hair done this afternoon—something different and stylish. Syd wants her hair done too, so you get two beauties tonight instead of just one."

"You'd look great stepping in from a rainstorm, Serena. You don't know how to look bad."

"Flattery will get you everywhere."

"You think?"

"I know."

× × ×

MACK HAD FOUR RARE vintage cars he cherished. His father had left him three of them as part of his estate, and the fourth was bought by Mack at a large estate sale for a mere fraction of its market value. He was planning on adding a fifth someday, when the right one came along. He kept them in his large, well-equipped garage attached to his unique home, spending time with them as if they were his good old friends. When he expected he could work for a while uninterrupted, he'd get started. He always wore mechanic's gloves to protect his hands and keep them clean. Once he got greasy and grimy, though, it took a while to clean up, so he didn't like to be disturbed.

Time flew by as Mack became absorbed in doing what he loved. In the late afternoon, he took a shower and then put on his custom-tailored dark blue sports jacket with a light blue dress shirt. He had polished a pair of dress shoes the last time he had worn them, so they looked crisp with his black pants. A touch of his favorite cologne, and he was ready to go on his date with Serena and Sydney.

He dropped off Woof at Hailey's and arrived at Serena's condo in good time. Serena looked fantastic in a turquoise dress, supplemented with silver and turquoise jewelry. She had purchased the jewelry pieces from New Mexico Native Americans when on a trip there a few years ago. She completed her look with turquoise leather high-heeled shoes and a large white flower on the side of her new stylish hairdo.

"You're a goddess—I'm breathless!"

"Thanks, and may I present my lovely goddess daughter?"

"Oh, Mom, it's no big deal."

Mack knew it was though. This was a big event for young Sydney—it was her date with Mack, too. Sydney had her black hair styled short like her mother's, and was wearing a tan dress with a string of dark brown beads and low-heeled black shoes.

"Sydney, you're beautiful!" Mack said, smiling. "If the boys in your school could see you now, I bet they'd all want to go out with you."

Sydney blushed and he could tell she was proud of her appearance.

"That would be too many dates for me," she said, laughing. "Most of the boys I know act way too silly."

Mack added, "But the not-so-silly ones would be thrilled to be with you."

"Mom, Mack's so nice. You should marry him."

Now it was Serena's turn to blush. "Um, we'll talk about that another time, honey. Right now, we have to go—we shouldn't be late."

Mack gallantly helped his ladies climb into the rental SUV and they drove off. It wasn't long before Serena spoke to her daughter.

"Syd, there's a special reason we're going out tonight. Mack helped the police catch thieves who were breaking into expensive homes and stealing things. An older couple who had their house broken into was so grateful for Mack's help, they gave him three free tickets for the dinner and show tonight."

"Gee, that was nice of them. Did they get their stuff back?"

"Most of it, yes," Mack answered. "They were lucky because a lot of it was still in an old warehouse."

"They were fortunate, but a lot of others weren't," Serena said.

"I'll say! Not many victims get their things returned," Mack said. "A few collect from insurance, but many valuable things get taken that can never be replaced."

"What kinds of things?" Syd asked.

"Paintings, antiques, jewelry, and much more," Mack said. "Sometimes things that were given to them by their parents who wanted them to remain in their family."

"Oh, that's so bad," Sydney replied, as if personally offended.

"Yes, sweetheart, it is," Serena said. "An entire gang got

caught by the police because Mack helped to catch them. They're in a heap of trouble now."

"What if someone breaks into our house while we're at the theater?"

Serena's eyes went wide and she looked at Mack. "Oh, honey, I don't want you to worry about that!"

Mack explained how the crime worked in more detail. "This time the tickets came from people we can trust, Sydney," he assured her.

The pre-performance meal was served and turned out to be a visual and taste sensation.

Mack enjoyed the dinner so much he proposed a toast to Chef Louis with Serena and Sydney. He was overheard by those at adjacent tables, and soon someone told the chef. A moment later, a rotund master wearing a white toque came out of the kitchen. Mack stood up and called out his toast again for everyone to hear, and the chef received a resounding applause.

Serena turned to Sydney. "Always remember to say thank you when someone pleases you. That's what everyone did by applauding after Mack's toast."

Soon, the diners entered the theater to enjoy the comedy routines. Three talented comedians were the entertainers—two men and a woman. As they performed, the laughter was plentiful and intoxicating. Mack was happy there was no foul language, for Sydney's sake.

"That show was so funny," Sydney said, still chuckling after it was over.

"I can't recall having laughed so hard for a long time—my sides will hurt for a while," Serena added.

"Worth the price of admission, that's for sure," said Mack.

"But you got our tickets for free," Serena noted.

"Oh yeah. Well, it's worth a lot more then! I'm glad you two enjoyed the show so much. Let's get back into the dining room for scrumptious desserts and drinks—I'm thinking a margarita or even two."

"Mack, you find our table with Syd while I freshen up in the restroom. I'll see you in a few minutes."

CHAPTER 26

"A STRANGE WOMAN HANDED me this envelope," Serena told Mack on returning to their table. "Then she hurried straight for the exit! She knew both your name and mine. She told me to give this to you, but why here? Who knew we'd even be here?"

"Who indeed." Mack did his best to hide his anger.

"It's got to be work-related, Serena. But this is a special night for the three of us. I refuse to let anything get in our way and disrupt our fun. Besides, it's Saturday night, so I'm sure it can wait until Monday morning when my office opens." Feigning a casual attitude, he took the large brown envelope from Serena.

Mack wanted to appear casual, but was concerned and tense. He was careful to pinch one corner with the side of his index finger and thumb because he knew he wanted to have it scanned for prints.

"Without opening it, I'm guessing there's a few sheets of paperwork inside. The last thing I want to see right now is more paper. It's probably something from Whiting. I'd rather be spending my time looking at you two beauties instead."

"Ah, that's so nice. Remember what I said about flattery?"

Serena teased, appearing relieved.

"I'd have a tough time forgetting that."

He set the envelope on an empty chair beside him. His mother Josephine had taught him: *"Out of sight is out of mind."* He hoped Serena would think about other things as he made an effort to distract her, but he wondered what the envelope contained. He hadn't told a soul he would be here—not even Hailey when he dropped off Woof. Who was this strange delivery woman? How did she know he had a date with Serena?

Mack asked Serena only one question: "What did the woman who handed you this envelope look like? What did she say? Maybe I can match her up with someone from Whiting's office."

Serena shut her eyes as if picturing the encounter. "Attractive, mid-thirties, tall and slender, bright red lipstick. Very black hair, partly covered by a dark-blue fedora style hat. And she also wore a long dark-blue trench coat with the collar turned up, black gloves, and a red silk scarf that matched her lipstick. The coat had a red rose pinned to the lapel." Serena laughed. "In fact, she looked like a female private eye out of a TV show. She said, 'Is your name Serena? Are you Mack Sampson's girlfriend?' When I nodded yes, she said 'Give this to Mack.' And the next thing I knew she was gone."

"Doesn't ring a bell," Mack said, "but my best guess is she's a Royal Ransom employee. She must have seen me when I was there. She probably just happened to be here and spotted us together, so went out to her car and grabbed the envelope—no big mystery." Mack didn't believe the words that had just come out of his mouth, but he wanted to dissipate any fear this strange occurrence might have instilled in Serena.

"That envelope must be important, Mack, even urgent," Serena said, concerned. "And how would she know my name?"

"Whiting would have called me if it was urgent," Mack

said, ignoring Serena's second question. "I've been available all day working on my cars. Who knows, John may own this place—or the owner might be a good friend of his. I'm sure there are things he wouldn't put in the mail, and no way he'd do his own deliveries. Could be he sold his company, who knows? Let's just enjoy our desserts."

Serena frowned, but let it go. "Okay...you're right. I should stop worrying I guess, but it's so strange. Make sure you tell me what's in it when you open it."

"Sure—count on it."

Chef Louis's special desserts arrived and everyone's attention turned to the grande finale—Sydney most of all. It only took a minute for her to get chocolate sauce on her dress. Serena decided not to reprimand her because she didn't want to spoil the great evening her daughter was having. "Nothing a little dry-cleaning won't fix," she told Sydney. Mack chose not to have a calorie-laden treat and ordered a margarita instead. He had started on a second one by the time Serena finished her slice of chocolate-covered heaven.

"How much did you love it?" Mack asked.

"I'm still floating on a cloud. I can hear angels singing. How was your margarita?"

"I can't remember ever having a bad one. In fact, the more I have, the better they taste," he said, starting to laugh.

× × ×

WHEN HE LEFT THE restaurant, Mack had made sure he picked up the envelope off of the chair beside him by the same corner he held it with the first time. He slipped it under his sports jacket, then into a storage compartment in the SUV.

They arrived at Serena's place contented, chattering about how the evening had been such an enjoyable experience—despite the strange envelope that distracted them. Serena invited Mack into her condo and told a very tired Sydney to get ready for bed. It was way past her bedtime and Mack soon heard the start of the *Sydney-getting-ready-for-bed* ritual. He figured mother and daughter shared those moments the same way every evening. Sydney came out in her pajamas to say goodnight and thank you to Mack. She made sure to give him a big hug as she headed upstairs to her bedroom.

At last, he and Serena were alone. She asked if he wanted a drink. He smiled and told her good liquor should never go to waste, so sure. Serena brought him the drink and then cuddled up next to him as they sat quietly, relaxing in the dim light. Mack wrapped his arm around her and they held hands as the moonlight and restful glow from the streetlamps streamed in through the large living room window.

It had been a while since they had enjoyed any private time together. They cherished each special silent moment as it passed. After becoming confident Sydney was sound asleep, Serena stood. She held her hand out for Mack's, smiled, and led him into her bedroom at the end of the main floor hall. Then she quietly locked the door.

× × ×

Sunday

MACK GOT BACK TO his place at 2:00 a.m. and headed straight into the den. He was very tired and feeling mellow after the warmth, affection, and love he had shared with Serena. Those wonderful thoughts and feelings remained with him, but he couldn't wait to see what was in the envelope.

He took off his sports jacket, not bothering to change. Using the sharp knife on the micro multi-tool he always carried with him, and holding the envelope with a folded piece of paper, he slit it open. Then he took a pair of tweezers out of a small drawer next to his recliner. He slid the contents of the envelope onto the surface of his lap desk.

What he saw shocked him: five 8″ x 10″ photos and a white sheet of paper with words pasted onto it. The photos had obviously been printed on a low quality black-and-white printer. The first was of Serena and Sydney leaving their condo; one of Serena dropping Sydney off at school; a third showed Serena shopping at the mall where she often went; then a shot of Serena coming out of the medical building where her office was; and finally, a photo of Sydney and her best friend, Heather, playing on the street in front of Heather's house.

The words pasted on the sheet of paper had been cut from newspapers and magazines:

These im**perfect** photos
COULD have been **left**
Next to the sculpture
On **her DINING** room table
Get **THE** picture?

Mack felt sick as he read the words over and over again while absorbing the implications. Then he became fuming mad. He knew he needed to approach things in a cautious and well-reasoned way, but his heart was heavy and filled with pain. *How dare someone threaten Serena and Sydney!*

Mack had always believed that when confronting evil, you examine the details—that's where the devil will be lurking. Serena had told him the woman who handed her the envelope wore gloves, so that would avoid leaving fingerprints. The implicit threat in the pasted words referred to someone illegally entering Serena's condo; he knew the sculpture on the dining room table the note referred to. He could find no direct threat, but Mack understood the veiled message to drop his Whiting case or suffer the consequences.

The word "imperfect," though rarely used in conversation, reminded Mack of the note he had received by email—the one he suspected came from Eddie Venn: *An imperfect plan failed: there will be another*. Had someone written the note for Venn? Mack now believed a hidden force *did* exist behind the evil events he faced, as Jake had suggested. Strings *were* being pulled behind the curtains and Jake helped to solidify Mack's thinking on that.

Who was the mysterious tall slender woman who delivered the envelope to Serena—was she a friend of Drago's son, Marco? Maybe his girlfriend or fiancée? He was known to help his father with the dirty work of the Mob. And why deliver the envelope at the theater? Why hand it to Serena? Because she was far less likely to ask questions? Or was it because the Puppet Master thought she wasn't trained to remember details like Mack? The most likely answer to these questions was probably that the message would have a far greater impact if Serena was the one to receive it.

The most frightening part to Mack centered on the implicit threat to Serena and Sydney. Had someone sneaked into her condo while she was at work? He knew Serena would have told him right away if anything was missing or out of place. And how did they know of his dinner-theater plans?

Mack pondered the possibility someone had planted a bug in his home, but his security system was state-of-the-art. Twice he had thoroughly scanned for bugs since he had the system upgraded recently. *Did they plant a bug while in Serena's place?* He became certain a bug was the problem, so he needed to search Serena's condo and remove it immediately.

Could the threat in those few cut-out and pieced-together words in the message backfire on the sender and reveal the source of the information? Mack grabbed a bottle of bourbon and downed a few shots. Then he paced around the room, thinking about the words and photos in the envelope. In the early hours of Sunday morning, he felt completely frustrated, mad as hell, and unable to sleep.

The way Mack had it figured, if the person or persons who concocted this lowlife threat really meant to do harm, it would have happened by now. Apart from the questions he wanted answered right away, one was foremost on his mind—what was he going to tell Serena in the morning?

CHAPTER 27

MACK WOKE UP TO the sound of his cell phone ringing beside his head. How it got there, he had no idea. The call turned out to be from Hailey.

"Hi, Mack, I hope I didn't wake you. You sound groggy, so if I woke you, I'm sorry."

"No problem—late night, Hailey. What time is it?"

"It's around nine. I need to go shopping, so I have to return Woof. Can I drop him off on my way, or would you prefer to come and get him?"

"I'd appreciate it if you'd just drop him off since you're on your way out anyway."

"See you in twenty minutes?"

"Sure."

Mack hung up. He had a lot on his mind and knew nothing could hit you as hard as real life. That's why it was important to get back on his feet and keep moving forward. To him, that was what distinguished a champion from the rest of the pack. He got up and made some strong coffee, and a few minutes later the doorbell rang. Mack answered, taking Woof from Hailey as she told him yet again what a great dog he was. She left happy with her usual fee and tip.

The first thing Mack wanted to do was go for a run to clear his head. Woof spun and jumped as Mack put on his runners. A couple of minutes later, they were out the front door. He'd been taking a different route each time he ran since the Checkerboard Park incident, but Woof didn't care. He enjoyed the variety of sights, sounds, and smells—happiness was running with his master.

Mack returned from his run feeling refreshed, but sweaty due to the high humidity. Despite the discomfort, at least he didn't need to shovel tons of snow. He finished a cool shower, toweled off, then threw on a baseball team shirt with well-worn jeans. Today was the day he had to pick up Lewis and his boys at noon, then head out to Fenway Park. They had spoken about the game a few times after Mack first suggested it, but time has a way of flying by and then suddenly it hits you.

It was a great stroke of luck and a welcome coincidence he and Lewis loved to discuss what they did for a living. Mack had heard him repeat an old saying so many times: *It's not just a job, it's an adventure,* with that wide toothy grin of his. Lewis repeated that whenever anyone asked him if he liked being a detective. Mack wanted to give him the brown envelope for analysis, then update him on what happened at the dinner-theater. He also needed his help to get Serena's place scanned, but there was one other important matter on his mind.

Mack fed Woof and, while he did so, he decided to tell Serena the truth about the envelope. He wanted to do it with no-holds-barred. There was also the pressing matter of security for Serena and her daughter, and he wanted to get her protected and her condo assessed fast, so first he called M and briefed him on the latest.

"I'm asking for your help to watch Serena's every move—we have to keep her and Sydney safe." Mack said he planned to brief Lewis since they were going to a ball game together:

he planned to leave around noon.

"I'm glad you called when you did because I was just heading out to the shooting range with a couple of friends," M said.

"I regret spoiling your outing on a Sunday. I know you love the range."

"No big deal. Priorities are priorities. Have you called Serena yet to tell her what you found in the envelope?"

"I wanted to call you first to make sure you can be on this. I'll tell her the truth, but before I do, I need her to believe I've got a good plan for her safety worked out. Besides, she knows and trusts you, and believes you're damn good at what you do. That ex-special forces rep of yours goes a long way with her."

"Thanks—you know I'll do what needs doing."

"One more thing. I believe whoever is behind this probably planted a bug in her place. I need to get the entire condo and her phone line scanned, so let's see if I'm right. If I am, then we play whack-a-mole. Over and out, buddy."

Mack hung up, then called Serena on her cellphone. He felt fired up and ready to talk.

"Good morning. Ms. Contented speaking..." Serena teased, the words rolling off her tongue.

"Your name should be Ms. Universe, because I saw so many stars last night. Have I told you how beautiful you are?"

"Yes, a thousand times...but you can tell me a few more times if you like."

Mack smiled, then became more serious. "I'd like to talk to you in person. When can we meet in *friendly surroundings?"* Serena always called her place *friendly surroundings* because she loved her neighborhood so much. They both knew he meant to meet at her place.

"I'll see you in a half hour? Don't hang up yet...I want to know if this has to do with the envelope?"

"Not over the phone, Serena. Please wait until I see you in

person—I need you to do that for me."

"Did I ever tell you you're not an easy person to love?" With that, she ended the call.

Mack felt sorry Serena was worried, but he had to get his ducks in a row fast. He called M back.

"Hey, M, where are you?"

"I'm outside your front, pal. I wanted to come over and talk to you, so I just finished driving up when my phone rang."

"What do they say about great minds?"

"I hope we're thinking alike, Mack. So, can you cut the crap and open your front door?"

Mack laughed. "Sure, be right there."

After Mack let M in, they headed for the den where he showed M the contents of the envelope.

M narrowed his eyes and his nostrils flared like an angry bull's. "Someone will get their heart ripped out for this shit. I can see why they used a cheap black-and-white printer. It's much harder to trace than a color one because with color they can match the tones of the print to the source where they originated. I'll bet you there aren't any fingerprints on it."

"I won't take that bet because I believe you're right. Anyway, let's get over to Serena's. I'm squeezed for time because I've got to pick up Mr. Lewis and his kids by noon for the game. Take your car so I can leave when I want. Poor Woof will have to stay here because I can't take him to the game and it's not a good idea to leave him at Serena's with everything that's been happening. Where's Paul when you need her, huh? Woof loves Paul!"

It wasn't long before he and M were both at the curb in front of Serena's condo.

"Nice to see you again, M," she said in surprise as she opened her door. She turned to face Mack. "This must be serious if you're *both* here. Good thing my darling daughter is at her friend Heather's house."

"It is, and I won't candy-coat it. It's best if we talk outside. Let's sit in my SUV for a few minutes. Please do me a favor and try your best not to show any facial expressions in case we're being watched," Mack emphasized.

"Okay, but what's this about?" Serena asked, squeezing his arm in consternation.

"There's no easy way to say this—I believe your condo is bugged." He helped her into the passenger seat of the SUV while M got in the back.

"Are you kidding me? That's crazy. Who would do such a thing—and why me?"

"We'd like to find out. M and I are here to hunt for the bug and whack it. We have a scanner we'll use, but the Lewis team should check your place out as well, just to be sure."

"This entire thing gives me the creeps—do whatever you need to."

"Count on it. I'll call the security specialists who set up my place. They'll come over and set up yours and I'll cover the cost. The job will need to wait until tomorrow though, because they won't do your installation on a Sunday. In the meantime, I've asked M to keep an eye on you because I can't stay."

"I know you wouldn't be suggesting this if I didn't need it, Mack, but you're scaring me."

"You're in good hands," M assured her.

Mack placed a hand on Serena's shoulder. "Not long ago you told me you're a big girl—not a fraidy-cat—and that's what I need you to be now. This isn't about being scared or mad, it's about catching the culprits responsible, and that's what M and I will do—I promise. It's clear they want me off the Stewart case, but they're pushing this whole thing to dangerous levels."

Serena froze, and her lips tightened. "What was in the envelope?"

Mack met her eyes. "Black-and-white photos of you and

Syd. There was a note with them."

"That's so terrifying! I can't look...I can't!"

"Yes, you can. I'll show them to you, but before I do, I suggest you call Pamela on your cell while you're outside here. Ask her if Syd can stay over there with Heather for a few days. Don't get into any detail—just tell her you'll explain later. Say you need a big favor. What are friends for, right?"

"Sure, she'll be glad to help us, but now I'm scared for them, too."

"The strategy of these creeps is simple, Serena," M said. "They want you to be afraid and pressure Mack to drop the Stewart case. It concerns Mack and me, not you and your daughter. They're afraid of us because we've got the upper hand—but we still have to play our cards right."

"How can you be so sure?" Serena asked, as she started to shake.

Mack removed the envelope from the large plastic folder he had been carrying as M stood and watched. There were big white labels on the front and back of the folder Mack had slapped on, marking it as evidence so it couldn't be thrown away or misfiled by accident. He showed Serena the photos and the note while telling her not to touch them.

"Oh my...oh my," Serena whispered, while continuing to shake.

Mack spoke in a low voice. "Photos such as these could have been taken with any camera and a decent telephoto lens. I realize it's frightening to find out someone followed you around and photographed you, but remember it's meant to scare *me*, not *you*."

"That's not reassuring at all," Serena said, sounding disheartened. "I'm the one being stalked!"

"Right now, we need to secure your home so you can get a good night's sleep."

"If someone entered here without my knowing it, I'd feel

violated," Serena said, her voice rising. "How am I going to get *any* sleep?"

Mack tried to hush her again. "It's perfectly normal to react that way, but we must know if someone entered and bugged your place."

"Do whatever you need to! Please, Mack—Syd and I are depending on you!"

"The thing that stands out the most to me is the comment on the sculpture," Mack said quietly. "There are a few ways someone could have seen the center of your dining room table. Let's say a person came to your door and spotted it, say a pizza delivery guy or a courier. It's visible from your front door. You, or one of your friends, may have mentioned it to the wrong person without remembering. Maybe it was seen through your window, or they broke into your place. A break-in is the one I'm most concerned about, Serena. It might not have happened, but we'd be foolish not to consider that."

Serena nodded numbly. "I understand."

"Your place will be much safer with high-grade security like Mack's," M said. "You'll have the peace of mind of knowing it'll protect you for as long as you live here."

Mack added, "How did someone know where we were going last night? We told no one we had tickets to that show. It's impossible to accept that the person who gave those tickets to me had anything to do with this. But someone handed you that envelope in the theater as slick as you please. Damn it, I've got to figure out how and why that happened. If there's a bug in here somewhere or on your phone, we have to find it."

At that point, they went into Serena's condo so that Mack and M could sweep the condo and phone line with their scanner. They went over the place and completed tests on Serena's cell phone, but found nothing. Mack approached her as she was sitting on the couch, sipping tea. M had decided to re-scan a room in the rear of the condo to be extra careful.

"Good news, Serena. There are no bugs we can find. It's unlikely anyone was in here, but I still want to ask Lewis to send someone to scan again. A second opinion is always best where advanced technology is involved. I'm taking Lewis and his boys to a ball game today, so I'll give him the envelope and a briefing. I'm sure he'll help us out."

"You never mentioned you were going to a baseball game *today*, Mr. Mackenzie Sampson. That's crappy timing! How can you do this to me?"

"Let's just say it's a fun way to discuss business. Besides, it's been in the works for a while, Serena. I have to admit the timing is far from the best, but it's a great opportunity to talk to Lewis. To compensate, I've asked M to be your bodyguard and keep an eye on things. As for the game, I was lucky to get good tickets. So often when you try to buy them on or near game day you only get crummy ones—unless you pay a scalper. As a member of the medical profession, I'm sure you know how important it is for men to play with their favorite balls every so often."

"Is that what you're up to?" Serena asked. Mack caught her starting to smile.

Mack laughed out loud. He could see she was coming out of her slump. Maybe she'd even be able to get a good night's sleep after everything that had occurred—he sure hoped so.

CHAPTER 28

MACK AND M WERE RELIEVED they hadn't found any listening devices in Serena's condo. Mack told Serena and M he would call them when he got back from the game with Lewis. He swung by the large Lewis bungalow and was pleased to see Nik and his boys waiting on the front steps. They waved and smiled as he stopped in the double driveway. Mack wasn't used to seeing his friend dressed in jeans, a navy T-shirt, and runners. He appeared to be carrying his own light jacket as well as one for each of the boys.

"Nik, before we get going, please take this folder," Mack said. "It has an important envelope inside—be sure to put it somewhere safe. I'll tell you about it while we're waiting for the game to start. We should be in our seats early enough to have some spare time."

Lewis took the folder into the house, then climbed into the front passenger seat of the SUV. "Okay, done. Did you remember the tickets, Mack, or do you have to go back and get them like last time?"

Mack laughed and winked at the two boys riding in the back. "You had to get a dig in, didn't you? I've got them. Since that last goof-up, whenever I get any tickets to anything, I stick them in the glove compartment. That way I can't leave home without them. Luckily, I hadn't done that before my own car got stolen."

Lewis nodded. "I see you're still driving a rental. Any word on your missing SUV?"

"Nope, but I'm not worried about my insurance—I'm confident they will pay as expected, so I'm thinking about buying *this* vehicle. It has less than forty thousand miles, one owner, beautiful shape, no accidents, and comes with a warranty. I'll save quite a bit of money buying used, so I think I'm going to do the deal sometime this week. Good thing I know a lot about cars since I work on them as a hobby. I'm also fortunate the owner of this rental and the dealership it comes from was a good friend of my dad."

Mack glanced into the rearview mirror at Lewis's two boys, who were now ten and eight. "Hey, how have you two guys been doing?" he asked. "Any offers to play pro ball yet?"

"I'm really good," Joey said, while the younger Jeremy shouted, "I'm great!"

"They've been fine, but no MLB or NFL offers yet, Mack," Lewis added. They all laughed.

The Lewis brothers had brought mobile devices with them, so were keeping themselves occupied playing video games. Mack could hear a variety of musical sounds as well as bings, bangs, booms, and clangs, emanating from the back of the vehicle as they headed toward the baseball stadium.

"Haven't been to Fenway for a while, and I must admit I've missed the old place. In fact, it's the oldest ballpark in Major League Baseball. Did you know that, Mack? I think the last time I went there was with you. Come to think of it, that was when you forgot those tickets."

"Dig number two, Nik," Mack said with a grin. "It's always amazing to me how fast time flies. Last time I saw your boys, they were both a foot shorter. Man, they're sprouting like dandelions. I guess you and the wife must be taking good care of them 'cause they sure look healthy."

"I'll trade food bills with you anytime, single guy. It makes my head spin what things cost these days. It used to be a man could take his kids to a ball game, and it wouldn't break the bank. Now, when you figure the cost of gas to get there and back, decent seats, snacks, souvenirs, and parking, it comes to hundreds! I'm glad I'm paid well and my wife works part-time, but the average joe on a single income can pretty much forget about that old *'Take me out to the ball game'* crap."

"That's for sure. So, what's your prediction for today's game? The Blue Jays and the Red Sox are reasonably well matched, wouldn't you say?"

Nik paused a moment to think, then said, "Maybe in your mind they are, but I've got to go with the home team."

"What say we put five bucks on it? I'll go with the foreigners—hard to do, but one of us has to. Besides, it adds some spice to the game."

"You're on," Lewis said with a broad smile.

Soon Mack entered Boston's dense Fenway-Kenmore neighborhood and pulled into a driveway quite a distance from the stadium. He asked the boys to stow their devices under the seats, and showed them how to do that in the rental SUV. Nik told his boys that too many *smash and run* crimes happened because people left desirable items visible to others in their unattended vehicles.

"An old buddy of mine owns this place and lets me park here whenever I need to, so we walk from here," Mack said. "It's about three-quarters of a mile to the stadium."

When they arrived at the stadium, Nik bought ballpark dogs, fries, and drinks for the kids since it was lunchtime. Mack grabbed a couple of dogs and beers for Nik and himself, feeling happy to be going to another game with his friend and glad his kids were along. Then they all went to their seats.

They were down near the front along the first base line, Mack's favorite spot.

"Glad we got our eats before the start of the game," Mack said. "The minute you get up and go for a beer or a quick pee, that's when the greatest play of the year happens. It never fails!"

He had a sip of beer, then turned to the boys.

"Do you see that high left field wall out there?" he asked them.

"Sure do," Jeremy answered.

"Yep," said Joey. "What about it?"

"Well, that's called the *Green Monster*. It's just over thirty-seven feet high. Many hits that would clear the walls in other stadiums can't get by the Green Monster. That's why Boston's team mascot is a furry green monster. His name is Wally."

"Wow," Joey said.

"This place has its own monster," Jeremy added. "Cool."

They had all been munching on their snacks and watching as the stadium filled up. The boys seemed distracted, so Nik nodded to Mack. "So, what's in the folder you gave me?" Sparing no details, Mack described what was in it and the strange way the envelope had been delivered.

"I'd like you to have your crew check it out for prints, DNA, or anything else," he concluded. "My thumbprint is on one corner of the envelope and Serena's prints are on it as well, but the person who delivered it was wearing gloves. Neither Serena nor I touched the contents."

"I'd be glad to get on that for you. Let's see what we can find."

The game started, and Mack put things on hold so that they could enjoy the action. It turned out to be a close game. There were two home runs, one by each team, and a fly-out to right field that a Boston outfielder caught as he slammed into the back wall.

"Did you see that unbelievable catch for my team?" Nik shouted at Mack amid the crowd's roars. "Man, what a thing of beauty! That guy can high-jump even better than you, Mack!"

The final score was five-four for Boston. Mack lost his $5 bet, but felt great. It had been so much fun. On the way back to the SUV, Nik bought each of his boys a Boston baseball jersey, which they were thrilled to receive.

"Cop wages being what they are and the price of everything always so high, I'm sure glad you sprang for the tickets, grub, and transportation, Mack, or I couldn't have bought these jerseys."

On their way home, the boys resumed their gaming.

Nik kept his voice low. "It seems obvious to me someone's trying to scare you away from the Whiting case, Mack. Eddie Venn is still caged up with us, so what do you think is going on?"

"I rented a small cabin in the woods for a couple of days this past week. I needed to clear my head and try to see things from a different perspective. I told the basics of the case to my trusted buddy, Jake, who owns the place. He said it sounded to him like there's some force pulling the strings behind the scenes—called him the *Puppet Master*."

"Sounds like he might have something there."

"Yeah, it rang true to me right away. My first thoughts after he used words like *force* and *Puppet Master* were of Drago and his son, Marco—the Vitales. I started to think Drago has some interest in Royal Ransom. I can't guess all of the cards in his hand, but from what I've gathered, Drago wants to get his dirty paws on a reputable North American and international importing firm to use as a front of some kind."

"Anything you need from me right now?"

"Bill's wife, Maggie, is obviously tied up in this somehow, Nik. Her brother, Lenny Mitchell—you know, the felon—is about to start working with Whiting at Royal Ransom the day after tomorrow. Maggie pressured Whiting to hire him; he didn't want to, but I convinced him to go ahead. He's making a big concession to me by taking this gamble, but hopefully it will appease Maggie for now."

"That could get you some useful info too," Lewis said.

"That's what I was thinking. Lenny Mitchell and a guy named Royce Tomlinson are going to be working side by side. We already suspect, as you do, that Tomlinson was connected to fencing goods with Bill Stewart for that gang that just got jailed. You know, the one carrying out heists from wealthy homes by buying theater tickets. I'm arranging for both Mitchell's and Tomlinson's office to be bugged. That way, we'll have every word they say digitally recorded."

"Have you spoken to Whiting about this? Is he okay with it?"

"Whiting's aware I plan to do it with Mitchell's office and he's agreed. I still have to clear Tomlinson's with him."

Nik gave a considered nod. "Mack, you asked me earlier about the potential need for warrants. I'll have to think about those and get back to you with an informed opinion. Whiting is the primary owner, and he makes the rules for his company. So, as far as I'm concerned, he can listen in to anything he wants. Admissibility in court is another kettle of fish, but warrants should be easy enough to get, given this is part of Stewart's murder investigation."

"Good, Nik. I was hoping you'd say that, and I sure appreciate any help you can provide. Here are a couple of my thoughts: They must discuss some crime or crimes so we'll need that evidence to be cleared for use against them, and that also goes for others they mention, so it will be useful in a court of law. On another point, I'd like one of your guys to scan Serena's condo for bugs. M and I worked on that this morning, but I'd feel better if I have an experienced second opinion given all the new high-tech equipment available out there. It would help to settle her mind and mine."

"Okay, but it'll take me some time, especially on the matter of Serena's place. There's little expectation we'd get anything from Serena's on the Stewart murder we could actually use. That's why I'll have to ask for a favor from one of my guys; but it's doable. I'll see if I can get an unmarked to swing by her place every evening for a few days as well. I'm sure the guys will be okay to help you out on this."

"Thanks, Nik," Mack said as he pulled up in front of the Lewis home.

"My boys had a lot of fun and I'm sure they'll be telling their friends all about it. It was good to get an update from you as well, and we didn't have to sit in a stuffy office to get it done. Oh, and don't bother about our bet. Keep the five dollars as a reminder of the fun we had together. Seriously, huge thanks for the great seats and treats, my friend."

"It's *you* I need to thank, Nik. I'll be in touch—and oh, one more thing before I forget." Mack pulled out a small plastic bag from under his driver's seat and handed it to Nik, who looked surprised.

"Huh?"

Mack broke into a laugh. "Here's a pair of stuffed Wally Green Monsters for your boys to show off to their friends. Ciao for now," he said, then waved and drove away.

CHAPTER 29

MACK WENT OUT WITH Woof after he got home from the baseball game, but felt a vigorous walk was all he needed. When he returned, he felt refreshed but hungry. He spent a few minutes preparing a strip-loin steak and Caesar salad. He shared part of the steak with Woof, then called Whiting. There was no answer, so he left a short message saying he'd call again in the morning.

In the den, he settled into his favorite recliner, then called M.

"Hey, I'm back from the game. How'd things go?"

"No issues—I'm still up the street from Serena's condo. She called a neighbor of hers and asked if I could park my car in their driveway—cool idea, wouldn't you say?"

"Serena is gradually turning into a PI. I told her there's no way I could be a doctor though—I'm a big chicken who gets woozy at the sight of blood."

"Serena told me I'd be more than welcome to make myself comfortable in her living room. She even offered to make me a snack, but I thought it would be better to be out here. I figured you'd be jealous of my ass sitting there with your little Suzie Q, munching and watching sports."

"Or listening to funky music and expecting to get paid?"

"Sure. Hey, Momma didn't raise no fool, as they say."

"Listen, M, I had a good time getting together with Lewis and his kids. Boston won five-four over Toronto. It's good to feel like we're friends again."

"That's good to see after all the issues you've had between you. What's with the envelope thing? Did you discuss that?"

"Yes, but I'll tell you more about it in person. It's getting so that if you're talking on a phone or sending email, you'd be smart to assume you're not alone. Ever."

"Ain't that the truth! Nowadays one never knows, and it's a crying shame."

"I'm confident we'll get what we want, and soon. I'll get hold of Whiting, right after I call my Suzie Q tonight."

"Good. I'll hang tough for a while, but I'm gonna head out at sundown. I told Serena to call me if she so much as hears a peep in the night. I reinforced that it's *you and me* they want, Mack, *not her*. She's okay, but I promised her I'd be close by just in case she needs support."

"Thanks, M. Let me know when you leave her neighborhood because I might swing by later and keep watch on her place for a while, too. Knowing Lewis, there'll be a cruiser nearby her home each night for a few days. He told me at the game he planned to do that. After all, he wants to solve this crazy case as much as we do."

Once finished with M, Mack called Serena. He wanted to keep his conversations with her brief until he was positive there were no listening devices to worry about.

"Hi. How was the game?" she asked when she picked up.

"Boston won, but only because I bet on Toronto."

"So, it's your fault the Jays lost?"

"Yeah, totally. It's guaranteed that if I pick a team and bet on it, they'll lose. It was a close game though, and lots of fun. Hey, did you know your new nickname is Suzie Q?"

"No. How did *that* happen?"

"M used it. He's a huge fan of southern bayou rock–especially old tunes by CCR."

"I like Creedence too! And M is a great guy. So, are you jealous we like some of the same things?"

"Suzie, the man is only five-foot-five. Nuff said!"

Serena laughed. "He looks short only because you're so tall. Besides, he's cute, has a solid physique, and happens to be a great guy. Height isn't everything, you know."

After a pause, Mack said, "Okay, okay, you're right. Besides, you know I love the little guy."

Serena replied, laughing, "You *never* stop, do you? Most of the time we women *are* right. You men just need to take the time to listen–"

"Suzie Q, so be it. Did you and Nik make any headway on your case?"

"Yes, but I'd rather tell you in person. I've called the troops out for you from everywhere. Don't worry, because the covered wagons are in a circle around you. You can sleep tight tonight, sweetheart."

"Thanks for taking such good care of me–I appreciate it."

"I know you do, but I regret involving you in this mess... and for the stress it's caused."

"What's a friend for?"

After hanging up, Mack tried twice to call Whiting at his home, but all he got was his voicemail. As always, he was reluctant to leave a message or call late. He didn't want to discuss much over the phone. Whiting would get a call from him in the morning–he had done what he could for one day. It was time to kick back and enjoy some boxing.

Though boxing could be a brutal sport, Mack liked it because it was one-on-one, man-on-man in the ring. There was nowhere to run or hide–a fighter can't sit on the bench when he's tired or hurt as in hockey or football. You're either ready and in condition, or you're not. It was a physical and mental sport, and you had to be strong in both categories to come out a champion. Mack's father, Matt, had taught him that when you're boxing and you hear your opponent swear under his breath, that's when you know he's starting to lose. It was that way in other situations in life, too. Sometimes the art and science of boxing reminded Mack of some dilemmas he faced while fighting crime.

After dark, when the boxing match had long since ended, Mack decided to swing by Serena's. All appeared quiet, but it allowed him an added measure of safety and peace of mind—much better to be safe than sorry.

× × ×

Monday

MACK WAS PLANNING A meeting with John Whiting on this bright, clear Monday morning, so he dressed well. The temperature had climbed to seventy-five degrees by the time he got to his office at 8:00 a.m.—the weather channel predicted a humid, hot day.

As soon as Woof jumped out of the SUV, he raised his hind leg and watered the low scruffy weeds along the fence at the back of the office property. He kept looking up, searching for gray squirrels in the large shade of trees overhead.

In the office, Mack turned on the air conditioning, then headed straight for his phone with Woof close behind. He called Whiting, pleased to arrange a meeting in an hour at a coffee shop about halfway between them. Mack intended to update him and answer any questions he had at this point in his case. A few minutes later, M came into the office with Pauline.

"Wow, Mack, did you get a new tailor? You look too good

to work here," Pauline teased.

M winked at Pauline. "His tailor must be Italian—has to be. That's why his suit fits so nice."

"You guys got it wrong, Paul," Mack said, grinning. "You and M are too qualified and smart to work here. All three of us know that. That's why I have to use management tricks on you every day to convince you to stay. I don't want you to ever think I'm an ogre, so my slick approach has been designed as a sly strategy to keep you both coming back for more punishment at modest wages day after day."

"Hmm, last I looked, you didn't have an eyeball in the middle of your forehead and your teeth were clean and straight," Pauline said, smiling. "Those things mean a lot to me."

"And you don't have warts all over your face," M kidded. With a wide smirk, he added, "Mind you, sometimes you smell bad because your aftershave or cologne sucks. But that's an issue to discuss another time."

"Ha! But I've hidden under a few bridges in my time. Don't ogres do that?" Mack said, chuckling.

Pauline laughed. "No, that's what trolls do. I must admit there were days in your recent past when you had a troll-like look. But today in those clothes you don't look like a troll, and at least you smell nice despite what M may think." She headed to her desk.

"Hang on one sec, Paul. I wanted to tell you that M and I are heading off to see John Whiting in a few minutes—we're meeting with him at nine thirty."

"We are?" M asked.

"Yes, I'd like you with me. After we get back, I'd appreciate it if you'd swing by Serena's office. We should return with time to spare so you can be outside her clinic when she leaves for lunch. She goes out every day for an hour at noon. It might reassure her to see you around there, so please make yourself obvious."

"Okey dokey."

"Oh, and would you also swing by Sydney's school when it lets out this afternoon? It would mean a lot to me if you'd watch her until she gets home."

"Better double that okey dokey," M said.

"Did I miss something?" asked Pauline.

"Paul, I have to update you on a few things. Order lunch for the two of us for noon, please. We can sit in my office together and talk; maybe chomp on deli food or whatever. Just promise me you won't say okey dokey."

"Okey dokey, then," Pauline said with a wink. "I wanted to take Woof out for a brisk walk on my lunch because I need to hone my fabulous figure—but sure, you've got a date. I'll go for my walk *before lunch* instead."

Mack smiled. "Good, so I'll see you when I get back and bring you up to speed. There's important stuff I need to share with you."

CHAPTER 30

JOHN WHITING SAT AT a small table near the window in the coffee shop. He was dressed in a dark gray suit reading a paperback as Mack and M entered.

"Oh, hello there," Whiting said, as he looked up from his book. He eyed Mack up and down. "Nice suit, Mack—I might have missed you if M wasn't with you."

"Are you an avid reader, John?" Mack asked.

"I used to be—I'm getting back into it, hoping it will take my mind off the crap I've been dealing with lately. My favorite kind is murder mysteries, though heaven only knows why with this Bill thing hanging over me."

"What about you, Mack?" Whiting asked.

"I'm not much of a reader. I live with murder-mysteries, detective investigations, and suspense in my life every day, so I find it relaxing to work on my hobbies."

"And what are they?" Whiting asked, setting his novel on the table and leaning forward with interest.

"Taking good care of my dog comes first; training to be ready for the Boston Marathon next year; maintaining a few antique cars; and then comes the outdoors—hiking, canoeing, and Mother Nature. Those are the main ones."

"John, don't let Mack fool you," said M. "He also appreciates the company of beautiful women, but I think he'd be a mountain man living with his dog somewhere in the backwoods of Vermont if he wasn't with us chasing criminals. He's a woodsman at heart."

Whiting broke out laughing, "And how about you, M? What turns your crank?"

"I go to the gym a lot and work at my martial arts and shooting sports skills, but shooting pool is at the top of my list," M said.

"And he's incredible at all of them," Mack assured him. "I think he paid cash for the souped-up machine he drives from his winnings off a few well-worn pool tables."

"Impressive. I don't mean to sound nosy, but I always like to know about the people I do business with. My wife, Joanie, is the real people person—curious as hell. Always asking me questions I can't answer about the people I meet. I try to head her off at the pass and have a few answers ready, but I'm never quite prepared."

"Speaking of heading someone off at the pass, John, I'd better tell you what happened Saturday night when I was at the dinner-theater with my girlfriend, Serena, and her daughter. A female stranger shocked the hell out of Serena by handing her an envelope meant for me." Mack described the photos and the pieced-together message in the envelope. "The word *imperfect* struck me. I'm certain it was Eddie Venn who set up this scare. He used the same word as part of a threatening email he sent me right after he tried to kill me with his truck. The bastard knew I'd remember that unique word."

"But Venn is behind bars—" Whiting stopped in mid-sentence.

"He has slimy friends," M said. "That's not too complicated."

"It seems there is someone behind this case pulling the

strings. I've come up with a theory that the underworld boss, Drago Vitale, must want control of your importing business. My suspicion is he plans to use it as a front for his own business dealings throughout America, Canada, and even Europe. I think that offer to purchase for fifty-five million came from him."

"That's one hell of a scary theory. If that's true, my life could be in grave danger!" Whiting said, his voice cracking.

"John, you're safe for now, so try not to worry. Someone has to run your company, and that's you—no one else can do it, at least not for the time being," Mack assured him.

Whiting nodded but paled. "Listen, what I haven't told you yet is that Maggie wants to sell one-third of her shares to a corporation she says contacted her through lawyers. This happened right after I told her I turned down that inflated offer."

"But why not sell her shares back to you at fair value?" Mack asked. "You guys have known each other for a long time and she knows and trusts you, doesn't she? She must know you'd want to keep things under *your* control."

"Nothing is certain anymore, Mack, and I'm very disappointed in her. I told Maggie I'd buy the shares back from her on fair terms, but it's obvious she wants more than what's fair. It's clear she's angry as hell because I refused that big offer. Maggie is a person I've known for years, and now she says she has no time for me. What the hell is going on?"

"Maybe the Vitales are pressuring her. Who knows?" M said. "You guys were good friends until now, so I don't suppose it's just the money—do you?"

"It was as if she planned to sell to someone long before we even had our discussion," Whiting said. "Now you've got me worried Drago Vitale will be my new business partner! What bloody nonsense! I'm so worried and scared—I mean, who wouldn't be?"

"Before we assume Drago's behind this, did she say who's buying her shares?" Mack asked.

"All I know is the sale was going through Marino, Hawthorne & Sharp. That's the same law firm that the original offer came from." Whiting's eyes narrowed. "It's damn suspicious. When they say, *'The devil is in the details,'* that may be the situation I'm facing here—Drago Vitale is the devil himself."

Mack and M could see Whiting was filled with fear about a new unknown business partner who could mean a heap of miseries for him beyond imagining. After a moment of silence, Whiting said, "Look, I want to thank you for updating me on my case. Anything you guys need, just let me know—I mean that!"

"Sounds great, thanks," Mack said while M nodded in agreement.

"Look," Whiting added, "I'm done with pussyfooting around. When you're at war, you need a battle plan. Come by my building at seven tonight with your listening devices and video-surveillance equipment and whatever. I'll tell security to make sure we're not disturbed for several hours so you'll have whatever time you need and we can talk then. Also, I have another check for you. I'll give it to you tonight."

Whiting's comment brought a smile to Mack's face. "Sure, that'll be great, John. M will be with me and I'll want a police surveillance specialist in on setting up the equipment."

"Now you're talking," M said, pleased with the outcome of their discussion.

"Not so fast! One problem—no police. No way! I want this to stay between you two and me," said Whiting.

"But why not, John? If we gather any important information, we want to make sure we can use it as evidence."

"I've been considering that and what worries the hell out of me are the actions of those two unknowns—Lenny and

Royce. I need to make sure I'm always in control of everything at Royal Ransom—no exceptions!"

"But I'll be reviewing our findings with you..." Mack implored.

"Not good enough! I've worked too damn hard for too long building a sterling reputation and an enviable list of wealthy clients. Our clients are hypersensitive to any negative publicity. Even the slightest suspicion of anything bad could mean we're headed for a load of trouble. We've already been mentioned in the reports on Bill's murder and Eddie Venn, even if the story is being spun as connected to a car theft and not connected to the import business."

"I can understand your reluctance, but—" Mack didn't get the chance to finish his thought when Whiting cut him off sharply.

"No!" Whiting said, with his voice raised. "Let me make it crystal clear for both of you. I don't want to be implicated in any criminal charges leveled against our people, or see nasty media headlines with Royal Ransom's name plastered all over the place. That outcome could ruin our company prospects and me! Am I clear?"

"All right—I can see where you're going with this and why, so we'll play by your rules," Mack said in his most soothing tone. "We'll do our best to make sure it works within your parameters; how does that sound? It might work out better. Who knows? It's worth a shot to do it your way, so I'll handle things with Lewis and try my best to obey your wishes."

Whiting appeared pleased. "Good—now you're talking! That's the attitude I wanted to hear from you."

"So...when does Lenny start work?" M asked.

"Tomorrow morning."

"Then our timing couldn't be better, John. We'll see you in the lobby downstairs at seven sharp this evening." Mack was feeling somewhat re-energized after having his plans shot down in flames.

"Count on it," Whiting confirmed.

"Thanks, John. Well, M, let's get going."

They walked away as Mack said, "Hey, that reminds me, you've got a date with Serena and I've got one with Pauline."

"No offense, Mack, but that really sounds weird," M said, as they broke into laughter.

CHAPTER 31

PAULINE RAISED AN EYEBROW as Mack returned to the office late in the morning.

"Paul, you look anxious about something—am I right?" Mack asked.

"We got a call about another case. Someone named Randall wants you to call him back. He left a number."

Between major cases such as the Stewart murder, Mackenzie Investigations often received requests on matters like a missing person, infidelity, theft and property damage, and others.

"What time did he call? Did he say what it's about?"

"He called right after you left with M and didn't tell me anything—not a word. It's clear he doesn't know how important I am. Anyway, I told him you were out and would try to call him back this afternoon."

"You are important, Paul—so important I want you to join me in my office in about five minutes. I plan to bring you up to speed on the Whiting case."

"Meetings, meetings," Pauline mumbled as she walked away.

Pauline had ordered lunch for them and made sure to

include something for Woof, as Mack suggested. They sat in his office eating together and talking.

"I'll check out the Randall thing," Mack said. "If possible, I'd like you and M to handle it without me, though. I'll be tied up for a while with the Whiting case."

Mack finished his sandwich, washed it down with a cold fruit juice, and told Pauline about the wonderful date he'd had with Serena Saturday night—disrupted by the mystery woman with the large envelope that was handed to her. He took his time describing the photos and message, the threats they represented, and his suspicions concerning Serena's condo being bugged. Then he told her about his time with Lewis and his boys at the ball game, and mentioned what was discussed. Finally, he briefed her on the meeting just completed with John Whiting.

"No police involvement? Is Whiting hiding dirty laundry?" Pauline asked.

"I'm not sure; perhaps he has some worries about old smelly gym socks and other clothes that might have missed the corporate hamper. It's not good to have dirty laundry lying around."

"What I hear you saying is he's nervous."

"Yes, he seems afraid some things may come to light to threaten the reputation of his company—maybe even kick him in the butt. He spent years building that reputation and doesn't want it soiled."

"Can you blame him? He lost his partner and good friend when Stewart died."

"Nobody can blame him for feeling the way he does when you think about it. He wants to be in full control of all the information. He plans to filter it and he wants us to help him. I don't like his avoidance of the police, though. He mentioned something about avoiding them right from our first meeting—even before Eddie Venn came into the picture. It was as if he already knew that Bill Stewart's murder had some connection with Royal Ransom."

"Well, his sidestepping got us a nice fat contract, didn't it?"

"One that almost got me killed. It's hard to put a price on that."

"This case has been a roller-coaster ride we'll never forget," Pauline said, frowning. "I hope we get it resolved before anyone else gets hurt or killed."

"That's one good reason I'm updating you now, Paul. I need to make sure Serena and Syd are okay and I solve this case before another bad event occurs. I may have to ignore other work, and that's where you come in."

"Can you do what's needed given Whiting's restriction on police involvement?"

"I sure hope so. He doesn't disrespect police—it seems he figures their other duties demand too much attention, leaving no time for his case. He could be right. Who knows? He has ample resources to get help—and we're it. Anyway, I can't blame him for feeling nervous and scared."

"That means you have to tell Lewis his surveillance specialist is not welcome at Royal Ransom tonight. Will that upset him?"

"Lewis is so busy I don't believe he'll care. He knows we're on it and trusts us well enough to know we'll keep him in the loop. I want to remain positive this could work out even if we do it Whiting's way."

"That's one thing I like about you, Mack—that great positive attitude of yours. I've seen that work so many times; no reason it won't work now."

Mack called the number Pauline had given him for Randall and got him immediately. After a brief discussion about his wife's marital affairs, Mack said he'd be happy to lend his assistance. He suggested Randall come into the office to meet Pauline, discuss fees, and sign a contract so they could get started on his case.

As he had done so many times, Mack said his business partner, M, would take the lead on the case and his office manager, Pauline, would assist. Others would help as needed. Mack assured him he would review the case file, and the progress made on it regularly. Randall seemed satisfied, so Mack ended the call. Then he called Lewis, and after two tries Steve Drakowski came on the line to tell him Nik was all tied up. Mack explained the matter of surveillance at the Selector Tower was off for tonight, and he would explain everything later. He made sure Drakowski knew it was no big deal, so he would pass that on to Lewis.

Moments later, M called in to say Serena and Sydney were okay.

"Super—so I'll meet you downtown at Whiting's office at about seven. I've got some running around to do."

"Works for me."

"Tomorrow, I want to scan all the phone lines in our office. When we scanned Serena's place, I remembered we should do our office again. I keep putting it off, but I'd feel much better knowing we're on top of it."

"Great idea," M said. "I'll make sure you don't forget. Failing that, I'll tell Paul to remind you."

"She'll have me duct-taped to the scanner each time we're scheduled for a checkup! You can't do that to me, M! I'll tell you what—I'll put *you* in charge of looking after the quarterly scanning if you're not careful. Then *you'll* have to explain things to Paul whenever you forget—how does *that* sound?" They both laughed.

"You know this means we're doing the scanning together from now on, don't you?" M said.

Mack chuckled. "It sure looks that way, doesn't it?"

× × ×

MACK MET M AT THE Selector Tower at 6:55 pm. John Whiting was already waiting in the lobby ready to clear the special after-hours request with security to let them onto the tenth floor and into the offices of Royal Ransom.

"I didn't want to forget to give you this," Whiting said, smiling. He handed Mack a $25,000 check.

"But we haven't earned that much yet, John. Are you sure you're okay with this?"

"You'll be needing it and you're here right now. Besides, I told you I wanted the best from you and was willing to pay for it. I just saved you an invoice and a stamp for a payment I'd make anyway."

Mack and M smiled at the kind gesture, but Mack felt wary because it seemed too easy—too calculated.

They finished with the installations two and a half hours later. They had installed discreet and well-hidden motion-activated video cameras, along with voice-activated audio devices, then tested the system twice to make sure everything worked as it should. The system would record video and audio whenever there was movement in the office of Royce or Lenny. The information would be sent to a central server where it would be retained in separate digital files for evidence retrieval purposes. The server housed a powerful system capable of storing up to two hundred hours of video and audio.

The data they collected could be accessed and transmitted at will to Mack's receiver within a range of about one mile. They had used a short range to minimize the chance of any interception from an unwanted party. Mack could download all the data he wanted fast. After that, he could review either the video, audio, or both, whenever and wherever he wanted.

The technology was expensive and state-of-the-art, and Mack and M agreed it was perfect for this intended use. All they needed now was Lady Luck. But one thing was certain—they had set the trap.

CHAPTER 32

Tuesday

"SO, HOW DO I RATE a call from you this morning, Nik?" Mack asked, pleased to hear Lewis's voice.

"I spoke to Steve. I assume you got things worked out with Whiting last night?"

"We managed to get that new system of ours up and running. After all, you were the one who recommended it to us after our other one broke down. I've only used this new one once before, but it worked great. I'm sure it will do the job we need it to do in Whiting's offices. It tested out at one hundred percent last night, and come to think of it, it should be working right now."

"Mack, I'm wondering why we weren't needed down there to help you."

"Whiting apparently doesn't want you to find something in his dirty laundry hamper he'd be embarrassed about or have a tough time explaining. He wants to make sure he knows all of the issues before he has to deal with the police or anyone else."

"Well, tell him he's damn lucky I have too many other things to worry about. Besides, he'd have a tough time finding someone to work harder on his case than you."

"Thanks, but if I tell him you're too busy, that will just reinforce his belief the police have no time for him."

"Good point. Anyway, I heard back from our people about your envelope. As you suspected, there were no unknown prints anywhere. Your big thumbprint was on one corner of the envelope, of course. Several were from another person on the outside—likely Serena. I know you'll be disappointed, but there weren't any fingerprints on the pictures—not one—and no DNA or anything else. Nada."

"Damn."

"The photos were taken with a cheap digital camera using a zoom lens—not a cell phone. As you mentioned, they were printed on a low-end black-and-white laser printer. We're sure we know the makes and models since all cameras and printers leave signatures. Our pros knew what to look for. They're going to do further analysis on the images and the note, but so far there's squat to go on."

"Pretty much what I expected, Nik. Just a cheap boogie-man type of scare-tactic to get me off the Whiting case. Somebody's afraid of me and wishes I'd disappear."

"As if wishing would make it so. We know they'd have to kill you to stop you, Mack, and they've already tried that."

"Let's hope they don't try again, shall we?"

"Yeah, right you are. Oh, and before I forget, I can have someone over to Serena's condo by eight tonight to do a scan? Does that work for you guys?"

"I'll say yes, Nik, and if there's a problem, I'll be sure to get right back to you."

"Good. I know I can count on you to keep us informed about what you're planning. I hope your surveillance at Whiting's offices gets us the answers we want so we can clean up this festering cesspool once and for all."

"In the loop you shall be. It may take a while, Nik, but these scumbags are about to find out I run one hell of a cesspool cleaning service. I have only the best solutions in my bag of tricks to make sure my clean-ups stay cleaned up."

"Knowing you as I do, Mack, I don't doubt that for a minute."

× × ×

Friday

THE EVENTS OF THE week had flashed by, with Mack hopeful something exciting would happen to set the Stewart murder on a new and productive course.

The Tuesday night search of Serena's condo for a hidden bug didn't turn up anything, and neither did a check of her landline and cell phone. Mack was pleased the search was completed as requested, because it gave Serena peace of mind.

Pauline and M had met with their new client, Randall, in the Mackenzie office on Wednesday afternoon and started on his case. Mack stopped by the conference room for a few minutes to meet Randall and assure him he would be reviewing their progress regularly. Mack did this with all new cases anyway; but sometimes an insignificant case could turn into a much larger one, so Mack wanted to be up to date on the meeting.

Lewis's crew found nothing new regarding the mysterious envelope Serena had received the previous Saturday night. Both Mack and M continued their surveillance of Serena and Syd, making sure to swing by often, especially at night. They also kept an eye on Sydney's trips to school and back, and the recess breaks and school-ground activities. True to his word, Lewis had unmarked cruisers complete due-diligence surveillance on Serena's condo and office.

Mack hated to sit and wait. He described his frustration to

others by telling them it made his gears grind, but he had no choice. In the first few days since planting the surveillance equipment in the two offices at Royal Ransom, nothing useful had emerged. The only interactions in Royce and Lenny's offices concerned the regular business of the company.

By viewing the video of the men as they worked at their desks, Mack was able to match the voices of Royce and Lenny to the phone taps. If he heard a voice he couldn't recognize as belonging to John, Lorne, Bethany, Angelica, Royce, or Lenny, he planned to ask Whiting for input. He also typed up the critical audio portions on his laptop to have a hard copy available, just in case he needed it. Mack didn't trust computer auto-transcription features for fear of an error. He preferred to do the transcribing the old-fashioned way.

Mack had told Serena he would try to see her later Friday evening, but it was critical he first do a digital download close to Whiting's building. He had done that after dinner each evening, ever since the Monday they had first installed the equipment. He made sure the staff had all gone home and business had shut down before completing each download. Later, he would review the material he'd collected and continue his review into the following day if necessary.

Mack sat with Woof in his newly purchased SUV to collect the Friday evening download, then headed home. He was hopeful there might be something different in this material. Often, employees would kick back and relax at the end of a Friday afternoon in anticipation of the weekend. After about an hour of watching the video surveillance, Mack heard a casual conversation. Royce Tomlinson and Lenny Mitchell were together in Royce's office with Royce behind his desk and Lenny seated in front of it.

Lenny: "Got any plans for the weekend?"

Royce: "I'm gonna get the hell out of here and do something wild, but I'm not sure what or where. Got nothing steady to play with, so need to find a curvy piece to amuse myself."

Lenny: "Bit different now that there are no new items coming your way from the moving company, huh? You got a lot more time on your hands to play with the ladies, right?"

Royce: "Never mind the ladies; it's the income I miss. Man, I was headed for millionaire status until now. Where am I gonna find another sweet deal like that? I'd like to see those two private-eye freaks Whiting hired floating facedown somewhere."

Lenny: "They sure pissed off my sister, Maggie, when they came to talk to her. I heard from Marco they're the ones who put Venn out of commission. Word has it he's really stressed in jail, even though Lupino said he'll get him a good deal."

Royce: "Cop problems are only minor when they involve someone else. When it's *your* dick on the chopping block, it's *never* minor. Easy to understand why he's scared shitless."

Lenny: "If Venn keeps his mouth shut, everything should work out. I don't wanna think about what'll happen to him if Dragon Man or Marco gets nervous about him blabbing."

Royce: "I hear Eddie's solid. [Pause.] After all, he's been around for a lot of years. By the way, word has it your sister unloaded a big chunk of her shares."

Lenny: "Had to—no choice."

Royce: "Yeah?"

Lenny: "Billy-boy was up to his ass in gambling debt. You didn't know? The interest was like fifty grand a month! Bill was hanging on as long as he had the moving company income to help finance his little hobby, but when the police shut that down with the help of those Mackenzie fucks, Billy was up to his neck in shit."

Royce: "I knew he was super-stressed, but I had no idea his gambling was out of control like that."

Lenny: "The Vitales played him like a violin. Search the

words *gambling sucker* on the internet and Bill Stewart's smiling face comes up."

Royce: "That's why I never gamble."

Lenny: "But you did with that moving scam, didn't you? You could have got caught, right?"

Royce: "Yeah, I guess but—"

Lenny: "All I can say is my sister was damn lucky she happened to know Drago from years ago, so he gave her a break. She said knowing him from before went a long way. He agreed to take a third of her shares to wipe out Bill's debt, and now I think he wants the rest. She was lucky he was interested in Royal Ransom, but he had his own reasons he wouldn't discuss with her."

Royce: "I'd say she's one lucky girl to get that debt wiped."

Lenny: "No kidding, and she still has two-thirds of her shares, which is worth a fortune."

Royce: "Fifty grand a month just in interest? How much did Bill owe?"

Lenny: "That crazy bastard was into Drago for over two mil! The way I heard it, he owed half a million, so decided to bet on two double-or-nothings in a row. He lost them both—I mean, talk about crap for luck. The man was an idiot. Or an addict...I guess all addicts act like idiots. Thought he could work his way out of his debts by playing double or nothing with the Vitales. Where's a brain surgeon when you need one?"

Royce: "Gotta admit it does sound nuts."

Lenny: "You get some first-class liquor in you and some sexy chick's tits rubbing up against you, and before you know it, you're feeling like a hero on top of the world. One minute you're smiling and then *bam*—you get sucker-punched below the belt. I mean, when you're gambling in a Mob-run casino with the champions of crime, you don't stand a chance in hell of getting out of the pit you're in—no chance at all. Man, when you're looking for a lucky break, the Vitale boys just hand you a bigger shovel. That's exactly the type of digging Bill Stewart did."

Royce: "It seems like all that digging was for his own grave in the end. I had no idea he was in it that deep. [Pause.] Even so, Maggie's shares were worth a helluva lot more than Bill's debt. What about that?"

Lenny: "You think you're going to get a good deal from the Mob when you sell something to them? If you do, I've got a nice shiny new bridge for sale you should have a look at."

Royce: "Yeah, okay, Lenny, forget I even mentioned it. Still, I had no idea it was that bad for Bill."

Lenny: "I have my suspicions the entire thing was what got him killed. Anyway, I've got to get going, so have a great weekend chasing the ladies! Be sure to share the uncensored details with me when I see you Monday! Catch you later, Royce!"

Mack sat back in his chair, flabbergasted and triumphant. Finally, a break in the case! He knew he would have to tell Whiting, but wanted to be careful how he did that. One thing was sure: It had been a great idea to plant surveillance devices in the offices of Royce and Lenny.

× × ×

MACK DECIDED TO SPEND a quiet Friday night at Serena's—just the two of them and Woof. Sydney was still at Pamela's place with Heather. It was nice to see things almost back to normal with Serena after all the trauma of the previous week. He didn't discuss the Whiting case, except to say he was making progress. No way he wanted to talk shop with Serena and end up seeing her full of worry again. Besides, it would have been unprofessional to divulge such business.

But even though he was spending time with her, his mind

was racing. He couldn't help thinking about the revelations he had just uncovered while listening to Royce and Lenny. *Finally, we're getting somewhere,* he thought. Mack would never give up on a case—never. But on this one, he was starting to feel much more optimistic that a solution might be just around the corner.

CHAPTER 33

Monday, End of June

MACK COULDN'T BELIEVE HOW fast the weekend flew by, though it had been uneventful. He smiled at the memory of the intimate time spent with Serena, and how their blossoming love had lifted the massive weight of stress off of their shoulders.

Mack had been in his office for about a half-hour when M and Pauline arrived within a minute of each other.

"Nice to see you on this fine summer morning—I have good news for you. Hope you guys had a good weekend," Mack said, as Pauline and M sat in front of his desk.

"I did." Pauline said. "Keith finally got back from his road trip, so we went out for dinner on Saturday night."

"I ended up winning over five hundred dollars with that great cue you gave me, Mack," M said, grinning. "What better weekend could I possibly have? How was yours?"

Mack smiled and leaned back in his chair. "It was nice and relaxing, so thanks for asking. I'm going to tell you right off that I misled you both a moment ago. I don't have good news for you...I have is some great, fantastic, awesome news for you!"

"Don't tell me; let me guess," Pauline said. "The spying on Lenny and Royce is paying off?"

Mack laughed. "Paul, you win some free health food! I already ate the cinnamon-raisin bagel, though." Mack picked up a box of donuts, muffins, and bagels from a small side table in the corner of his office and let Pauline have her pick, then handed the box to M. Luckily, she had brought a cup of coffee in with her.

"This Boston cream donut will taste so good with my coffee—it's chocolate-covered heaven," Pauline said. "I feel like I just won a prize."

"I've been on the verge of bursting waiting to play you this audio tape," Mack told them. "It's a conversation between Royce and Lenny while they were sitting in Royce's office on Friday afternoon. You just gotta hear this!"

"Must be really good if you've been bursting," M said, grinning.

Mack played the recording and high-fived both of them when it finished. Now you two look ready to burst, just as I was! He handed them a photocopy of some notes he had made from the conversation, with yellow highlights.

"Here's my summary of what was said between those two slimy losers. If you think I need to add anything, please say so. Any first reactions?"

"You better believe I have a first reaction!" Pauline almost shouted. "I mean, if I was married to that rat-bastard snake named Bill Stewart and I heard he owed the Mob two million dollars of *our* money, and that it was piling up at the rate of fifty thousand a month in interest, I'd hit him with a hammer myself!"

"Would you really?" Mack asked.

"Well, *I* wouldn't—but I can sure see how someone like Maggie might. She's shocked to learn his solution to paying for a nasty gambling habit is to operate a theft ring? He's taking the huge risk of getting caught and going to jail—so much for the Sugar Daddy income. Plus, he's now essentially owned by the Vitales. He's basically thrown a lifetime of work right out the window...and speaking as his wife, that would put our entire future at enormous risk. I mean, how would I know that Bill could ever stop gambling? Maybe it would keep on getting worse and worse!"

"Wow, Paul, you *are* upset," M said.

"M, you haven't seen me upset and you don't want to. I'm just getting warmed up!"

"You've outlined something critical for us, Paul," Mack said. "Maggie Stewart could have had her husband murdered to protect her personal interests. It's certainly an option we have to consider."

"Maggie could have hired any number of bad people to do her bidding," Mack said. "In fact, she may have known Venn and several others from her earlier life when she was turning tricks."

"So, how do we prove it?" Pauline asked. "That's what we need to do."

Mack was quiet for a moment, deep in thought. Then he said, "I don't like her at all—in fact, I think she's despicable. But for now, I have to believe Maggie is innocent until found guilty. We have no evidence whatsoever that she had anything to do with her husband's death."

"Yes, I grant you that," Pauline said, looking dubious.

"I think we have two options open to us, Paul—at least as I see things now," Mack said. "One, we can wait and hope our daily surveillance of the offices at Royal Ransom provide more proof about who was behind Stewart's murder. Option two, we talk to Lewis and ask him to speak to the DA to see if he'll do a deal. We propose that Venn gets a lesser charge or maybe serves it in a better location, but only if he signs an affidavit on video that Maggie hired him to kill Bill. We'll need something tempting to offer him, though. Having a life sentence off the table is something he'd pay attention to."

"But what if Maggie didn't hire Venn?" M asked. "Probably a stretch, but it could be. Venn might accuse her just to get his sentence reduced."

"What other choice do we have?" Mack said, his voice raised. "Paul, based upon what you just said, Maggie is likely a main character behind Bill's murder. We know that someone put Venn up to it; he didn't act on his own. Who else has a clear motive? From what I can see, Drago and his Mob would want to keep super-salesman Wild Bill right there at Royal Ransom. They would want to continue collecting their massive interest charges from him, wouldn't they? Dead men don't pay any debts as far as I know."

Mack paused for a moment, then added, "Now that I know about his trafficking in stolen goods with Tomlinson, it's clear Bill was a shady crooked sneak like all the rest of those Mob racketeers. We know he was central to the success of Royal Ransom, and the Vitales had him by the balls. Every man knows that if you grip 'em tight enough, you help assure loyalty to your cause."

"Now you're talking my language," Pauline quipped, chuckling.

"Easy, Paul," said Mack.

Pauline winked. "Just sayin'."

"I'm thinking out loud here, but what I'm going to propose is a ruse—a bluff," Mack said, feeling like he was on a roll. "We'll ask Lewis to go nose-to-nose with Venn and make him believe someone ratted him out—sold his hide to the police for a favor. Also, we'll ask Lewis to tell Venn we know Maggie's as guilty as sin, but Venn is the only one who is going to rot in jail *because we have nothing on her*. And just to drive it home, Lewis will also remind Venn that Maggie will live the rest of her life in luxury at his expense."

"Pure genius," M said, elated.

"Well, I think we should thank Paul for putting us on this sensible new track, shouldn't we, M?" said Mack.

"Thanks, Paul," M said.

Pauline smiled. "Are you both telling me I'm a genius? If you are, it's important we cherish and remember this moment so we can recall it when needed. And pass the donuts."

CHAPTER 34

MACK BELIEVED HE AND his team had accomplished a lot in the action-packed three and a half weeks since they had started on the Whiting case. It was hard for him to believe it hadn't been longer. It was the end of the month and heading into the warmer weather Bostonians enjoy in July. Mack was thinking how fortunate he was to score a meeting with Nik Lewis on short notice once again. He drove along, admiring the sights of the city he loved as he headed toward the Boston Central Police Station. He also thought about his need to call Whiting and brief him, but he wanted to do that after seeing Lewis.

Mack knew the way he was planning to handle this situation could be problematic— it could even get him thrown off the case. Whiting didn't want the police involved unless he gave his permission, but that was unlikely to be forthcoming. Mack felt he had a higher level of responsibility to do the right thing, however, and the right thing was to give the police all the evidence he possessed.

The mutually trusting relationship he'd established with Lewis had grown stronger over many years despite a few bumps in the road, and he planned to protect it for the long haul at any cost. If there needed to be short-term pain from

Whiting in exchange for long-term gain from Lewis, then so be it. Mack hoped Whiting would change his mind about police involvement after he saw results, but he wasn't going to hold his breath.

"I hear you've got something for me. Is it good?" Lewis asked the moment Mack sat opposite his desk.

"Makes me want to get up and dance."

"Ha, well you can try, my friend, but you got no rhythm as we both know. You need some darker skin for that, and we both know a suntan isn't what I'm talkin' about here. Anyway, let's have a look-see at the cards you're holding—is it a good hand or a bluff?"

"Funny you should ask. I'm actually going to recommend that *we do* bluff, Nik, but I need you to agree so we can pull it off together."

"Man, now you've really got me puzzled!"

Mack played Lewis the audio. "We have the video of this as well," he reminded him. "To make a few more points: Maggie Stewart knew Drago from her sordid past on the streets of Boston, and likely quite well. Therefore, she probably knew Eddie Venn, his enforcer, and Eddie is stressed and nervous in jail. So, I'm thinking it may be an ideal time to pressure him to reveal who paid him to kill Bill Stewart. What can we use as leverage to convince him he should talk?"

"My compliments on some great work. I really mean that, Mack." He bowed and applauded his friend's efforts. Then he furrowed his eyebrows. "That tape is quite a story, and it's likely going to get Tomlinson sent to jail...but I'm missing your point on Eddie Venn."

"For clarification, we need Pauline."

"Excuse me?"

Mack grinned. "We should have Pauline here to repeat what she told me earlier. To put it in a nutshell, she said if she had been married to Bill—that 'rat-bastard snake' as she called him—and found out he owed two million of *their* money to the Mob plus fifty grand a month in interest, she would have taken a hammer to him herself."

"Mack, that's some woman you've got working for you—gotta love her spirit!"

"Isn't she something? I think she's great, and it could be she's right. Pauline visualizes a tough, street-smart, street-hardened Maggie Stewart, a woman who becomes upset that her financial future is being destroyed. Her husband has a crazy gambling habit that may never end, and one of his means of paying for it derails when the moving company scam goes sour. His stupidity is costing them millions. You tell me—what's Maggie likely to do?"

"Yeah, but Pauline could also be wrong," Lewis said flatly.

"Okay, I grant you that, but who else had a motive to kill Stewart?"

"What about the Mob?" Lewis asked, as if he already knew the answer.

"It seems the Vitales want control of Royal Ransom as a front for expansion plans. They already had Stewart by his twisted shorts, paying off his gambling debts. Why would they kill him? He was making Royal Ransom all kinds of money."

"Okay, I'm sold, Mack," Lewis said, sounding determined. "So, what's our plan? Where do you see us going with this?"

"You and I know we need to take some risks to get to the bottom of it, and we need some leverage to get Venn to talk. That little piece of slime knows he's cooked, but he still believes Lupino might pull off a miracle for him. He must be having serious doubts though, given all the evidence against him. You heard Lenny say Venn is stressed out at the prospect of remaining in jail—despite Lupino's promise to help him."

"I know I'd certainly be stressed about Stewart's murder if I were him. Plus, he's got your attempted murder to face as well," Lewis said. "Nice double-whammy to ensure he doesn't walk free—ever."

"Nik, what I think will work is if you go nose-to-nose with Venn. Tell him you'll do everything you can to make a deal with the DA to ease his life sentence if he fingers who paid him to kill Stewart. Come right out and ask him who gave him the money to do the dirty deed."

Lewis nodded thoughtfully. "Payment always results in some level of guilt on the part of the payer. At the very least, that makes the payer an accessory. I like your idea about asking who paid him rather than who hired him. Hiring him is just words, but *paying him* is the exchange of a tangible item—money."

Mack continued, "Tell Venn we know who hired him to kill Stewart. You could say someone just squealed on him—thus the reason for your meeting. Between you and me, there's a small chance Maggie is innocent. I mean, we can't hang her without a trial, but the hand we should play is to tell Venn the reason we know who hired him is he has been *betrayed*."

"*Betrayed* is a great word to use because it's hateful; but it's something all these rats understand."

Mack added, "If he doesn't cooperate, you tell him you and I will be in the front row enjoying every word of his sentencing. That ought to get him thinking seriously about our offer of getting him a break on his life term. His alternative is to die all alone in a prison cell while Maggie lives the high life at a tropical paradise somewhere. To many men, that would be a fate worse than death."

× × ×

Tuesday

NIK LEWIS DECIDED HE would go forward with Mack's plan after discussing it with the Boston Homicide Division head, especially since this was a big case that had been in the media. After the detailed twenty-minute discussion, he was cleared to approach Eddie Venn with the proposal recommended by Mack.

The well-lit room where the face-to-face with Venn would occur had video and audio in place. It had light-green concrete block walls and only a small metal rectangular table and two metal chairs. All three furniture pieces were bolted to the floor, so nothing could be used as a weapon. Venn was brought into the room in handcuffs. He was wearing a bright orange prison-style jumpsuit. He was five-eleven in height, slender, and sinewy, with short black hair, a clean-shaven face, and evil-looking piercing eyes set in deep dark sockets.

Lewis let him stew for a few minutes before he entered with an authorized officer who needed to be in the room to receive Venn's oath. After they were both admitted, the door was locked.

"So, Eddie, do you want your lawyer present before we talk?"

"No—I got nothing to say."

"I'm gonna keep this meeting short. As a courtesy, I remind you of the Miranda rights I read you before you were apprehended at your sister's house. Do you want me to repeat any of that to you?"

"No."

"Well, you don't have to talk to me if you don't want to," Lewis reminded him anyway. "This meeting is being recorded. I'm certain you'll want to pay close attention to what I have to say. You can still choose to meet with your lawyer later if you want—that's entirely up to you."

"I just told you I ain't sayin' nothin,' so take the wax out of your big cop ears."

"This is simple, Eddie. I want you to tell me who paid you to kill Bill Stewart. We know you didn't come up with the idea to smack him in the back of the head and shoot him all by yourself. For that information, I'm willing to go to bat for you with the DA to see if he'd be willing to give you a break on your sentencing. Any concession would certainly be a lot more than you deserve. It's a simple give-to-get trade I'm talking about here."

Venn was quiet for a moment, thinking about what Lewis said. Then he responded, "All you just offered me is the promise of nothing."

Lewis offered a sympathetic nod. "Look, we already know who paid you to kill Bill Stewart because you were *betrayed*—sold out, Eddie. You're looking at a life sentence for cold-blooded, premeditated murder and a second charge of attempted murder on top of that one. We've got video of you following Stewart out to the parking lot; we've got the murder weapon; we've got your prints; we've got your DNA. I'm giving you the opportunity to get back some of your life here, or at least live a better one. All I want you to do is write the name down and sign an affidavit. It's that simple."

"I know what you want, cop." Venn said, his voice tight.

"It's all about who paid you, so we can bring charges," Lewis added evenly. "The name is worth something to us and should be worth something to you—if you value a life out from behind bars someday. As I said, you've been *betrayed*."

"No one would squeal on me! No one would dare!"

"Someone did."

"If you know so much, why are you hassling me?"

"Eddie, don't play dumb with me. No one's afraid of you anymore because you're not gonna get out of here. You're not worth so much as a bent nickel to anyone because you're guilty of Stewart's murder, and everybody knows it. Old news; that's all you are now. You're going away for life, so you're of no real value—chump change."

"You're just tryin' to sucker-punch me—that's all this is..."

"The man you tried to run over with your truck at Checkerboard Park, remember him? Well, he happens to be a good friend of mine. He and I will be front-row-center at your sentencing, laughing at you for being such a fool. I'm much too busy to ask you over and over about this. Tell you what. On Friday, three days from now, I want you signing an affidavit on video—a statement of testimony with this authorized officer as a witness. It will be right in this room, same time, or life as you know it will be changed forever."

"Are you done?"

"Actually, it's you who's done, Eddie. Even Lupino can't save your skinny ass on this one, and the saddest thing is you already know it!"

With that, Lewis stood up and knocked on the metal door to alert the guard. Eddie remained seated in a sullen slump.

× × ×

WHEN LEWIS GOT BACK to his office, he called Mack to tell him how things had gone. He knew Mack would be dying to know.

"Venn didn't want to talk, but that was expected. He also waived having a lawyer present. I'll see him again this coming Friday. I told him I'm not going to waste my time, so he'd better be on board to swear an affidavit or say goodbye to the rest of his miserable life. I can't predict what he'll do—I couldn't read his eyes because they're dead. It feels eerie just to look at him."

"The man's an insect who needs to be exterminated," Mack said. "Look close enough at any bug like him, and your skin will crawl. Anyway, smart of you to let him know who's in charge of pest control."

"As you suggested, I told him we'd enjoy watching him get sentenced to life. It certainly got his attention. The likelihood of parole for him is less than zero. I could see he was paying close attention, despite trying to be Mr. Macho in front of me."

"Did you tell him we know who paid him?"

"Sure did."

"Did he believe you?"

"I don't think so...I could tell by his expression he wasn't sure if I was bluffing or not. He ended up telling me no one would dare betray him. Of course, I remained steadfast and unwavering like the super-cop I am."

"Kinda makes me proud to know you, Nik. Is your all-American chest swelling right about now?"

"Damn right."

"Yeah, that's what I thought."

CHAPTER 35

Friday, July 3rd

MACK SAT IN HIS office waiting for the results of Lewis's second meeting with Venn. He had briefed M and Pauline on the first meeting, telling them to fasten their seat belts. They were confident Lewis would succeed in getting Venn to admit he had collaborated with Maggie to eliminate Bill.

Lewis had called Mack earlier to say the document was ready for Venn to sign at 1:30 that afternoon; he had run things by the DA again just to be sure. Mack told him he wouldn't be able to focus on anything else until he was updated on Venn.

The surveillance at Royal Ransom had yielded nothing new since Friday's session. Mack was still reluctant to discuss anything further with Whiting. He had left a message on Whiting's phone late Tuesday, when he knew his client would be unavailable. He wanted to avoid telling him he had involved the police against his explicit instructions. Mack suspected Maggie was guilty and figured he was mere hours away from revealing that, but there was no telling how upset Whiting might be. Until Lewis and Venn met and he learned the outcome, there'd be no point saying anything to Whiting.

Ever since the installation of security in Serena's condo, she was much more at ease, and so was Mack. He and M continued their surveillance program day and night, but had seen nothing out of the ordinary so far. After revisiting the entire experience of the envelope with the photos and strange message, Mack still couldn't understand the ultimate intent. All he could think of was someone trying to force him to resign from the Whiting case.

Pauline was busy at her desk when the phone rang.

"It's Nik for you, Mack!"

Mack was excited as he answered the phone. "Hey Nik, thanks for calling. I've been sitting here filled with anticipation!"

"I finished up with Venn, and you won't believe what I've got to tell you. I won't do it over the phone, so how soon can you get to my office?"

"Damn! Okay, I'll be there within a half hour unless a cop stops me for speeding."

"Play it safe. What I have to tell you will knock your socks off while you're standing in them!"

Mack grabbed his jacket and burst through M's office door.

"Want to come with me to see Lewis? He says he's gonna shake us up on the Whiting case, but refused to say a word over the phone—it's about his second meeting with Venn."

He headed out of the office, calling back to Pauline, "Can you look after Woof until I get back, please? If I haven't returned when you want to leave, would you take him with you? I promise to pick him up as soon as I can—I'll make it up to you."

"Sure, but I have two questions—will you vacuum my car seat, and am I any closer to Hawaii?"

× × ×

NIK LEWIS WAS IN his office when Steve Drakowski walked in at the same time Mack and M arrived.

"Gentlemen, please come in and join me. You don't want to be standing when I tell you what transpired at my meeting with Eddie Venn. Steve, did you get the warrant?"

"Sure did."

Lewis turned to Mack and M. "Well, listen up. The four of us have a job to do, pronto!"

"Nik, what the heck is going on? Don't hold out on us, buddy!" Mack implored.

"As I told you, you're not gonna believe it. I met with Venn as planned. He had decided to try and get some relief on his sentencing. I put the affidavit in front of him with the video rolling and what did he do? Does he write Maggie's name as we expected? Nooooo. He told me it was...are you ready for this? He said it was the one and only *John Whiting* who hired him—paid him in cash. Then he wrote Whiting's name and swore his testimony on the affidavit. He said he'll swear the same thing in court. I couldn't believe it!"

"What? Tell me you're kidding!" Mack saw his astonishment mirrored back at him as he looked at M.

M said, "Venn should get the Academy Award for best deviant behavior in a supporting role. I don't believe this!"

"Hey, guys, I was so stunned I told Venn he was full of shit! I'm sure any judge will love to hear me say that on video to a prisoner headed for trial. I demanded proof about Whiting, so Venn told me that two of the five bundles of the money Whiting gave him were still in his sister's garage with Whiting's prints all over them. With that ugly grin of his, he told me where they were hidden. Then he asked, *'Is that proof enough, Mr. Cop?'* I felt like decking him!"

"I mean, how could this be true?" Mack asked.

Lewis shrugged. "I sure as hell wonder, but we'll find out. Drakowski got us a warrant, so we'll go have a look. You and

M want to come along?"

× × ×

MACK PICKED UP WOOF from Pauline's at 7:00 p.m. after calling ahead to say he was coming. Pauline answered the door, holding Woof by the collar. She was barefoot and wearing well-worn jeans. Her bright pink T-shirt *read I'm the Best!* in red lettering.

Pauline's small townhouse and its interior were as basic as she was. Mack had always felt the place suited her. He could smell pizza as he entered, so he guessed she had just finished supper. Mack was particular about what Woof ate, so he hoped she hadn't given him any of the people food—a no-no.

"Come in—so what happened?" Pauline asked excitedly. "Tell me, please! You can't leave without filling me in. This Eddie Venn thing is making my head explode! C'mon, Mack, don't leave me in suspense!"

"Okay, here's the short version—Venn signed the affidavit, but he said it was *John Whiting* and not Maggie who had paid him."

Pauline's mouth dropped. "What? It can't be! Is this a joke? He has to be lying!"

"No joke—I know it's unbelievable, but Venn had proof. Lewis and Drakowski drove us to Venn's sister's place. Eddie said he still had twenty thousand in cash as part of the payment he got to kill Stewart, and he told Lewis it was wrapped in bundles with Whiting's fingerprints on them. Venn said he'd hidden them in the bottom of an old toolbox underneath a workbench only he uses. Sure enough, there it was at the back of the barn. Good thing we had a search warrant because when we got there, Venn's sister started screaming while calling us every name under the sun. She has quite a well-developed vocabulary, but I'm not too sure what dictionary she uses."

"It's a good thing I didn't get my hands on her, that's all I can say," Pauline said.

"The money was right where Venn said it would be in the barn, and Drakowski had a hell of a time getting at it with all the stolen car parts stacked up everywhere. Anyway, he found the cash and bagged it for analysis. Lewis put a big rush on it because tomorrow is the Fourth of July, so we should know later tonight if Whiting's prints are on it. His guys want the weekend and Monday off to celebrate with their families. He also sent a crew into the barn to try and get VIN numbers off those chopped-up cars and parts. That way, we can see who they were stolen from. They wanted to do that sooner, but were tied up on some other huge job."

"Be nice to inform the owners. Getting back to the cash. What does Lewis and his team have to match Whiting's fingerprints to?"

"Great question. Remember that contract Whiting signed in our office?" Mack grinned. "Now it's in the same place as those two bundles of cash. That's why I'm so late–I had to swing by our office and pick up our original and get it to Lewis."

"Makes me proud to work with you," Pauline said.

"If the prints match, as we suspect they will, Lewis and Drakowski will be over at the Whiting residence to take him in for questioning. His quiet Saturday afternoon will be a visit to the famed police hotel. It's the one with bars on the windows and doors. It will be Independence Day for everyone we know, except Whiting and Venn."

"If his prints are on that money, then I'd say that's the clincher, wouldn't you?" Pauline asked.

"If the prints match, I doubt he'll be leaving police custody, despite all his money to hire the best lawyers in Boston. He'll likely be facing a murder charge by sundown. No nice quiet dinner with his wife tomorrow night if Lawman Lewis gets his way. As for us, Mack's steak and ribs—here we come!"

"Yum, I can't wait and neither can Keith. Whiting will deserve everything he's got coming to him," Pauline said. "What a nice man he seemed like when I first met him—he reminded me of my dad, for heaven's sake. We should remember he's innocent until proven guilty, of course, but it's so hard to do. Venn could be playing a cruel joke here, couldn't he?"

"Sure—I'm not sure *what* to believe anymore. It's good you always think about the good traits in people first, Paul. You make me feel there's still hope for humanity despite all the *inhumanity* out there. We've really been tested and rattled by this case so far, haven't we? Well, I should hit the road and call Serena. I've asked Lewis to call me the moment he hears anything."

"You won't get any sleep tonight, and I'm sure I won't either," Pauline said. "Please make sure you call me right after Lewis calls you. I won't be able to think straight until you do."

Mack took Woof by the collar, giving him a pat on the head and a scratch behind one ear.

"Thanks for everything, Paul, but I can't stay another minute," he said. "I'm exhausted and should get going. Besides, I still have to eat supper."

"I've been rude standing here listening to you without even offering you a slice of savory pizza. Double cheese! There was too much for me to eat alone and I have to watch my weight."

"No thanks, but I appreciate the offer."

"Well then, the least I can do is give you an assorted six-pack of Keith's beer. I know he'd want you to have it."

With much thanks, Mack went on his way with Woof.

"Woof, I'm having ribs at our barbeque tomorrow night, so we'll see if there's any meat-covered leftovers for you," Mack said as they walked toward his SUV. "In the meantime,

I promise you slices of roast chicken when we get home. Maybe there'll be leftovers for you tomorrow too—that's for being such a good dog. You'll like my roast chicken much better than her pizza, even with double cheese."

Woof bounded into the SUV as soon as Mack opened the door, wagging his tail and whining. He knew Mack had been talking about food. Smart dog.

CHAPTER 36

Late Friday, July 3rd

MACK HAD NO INTENTION of seeing Serena after he finished his late snack, but called her to see how she was doing. He was pleased she was looking forward to spending Independence Day with Sydney, Pauline, Keith, and M. Mack described the fun it would be and how eager he was to celebrate together. Since he wanted everyone to meet at his place for supper, Serena offered to come early and help.

Mack said goodnight and settled into his comfy leather recliner. His favorite pal was at his feet as he turned on his favorite sports channel. Beside him, he had one of Keith's beers. The beer was high in alcohol and tasted good.

He awoke with a start at 4:00 a.m., surprised to still be sitting in his recliner. There were three empty cans of beer on the side table next to him. The TV was off, and Woof was asleep on the carpet nearby. He didn't recall having turned off the TV or lamp, but knew he had been alone. After stopping at the bathroom, he headed straight to bed.

He awoke again at 9:00 in the morning feeling refreshed. Woof was beside him on the floor and started to whine at seeing him get up. He knew if Mack slept longer than usual it meant they were going to spend time together.

"It's Independence Day, Woofster. Let's go for a run." The dog liked the word *run* as much as he liked the words *food* and *steak*. He barked, then whimpered and pranced while wagging his tail.

It was a picture-perfect day—sunny and in the mid-seventies. Mack put on a Celtics shamrock-green and black team shirt, and a pair of black shorts. The two pals were ready to go. On his way, Mack made sure he grabbed his cell phone. *Be Prepared.* He had just stepped out of the door when his phone rang. The Caller ID told him it was important.

"Mack, it's Steve—Nik wanted me to call you right away. Our forensics people were working late last night so they could have an uninterrupted July Fourth break. They called him as soon as they had something for him on your case. It was a match on the prints lifted from your contract document signed by Whiting. They were the same as those on the bundles of cash I bagged up at Eddie's sister's place. Bingo, buddy!"

"That's fantastic news, Steve!"

"Mr. Whiting is in deep shit, Mack, and Nik's on his way to Whiting's house right now to read him his rights and take him into custody. The entire U.S. Cavalry followed him there. Too bad it's Independence Day, but Nik insisted on leading the charge personally."

"Holy smoke, Steve! This entire case has been strange, so it's good to see things coming together. There are so many questions I need to ask Whiting when I get the chance."

"You got that right—stand in line. Oh, and one more important thing. A search through those chop-shop parts in Venn's sister's barn yielded a Cadillac transmission with a VIN number matching your stolen SUV!"

"You've gotta be joking! That's unbelievable! They didn't happen to find my cedar canoe as well, did they?"

"Not as far as I know," Steve said. "But I'll make sure to

review the list of everything they found there as soon as it's completed. There was a hell of a lot of stuff."

"So...they were the crooks stealing vehicles from those highway pull-off areas? Damn! I was trying to figure how they stole my SUV with Venn being in jail, but then I recalled the police missed getting Drago's prime car thief, Rooney, when they arrested Venn and two others at his sister's place. Rooney must have kept working at stealing while waiting for his cronies to be released from jail. Maybe the police will find him—who knows? I sure hope so. I'll call my insurance company and make them aware. Great work, Steve! Be sure to thank everyone for me!"

"Will do, Mack. Hey, I gotta run."

"I might as well run too, Steve, but with my dog. There's nothing else I can do until Whiting is arrested. Thanks for calling to fill me in—be careful out there!"

After Mack returned from his run, he called Pauline, M, and Serena. He told them, while still feeling shocked, that Whiting would soon be in custody. He also told them the transmission from his stolen Caddy SUV was found in the barn behind Venn's sister's place.

× × ×

MACK ALWAYS ENJOYED BEING the host to friends, and his July Fourth barbeque was no exception. Everyone had a wonderful time together, topped off by a magician named Magic Man whom Mack had hired to entertain. Sydney loved magic, so the show was a special surprise for her. She oohed and aahed at the amazing variety of tricks Magic Man performed, especially when he waved his wand over a flowerpot filled with some kind of shredded black fiber and a large bouquet of flowers popped up with a live white dove on top.

After the barbeque, they all got into a limousine Mack had

reserved and traveled to the site of a huge fireworks display over the Charles River. Coordinated to music, the fantastic multi-color bursts sparkled across the sky. Afterward, the limousine drove everyone back to Mack's home to get their vehicles. As they departed, there were hugs all around. Mack wished everyone a great Sunday and Monday away from their offices. He smiled as they departed, content in knowing that he, M, and Pauline worked so well together, even though they were so different; and delighted that Serena and Sydney, and now Keith, had become treasured members of the Mackenzie Investigations family.

× × ×

MACK ANSWERED A CALL from Lewis late in the evening.

"Mack, I wanted to call you earlier, but with the ton of crap that happened today, there was no chance 'til now."

"I've been on pins and needles since Steve told me you were heading over to Whiting's house with a posse. What the hell happened?"

"There's no way to sugarcoat this, buddy—John Whiting is dead. He shot himself when we arrived to arrest him."

"What? I can't believe it! This is a nightmare!"

"I didn't want to make this call to you, Mack. As we arrived at the front door to the Whiting residence, we thought we heard a shot. I pounded on the front door until his wife answered. The poor woman was screaming frantically that John had just shot himself and needed an ambulance. As soon as we saw him, we knew the only thing John needed was a body bag and a hearse. I've never seen so much blood. I'll spare you the gory details, my friend, but what a helluva mess! He tried to swallow a nine-millimeter—musta been a hollow-point."

"Oh man. This case has been one smash-bang event after another, Nik, and here's the mother lode. I really regret what you had to go through. I'm glad you called, but I'm left speechless."

"Mack, I'm done—I've got nothing left—totally worn out. Gonna go hug my wife and suck on a bottle of rum. Let's talk Tuesday."

"Yeah, Tuesday, Nik. Thanks again for keeping me in the loop."

CHAPTER 37

Tuesday

ON TUESDAY MORNING, PAULINE and M were back in the office, chatting more than usual about the fun-filled Saturday night celebrations at Mack's and the incredible fireworks display. They fell silent and eyed one another as they watched Mack walk in and head straight to the conference room with his leather-covered notepad. Sensing something was wrong, they followed him in.

"Hey, guys, I should tell you that I spent Saturday night alone and miserable after we ended our festivities," Mack said, sounding frustrated.

"Why? Did you break up with Serena or something?" Pauline asked, concerned.

"No, but I got an unbelievable smash-in-the-mouth call from Lewis right after everyone left! I had to get my thoughts organized and figure things out as a result. I ended up spending every waking moment on Sunday and Monday on the Whiting matter and reviewing what transpired over the past month. As much as I wanted to, I didn't have the heart to call either of you. I left you alone to have a well-earned rest. Besides...I needed to think."

"I'm afraid to ask what Lewis told you," Pauline said softly.

M nodded. "I know this won't be good."

"It's hard to figure out where to begin with everything that's gone on," Mack said. "I'll get started by thinking out loud, so don't expect everything to be polished—I offer no apology for that. Consider this meeting a *post-mortem*."

"Uh-oh, gonna be nasty," said M.

"Nasty is an understatement. John Whiting is dead."

Pauline gasped. "When? How?" she asked, then paused. "Will we get the money we're still owed?"

"I don't want to discuss money right now—I'm way too upset. Whiting shot himself when he realized the jig was up just as Lewis and his gang arrived to arrest him on Saturday afternoon. So far, the police have managed to keep the incident out of the media. They want to get their facts straight first because they don't want to be accused of killing him."

"It's tough for the public to accept the police version of a story sometimes, so it's best they play it cool," M said.

"Damn it, may John Whiting rot in hell," Mack added. "He conned us from the start of this case, and I'm embarrassed to admit I've been such a dumb-ass chump! If it wasn't for all that money, I'd have told him to..."

"Mack, don't blame yourself!" M said. "There were so many twists and turns in this insane case. Hell...no one could have predicted *this* crazy outcome! Haven't we had our fill of surprise bangs? And I'm not talking Independence Day fireworks here."

"We're finally drawing to a close on this," Mack said. "There's been the death of two business executives—Stewart and Whiting; an attempted murder on me; a killer put in jail; and a bunch of unanswered loose ends with obvious criminal intent by others—even Mob involvement. What more can a private investigator expect to face in a single case?"

"When you put it that way, it makes me wonder if there's

another big bang just around the corner," M said.

"Better not be!" said Pauline. "We need to think positive!"

"It's all part of the business we're in—you know, this business we love so much?" Mack said. He sighed, reigning in the sarcasm.

"I called this meeting to draw out any more ideas you might have on this case. Maybe we can get some closure from Lewis and his department."

"How do the final pieces fit together?" M asked. "That's what I want to know."

"It will take time for the Venn issues to come to trial," Mack said. "There are still a few outstanding matters such as Royce Tomlinson and that trafficking in stolen goods fiasco which has yet to come to trial."

"I hate to be a party pooper, but are we ever going to get paid for the rest of our work on Whiting's case, considering he's dead?" Pauline asked. "Weren't we talking a hundred thousand as a total contract fee?"

"Yes, so thank you for being the business brains here. I don't check the company books as often as I should. It will surprise you though—I reviewed our records and time sheets on the Whiting case over the weekend. After adding things up from the beginning, I can confirm we've covered all our time and expenses with what's been paid, and there's quite a chunk of money still left over. We got two early payments and then another when M and I installed the recording equipment at Royal Ransom. I could go after John's wife, Joan, for the twenty-five thousand outstanding since it was a flat fee contract, but I don't have the heart. We came out fine as it is."

"Yes, I agree," Pauline added.

"So, moving right along," Mack said, "the first question I had to answer was why Whiting took his own life when the police arrived at his home. After all, he had the money to hire top lawyers to defend him. He was a seasoned businessman who had been through many tough situations. Look at what he and Stewart achieved—amazing! It took a while for me to discover the answer, but now I understand."

"So?" Pauline asked.

"I'm convinced when M caught Venn on our camera at Checkerboard Park and he ended up in jail, that's when Whiting started to become unhinged. He knew Venn could incriminate him."

"But why did he hire us in the first place if he was involved in his business partner's death?" Pauline asked. "Wouldn't he be afraid we'd find him out?"

"Great question! Whiting was an intelligent man, and it was a tactical move on his part. I'm convinced he had information on us before he hired us—much more than I figured. He knew my brief history with the Boston Police, for example, and probably knew I was fired and liked to drink heavily. Why would anyone suspect him of being involved with Stewart's murder when he hired our PI firm to solve it? There's no sense suspecting John Whiting, right?"

"I gotta agree with you there," M said. "That was a brilliant move."

"Sure, that's what Whiting figured, too. He hired a Mob enforcer to do the job for him, and Venn had proven himself. There was no way Whiting believed Venn could get tagged with Stewart's murder, especially given he had Lupino covering for him."

"But he did get caught, so it's starting to make sense. How would a successful exec like Whiting ever meet a slimy street snake like Venn?" Pauline asked.

Mack smiled and said, "That's right at the heart of the issue."

"Why?" Pauline and M responded in unison.

"Because he wouldn't," Mack responded. "My theory is Maggie and Venn got acquainted many years ago. When

Whiting found out Stewart had awful gambling debts with the Mob and insane interest piling up each month, Whiting and Maggie must have had a long talk. It most likely resulted in Whiting contracting Venn. He wanted Venn involved for several reasons."

"What reasons?" asked Pauline.

"We know that Whiting lived and breathed Royal Ransom; he wasn't faking that. I'm sure when he saw the Mob-related gambling disease moving in—and couldn't do a thing to stop it—he'd feel defenseless and fearful. Natural human emotions, right? If he found out Stewart and Tomlinson were having secret discussions, he'd wonder what the hell was going on. Whiting wasn't stupid, and he wasn't a sucker. He'd be very concerned!"

"So, those things lit his wick—at least that's what you're saying," M said.

"Yes, though it's pure speculation. One thing is certain: Given the right circumstances, some people will do anything—even kill someone. This might be an example of that."

Pauline frowned. "How does Maggie fit into all of this?"

"John Whiting was depressed and sullen when M and I saw him the first time we met. Little did I know he and Maggie had just killed someone—a friend and business partner to Whiting, and a husband to Maggie; good old Bill Stewart."

"Yeah, he was choked up and shaky when we spoke to him," M said. "I thought he might have a heart attack because he was sweating and shaking. I mean, if that was an act, it was incredible."

Mack continued. "He was genuinely upset—just not for the reason we thought. Having someone murdered can be very traumatic. But we were seeing guilt as well as grief. Whiting considered Maggie a good friend, and he was starry-eyed toward her for some unknown reason. My best guess is that Maggie told Whiting about Bill's gambling, and the ongoing threat it caused Royal Ransom. The two of them hatched a plan to end Bill's life with an eye to saving the company. Whiting knew nothing of Maggie's past as a call girl, and there's no way he knew Venn. It's important to note that if Maggie was the one who put Whiting in touch with Venn, then she's complicit in Bill's murder."

"You're supposed to be innocent until proven guilty—except for that horrible bitch," M said.

"I don't like her either, folks," Mack said. "Maggie wanted Whiting to end Bill's gambling habit permanently and pay the cost to boot. Who knows what other kind of favors she might have promised Whiting if he succeeded? She's a classic femme fatale—and convinced her friend Whiting to do whatever it took to fix things for his treasured company and for her. It was a brilliant plan, actually. They never expected that Venn would be identified. But if he ever was, they knew the murder would look like part of a car theft gone wrong. They would let Eddie suffer all the consequences."

"Well, it's certainly believable Maggie would have thought of all of this; she has quite the background," Pauline said.

"She sure does—you did the research on her, Paul. Once again, great job!" Mack said. "Here's another thing. Remember you told us how they found her first husband, Jack Schroeder, driving his white Porsche under fifteen feet of water a few years ago?"

"Sure do," Pauline said.

"Given what's gone on with Bill Stewart, I'm going to encourage Lewis to re-open the Jack Schroeder case," Mack said. He started drumming his fingers on the conference room table. "I'm thinking she had her first dear unsuspecting husband Jack murdered too. It might have been Venn who handled that hit as well. Who knows? If we can prove who did that, then she'll see jail for life with Venn. Lewis will try his best to make sure—you'd better believe it!"

"Why not establish her involvement with Stewart's death first? You said she might be complicit, didn't you?"

"Prove it," M challenged.

"What?" Pauline said, sounding annoyed.

"Yes, prove it," Mack added.

"How can I do that?" Pauline asked.

"That's our point, Paul. Whiting couldn't squeal on Maggie without implicating himself, and now he's dead. And will Venn talk? What's in it for him, and what more can we offer him? He already made his deal to finger Whiting. He has no reason to add in Maggie."

"Okay," Pauline said. "But answer something else for me."

"If I can," Mack said.

"Why did Venn try to kill you with his truck?"

"Because we're so good at what we do!" Mack said. "Whiting was getting scared we were achieving much more than he ever bargained for. Keep in mind, he was only using us as a cover to hide his crimes. He didn't *really* want us to solve Stewart's murder or anything else. He thought he'd hired a loser PI drunk who was fired by the police. The money he paid us was nothing to him—another corporate write-off. My guess is Whiting even offered Venn a bonus to kill me. I'd be willing to bet Maggie was pushing him like a toddler on a tricycle. With me gone, Mr. Whiting and Mrs. Stewart could dance through a field of daisies together. Sure, he knew the police would investigate Stewart's murder. But hiring me made him look innocent, and he probably truly believed the cops were too busy to work the trail of the case back to him."

"It's hard to believe he'd put a contract out on his long-time friend," Pauline said.

"Well, chances are he was pushed by his personal cheerleader. I'm sure Maggie knew Bill could never quit gambling. The problem would continue—even get worse. Add to that my belief Whiting had been living in the shadow of a good-looking athletic man—someone with charisma who got all the attention and the women. Bill had the gift of gab, the pickup lines, and the dance moves. He dressed like a movie idol and he even had hair! Bald, paunchy Mr. Whiting had a follicle challenge to worry about." Mack and M started to laugh.

"Are you making fun of bald men, Mack?" Pauline asked. "I'm disappointed in you—bald men can be sexy too."

"I'm not mocking *all* bald men. I'm just pissed at one particular bald guy named John Whiting who paid to have me killed and played me for a sucker. Plus, Venn could have run over Woof!"

"Yes, that was horrible!" Pauline said.

"Whiting likely had a boiling cauldron of envy because of Stewart and his lifestyle, stewed over many years. With his business partner out of the picture, Whiting had a better chance of securing all the company shares for himself and his wife, and so someday for his son."

"What about that inflated offer for Royal Ransom? How real was that? Who will run Royal Ransom now?" M asked.

"It's my guess that the offer never existed, and the Vitales never intended to take over the company. They were fine letting Stewart and Tomlinson use the company to fence stolen property, so Stewart's gambling debts got paid...and paid. Why would they need the headache of running the company? Whiting's story about Maggie pressuring him to take the offer might have been to throw some suspicion on Maggie—so he would feel they were even and neither could rat on the other."

"As for what happens next, Whiting's wife, Joan, will inherit his majority shares, but I can't even guess how things will work out. Unless she's incriminated, Maggie can still keep or sell hers. If I were Joan, I suppose I'd want to hire two top executives to take over the company and continue to build it. I don't believe Lorne Harris and Bethany Williams can do it. Bethany's great, but she's not seasoned enough yet."

"Too bad—what a great opportunity for a woman!" Pauline said.

"My head is spinning from this," Pauline said.

M nodded. "It's been crazy."

"There's even more," Mack continued. "There's the matter of the envelope with the photos and that pieced-together message handed to Serena at the dinner-theater."

"Oh yeah, that was strange...and frightening. So?" Pauline wondered.

"I don't think Venn or his crooked Mob friends had any part in that," Mack said.

"Then who did?" Pauline asked.

"Do you remember when M took pictures of Maggie and showed them around downtown hotels?"

"Sure, what about it?"

"I recall telling Whiting that M had taken shots of his dear friend Maggie and found a doorman who recognized her from her call-girl days."

"Oh, so Whiting told Maggie he knew about her past, and she went berserk and came after us—is that it?" Pauline asked.

"Well, he may have told her...but I don't think he could have told her he knew about her sordid past. Maybe one of those doormen or someone from the old days got in touch with her after M showed those photos around. She'd be the only one to hatch a plan to scare the crap out of us in retaliation, and she sure did a good job."

"Boy, you're not kidding," Pauline said, shaking her head. "I hate to admit it, but it all sounds plausible. I think she had Venn wound around her little finger, and I hope he squeals on her."

"It sure would be nice," said Mack. "Given her shady past, Maggie understood the power a woman like her can wield over men. She must have figured if she scared the heck out of Serena by including Sydney in the photos, Serena would try and force me off of the Whiting case."

"But how could she have known about the theater?" Pauline asked.

"She probably didn't. My guess is Maggie got a friend to follow me to Serena's and then to the theater. She either got a favor from the theater manager or bought her own ticket so she could deliver that damn envelope."

"What about the statue on the table at Serena's?" M asked. "That one has me mystified."

"Me too, M," Mack confirmed. "In every murder case, there's always an unanswered question or two that haunts you like a mystery of the universe. My theory, though, is that someone—maybe even Maggie—knocked on Serena's door and said, *'So sorry, must be the wrong house,'* or another excuse. That way, she could peek inside and take a mental snapshot." Mack shook his head in disgust before adding, "There's the matter of the shares Drago received to pay for Stewart's huge gambling debt. How will that play out? Has he got them in his possession? That share issue alone is a headful for any new executive to resolve."

"What about Lenny and Royce?" M asked.

Mack took a couple of gulps of coffee before answering. "Though he has a crime-filled background as we saw from what Paul dug up, Lenny Mitchell has done nothing wrong—not as far as I can tell. His only crime is he's Maggie's brother."

"Lucky guy," M said with disdain.

"As for Royce Tomlinson, I want to see him charged with trafficking in stolen goods. Given our work with the police in capturing the gang, the odds of that happening look pretty damn good. Since Lewis works homicide, I'll defer to other officers and am prepared to help them in any way possible."

"Are we going to sell the bat cave and the bat toys?" M asked, grinning. "As Robin, the incredible sidekick on your team, is my job finished now?"

Mack shook his head ruefully. "Whiting had me fooled, M. I feel stupid about the way he conned me, but I never claimed to be Sherlock Holmes. At least I work hand in hand with the police on my cases better than Holmes ever did. I admit I drink too much and take Xanax for anxiety now and then, but at least I don't inject cocaine like old Sherlock. Whiting failed to see my connection with the police, so that helped lead to his demise. Whiting said he avoided the police, but I think he detested and feared them—and he thought since I'd been fired, I did too. But he was wrong."

"He sure had us fooled!" M said.

"I admit I should have paid more attention to his every word. I recalled a piece of critical information: He told us he and Bill had studied acting in Cambridge when they were students; remember that? Well, the Massachusetts acting school they both graduated from is one of the best in the country—perhaps the world. During our first meeting I was feeling sorry for Whiting, but it turns out he was performing for an Academy Award. It was for *Best Actor in a Leading Role*—right there in front of us. Had those scenes been captured on film, I'm sure he'd have won an Oscar, hands down."

"The envelope please," Pauline added in disgust. "And the Award goes to...?"

EPILOGUE

The Hawaiian Islands
February of the following year

"I'VE NOTICED ALL THE women walking by here hesitate for a few seconds to look at you," Serena said while turning to look at Mack.

Mack and Serena were relaxing on padded recliners under a small beach sun shelter covered with palm fronds. They were on one of the amazing beaches on the island of Maui, the second largest Hawaiian island. He was wearing burgundy swim trunks. She wore a bright turquoise bikini with white daisies, and her hair was tied up in a bun. Sydney was playing in the fine white sand with another girl her age not far away.

"Isn't that your third margarita?" Serena asked.

Mack shrugged happily. "The first two don't count. They were what's known as Continental U.S. margaritas. This one is a Hawaiian margarita because it has pineapple and strawberries. I've only had one that counts—if you're counting—which I'm not."

"Oh, it's all clear to me now," Serena said, smiling.

"Besides, isn't that your second drink of whatever the heck that is?" Mack grinned. "It's rare for you to start a second drink—that's plenty of stuff packed into one highball glass."

"It's called 'Sex on the Beach.' What a lovely idea, huh? There's vodka and peach schnapps with orange and cranberry juice—so yummy."

"Wow, so doctors use the word *yummy* like the rest of us—who knew? Hey, here comes Paul and Keith. Pauline said they'd be back from their spending spree before we finished our drinks. That's not fair though, because they knew we'd keep drinking."

"Maybe that was why she was laughing when she said it," Serena said.

"Sneaky. Where did M go?" Mack asked.

"He rented one of those big paddleboards with a sail on it and he's been zooming around showing off his windsurfing skills. He's got a great sense of balance and he can handle it just fine. You can't get him off the water—I'm sure that's where he'll be until we leave. He looks great with his clothes off though," Serena teased. "His body may be even better than yours."

"Perhaps..." Mack said, "...but I'm taller." Serena laughed and shook her head.

Keith and Pauline approached. They wore shorts, T-shirts, and flip-flops with Keith's light blue craft brewery ball caps. He was holding a big shopping bag overflowing with items.

"So, what did you guys buy?" Serena asked.

"I bought a cool new bikini. It's iridescent pink, because I figure that way Keith can find me among the nearly naked beach beauties around here. Oh...that drink of yours looks so scrumptious, Serena! What is it?"

"It's called Sex on the Beach," Serena said with a wink.

"Did you hear that, Keith? We should try one of those," Pauline joked, as she poked Keith in the ribs. "We're going to our room to change now, so we'll join you here in a few minutes. We're pooped out from walking—time for us to sit and relax."

It was over an hour before they returned. Serena put down the novel she was reading. Now in bathing suits, Keith and Paul moved two beach chairs so they could be in the shade beside Mack and Serena.

"What took you guys so long?" Serena asked.

"You don't want to know," Pauline said, grinning slyly.

Mack laughed. "You look good in that bikini, Paul. Keith must have thought so too. That's the first time I've seen you so naked—no offense intended, Keith."

Keith said nothing. That was the first time Mack had seen Pauline blush—he didn't think it was possible. She always got the last laugh, so Mack had to be on guard.

Serena chuckled. "Pauline, he's ribbing you about being half-naked because he's trying to get back at me for saying M has a nicer body than he does."

"Yes, that might be true, but Mack's taller," Pauline said, laughing.

"What did you say? Do you guys practice rebuttals together? Is that what you do at work while I'm slaving to keep my patients alive?" Serena was trying her best to sound serious and not laugh. "M is so nice. You wish there was more of him to admire—is that what you mean?"

"Well said, Serena! Of course, that's what I meant! As for Mack's sexist comment mentioning my near-nakedness, I can assure you the fat lady hasn't sung her last tune on that one yet!"

"Uh-oh," Mack said.

"Let me be serious for a minute. Keith and I want to take this opportunity to thank you for this trip, Mack. For the longest time, I thought you were only kidding when you said I was getting closer and closer to Hawaii. Then you said you were giving me and M an extra week of holidays. Now you gave us this all-expense paid trip—how very generous!"

"You're welcome," Mack said. "You earned this nice bonus. That big Whiting payout helped a lot, but truth be told, I also sold my least favorite one of my cherished collector cars so this trip could happen. It hurt, but it was for a great cause. Besides, I have the rest of my life to collect cars and there's always a good opportunity to purchase another somewhere. One thing I've learned from all of this is I've managed my money better than I did before."

"I can't believe you sold one of your cherished cars for us," Pauline said. She walked over and gave Mack a big kiss on the cheek. "Thanks again."

"Hey Pauline, just a quick question while you're here. I need more photos for Sydney to remember this trip when she gets older," Serena said. "Would you happen to have some?"

"I've got lots of photos to share with you, so don't worry," Pauline said.

Keith chimed in. "The weather's been great; seventy-eight to eighty-two degrees every day. It's hard to believe we're still in America. Boston will likely get over a foot of snow again this week. Just think; we won't be there to pitch in with our shovels to help out. How sad is that?"

"Kinda breaks my heart," Mack said, smirking. "Wonder-dog will be outside jumping around in the snow and he'll love it—I can see him now! Woof likes to use his snout as a shovel; don't ask me why. It was great Hailey agreed to keep him at her place for the entire duration of our trip. I plan to give her a huge bonus for the favor, but something tells me she already knows."

Mack took a swallow of his margarita, and said, "Anyway, we had a good year last year—the earnings were up nicely thanks to the Whiting case. It was time to share with the ones who helped earn it. It all worked out even though Whiting left us short of a full fee. And hey, I just had an update on the Whiting case from Nik Lewis about an hour ago. He called the hotel and had them hunt me down just so I'd have the latest news. How thoughtful is that!"

"Do tell!" Pauline said.

"I'm pleased to report dear old Maggie will finally get what's coming to her. Lewis said Venn couldn't wait to throw her under the bus—just the opposite of what M and I figured. See, Paul, I'm not always right."

"I told you I thought Venn was sweet on her—so I was..."

"You were what?"

"Right. I was right, Mack. What do I win? I should win something!"

"Oh sure, Paul, you were right, so you get one point. Those points may only get you a free box of cornflakes...or another exotic all-expense-paid holiday like this one. One never knows. That's another reason why working for Mackenzie Investigations is so exciting and so much fun!"

"Gotta love those points!" Pauline said, laughing.

"Getting back to Eddie Venn, that evil snake; he was eager to cut another deal to get his charges reduced even more if he could," Mack went on. "Lupino has been stalling Venn's case over and over, trying to keep it from going to trial. The delay tactics wore thin, so Venn's been drooling at the chance to make something happen."

"But Venn's a known Mob contractor and enforcer. Why believe a single word he says?"

"I wouldn't, but don't forget that Maggie has a big problem too. Given her sleazy background, would anything she has to say be taken seriously—even be admissible? It makes sense Whiting wouldn't know Venn—but she would. There's supporting material in her file."

"Okay, I see how Lewis can make that work," Pauline said, sounding convinced.

"Yes, and Venn gave written testimony on another affidavit and on video too, that Maggie was the one who put him in touch with Whiting. As he did with his first affidavit naming Whiting, he claimed he would repeat his testimony under oath in court if necessary. As a result, Lewis charged Maggie as an accessory to her husband's gruesome murder."

"Yippee!" Pauline shouted.

"I'll second that," Mack said. "I'd have told you sooner, but as I said, I just found out—M doesn't even know yet. Why don't you tell him over dinner tonight, Paul?" Mack took a big gulp of his Hawaiian margarita, then added, "Oh, I forgot! There's even more to the Maggie story, folks."

"How can there be more?" Pauline asked, sounding surprised.

"Speaking of more, what about that mysterious woman who handed me that envelope full of photos?" Serena asked.

"You're not going to like this, but she remains a mystery," Mack said. "I'm hopeful we'll find out who she is someday, but so far, nothing."

"Damn!" Serena said. "I was hoping..."

Mack continued, "So, as I said, now that Lewis has got Maggie tagged as the accomplice to Bill's murder, he's sure to get the go-ahead to examine the mysterious death of her first husband, Jack Schroeder."

"Mr. Imperfect, Fast Eddie Venn, might be at the center of that one too. Oh, and I suspect he became attracted to the word *imperfect* because of his huge ego."

"Huh?" Pauline said.

"Well, the word *imperfect* has the words *I'm perfect* in it. Turns out Venn isn't so perfect after all," Mack said, smiling. "It took a while to catch on to his enormous Trump-like ego. I had to figure out why he used an uncommon word like *imperfect* in his email and note to me, but now I know."

Pauline said, her voice raised, "I'm perfect! Did you hear that, Keith? Well, Mack, thank you for proving Venn wasn't perfect, so now we get to rest easy in paradise thanks to you."

"Don't give me more credit than I deserve. It was you, M, Lewis, and me, together, who did that—it was great teamwork. And speaking of M, he just dragged his paddleboard onto the beach and...oh, good—he's on his way over here." After a moment's pause, Mack continued. "Say, M, nice you decided to join us. As I just mentioned, Nik called and Maggie will be charged as an accessory to her husband's murder. And though our role in the Whiting case is over, Lewis promised to work hard on the Jack Schroeder case until he nails Maggie for first-degree murder on that one too."

"That's great news! I'm so glad that Maggie Stewart bitch will finally get what she deserves," Pauline said.

"I should say!" M confirmed. "Glad I arrived just in time to hear that!"

"Yes, I'm sure we can all agree!" Mack said, sounding satisfied.

"What are you and Serena doing after supper to celebrate all of this wonderful news?" Pauline asked.

Serena had a naughty look—a coy smirk that Mack knew well.

"Why, sex on the beach," Serena said, as everyone broke into laughter.

COMING SOON!

Mack and M's Next Incredible Adventure . . .

NEVER LAUGH AT THE DEVIL centers on Jonathan Burke, a mid-thirties financial wizard who is fed up with a life he's convinced is destined for tragedy. He's a bachelor who wants to settle down but lacks any hope of a decent future while running a Ponzi scheme for an evil Mafia boss and his son. He decides to change his life for the better. The tragic and incredibly challenging consequences of his actions, and the intervention of Mackenzie Sampson and his team, are beyond anything Jonathan could have predicted in his wildest dreams.

ABOUT ATMOSPHERE PRESS

Atmosphere Press is an independent, full-service publisher for excellent books in all genres and for all audiences. Learn more about what we do at atmospherepress.com.

We encourage you to check out some of Atmosphere's latest releases, which are available at Amazon.com and via order from your local bookstore:

Dancing with David, a novel by Siegfried Johnson
The Friendship Quilts, a novel by June Calender
My Significant Nobody, a novel by Stevie D. Parker
Nine Days, a novel by Judy Lannon
Shining New Testament: The Cloning of Jay Christ, a novel by Cliff Williamson
Shadows of Robyst, a novel by K. E. Maroudas
Home Within a Landscape, a novel by Alexey L. Kovalev
Motherhood, a novel by Siamak Vakili
Death, The Pharmacist, a novel by D. Ike Horst
Mystery of the Lost Years, a novel by Bobby J. Bixler
Bone Deep Bonds, a novel by B. G. Arnold
Terriers in the Jungle, a novel by Georja Umano
Into the Emerald Dream, a novel by Autumn Allen
His Name Was Ellis, a novel by Joseph Libonati
The Cup, a novel by D. P. Hardwick
The Empathy Academy, a novel by Dustin Grinnell
Tholocco's Wake, a novel by W. W. VanOverbeke
Dying to Live, a novel by Barbara Macpherson Reyelts
Looking for Lawson, a novel by Mark Kirby
Yosef's Path: Lessons from my Father, a novel by Jane Leclere Doyle
Surrogate Colony, a novel by Boshra Rasti

ABOUT THE AUTHOR

STEPHEN WINN is the author of the Mack Sampson & M Crime/Detective Series. *Don't Look Back* is his first novel. He lives in St. Catharines, Ontario, Canada, about twenty minutes from Niagara Falls.

Visit his website at
www.stephenwinn.com

CPSIA information can be obtained
at www.ICGtesting.com
Printed in the USA
LVHW110044111022
730382LV00005B/131/J

9 781639 885800